Graham Pears (www.gpears.com) joined the police cadets in 1974 and retired as a Chief Superintendent with Northumbria Police in 2007. Whilst in the middle of a busy career he took an arts degree as a diversion from the day-to-day issues of policing, following on with an MA in creative writing. Although he had originally started work on his first degree to give him a break from police work, it seemed natural for him to write about crime. He has now dedicated himself to writing page-turning crime fiction.

He currently lives in Stocksfield, Northumberland, with his wife June and their many pets.

THE MYTH OF
JUSTICE

GRAHAM PEARS

CRIME

First published in the UK in 2009 by
Red Squirrel Press
PO Box 219
Morpeth
NE61 9AU
www.redsquirrelpress.com

Cover and text design, Ashbydesign
Cover image: Superstock

ISBN 978-0-9554027-7-7

Printed in the UK by Athenaeum Press Ltd.
Gateshead, Tyne & Wear

Dedicated to the memory of
my mother, Jane Pears.

Chapter one

March 1986

'How bloody stupid do you get?'

He ran as fast as his legs and scorching lungs would allow, and as he did, he heard his mother's voice in his head.

'How bloody stupid do you get?'

Normally when he stole from cars it was late at night, when streets were deserted and car radios begged to be stolen, but today he had taken a risk, on impulse, to get a gift for his mother. The street had seemed empty enough on this Sunday morning, but as soon as he had broken the window, reached into the car and grabbed the plant that was lying on the front seat, he became aware of a commotion in a nearby garden and instinctively knew that someone had seen him, and now he was being chased.

'How bloody stupid do you get?'

The thought kept repeating itself, and he knew it was exactly what his mother would say to him if she had to go to the police station *again* and sit through another interview with another stupid copper and hang around whilst he was being fingerprinted *again*.

'You take them every time that lad's in here; how many

1

sets of bloody fingers do you think he's bloody well got?'

She always said that to the coppers as they rolled his thin bony fingers on the ink that covered the brass plate and rolled them again on the white form which was clamped down on the bench beside the plate.

'He's only a kid; do you have to treat him like shite? You'd think he'd robbed a bloody bank.'

She always gave the coppers a hard time. Most of them said nothing as if they didn't mind, but she'd always tell Geoffrey on the way home how red their faces had been. But when they got home and were alone, away from the gaze of stupid coppers, she gave him a hard time as well, and made him promise he wouldn't get her dragged down to the copper shop ever again. He knew that if he got caught today, on Mother's Day of all days, he would really get it.

As he ran, he glanced back over his shoulder and saw that the figure behind him was catching up. At fourteen years old, running away was one of the few things Geoffrey Trent had practised regularly, but it looked like this pursuer was fit and determined.

'It's only a fucken' plant.' Geoffrey thought to himself as he ran, but it was not accompanied by the thought that the awkwardness of carrying the plant might be hindering his escape. In Geoffrey's mind the plant was now rightfully his, and given all the effort he had put into getting it, he wasn't going to give it up. After all, it was a present for his mother.

Geoffrey could now see the end of the street and knew

he was not far from the footpath that ran through this estate and would eventually take him across Newcastle's Town Moor back to his own house. He wondered whether, when he ran around the corner, he should try to find somewhere to hide in the few seconds he was out of sight, so his pursuer might run past him. This was a ploy he had successfully used before and he was always surprised at how people who were chasing him just kept on running, no matter how poor his hiding place. Geoffrey thought this was because they were so excited that even when they lost sight of him they didn't want to slow down in case they were losing ground. That or they were just stupid. Either way it usually worked and could be a good way of avoiding a lot of exercise when the person running after him was fit and attached to the article he had just taken, which appeared to be the case now.

Geoffrey's preferred tactic was to exploit opportunities where the chances of an enthusiastic pursuit were minimal. Two weeks ago he had taken a wallet from the hut at Wallsend Park bowling club and had been amused at the old man who had chased him through the grounds. The daft old codger seemed to be putting every bit of effort he had into running, but it was no faster than a brisk walking pace. Geoffrey actually stopped a few times when the old man was running out of puff and, maintaining a safe distance between them, shouted. 'Come on you daft old git; is that as fast as you can go?' This did seem to rally the old man, at least for a few seconds. When the old man slowed down again, Geoffrey stopped and shouted, 'Did you leave your running shoes at home Grandad? I'll wait here if you like, if you want to go and get 'em.' This caused the old man to mutter something and make another attempt to chase him. When he slowed down again Geoffrey shouted, 'I hope you haven't left your bus pass in your wallet cos you'll never make it home without it.'

At that he had run off leaving the old man bent over double, trying to catch his breath, his white bowling trousers looked baggy, as if they had slid down his waist during his pathetic attempt at pursuit. Once he was out of sight, Geoffrey had been disappointed to find the wallet contained nothing more than a door key and a black and white photograph of some odd-looking woman dressed in old-fashioned clothes and for some reason standing by a chair. He turned the picture over and saw faded slanted handwriting on the back of it which said 'Ever Yours, Love Juliet. 23rd July 1940.' Geoffrey had one last look through the brown leather wallet, which looked as old as the photo, and, finding no cash, couldn't understand why the old man had made such a fuss over losing it. 'Silly old twat,' he said as he threw it into the dark water of the burn that flowed through the park, watching for a few seconds to make certain the evidence of the theft had sunk without trace. He had been pleased he did that, because not long after a suspicious copper stopped him and accused him of stealing the wallet. He even had to go to the police station to protest his innocence. His mother had been furious when she got there and shouted at the coppers. 'Every time something happens you blame that poor lad; haven't you got owt better to do than pick on little kids?' His mother always gave the coppers a hard time.

'How bloody stupid do you get?'

His mother's voice pierced his head again. He continued running and as he did, quickly glanced back again. Geoffrey could see there was very little chance of his current pursuer running out of breath and, given the short distance now between them, it was probably too risky to try and hide around the corner. He still felt he had some running left in his legs, so he would keep going and hope his hunter would lose interest in the chase as he got further from his home. After all it was only a plant!

Geoffrey knew the pathways in Gosforth well as a result of his night visits. It was on the edge of Newcastle and very different to Cowgate, the council estate where Geoffrey lived, even though they were within running distance of each other. The gardens here were lined with hedges and high fences and many had mature trees standing in them, which made the place look very green. There wasn't much green at all on Geoffrey's estate, not that it worried him, as his mother often said, 'If we had grass, we'd only have to go to the bother of cadging a bloody lawnmower.'

He came to this estate because it was a place of opportunity. The hedges provided lots of cover, and there was usually something worth the walk there and the run back. He knew this was the place where some of the kids from school lived: the ones who wore neatly-pressed black cotton trousers, polished shoes and didn't talk to him. The kids who seemed compelled to go to school every day, as if it served some purpose. He wondered whether he was being chased by one of the posh kids from school, one of those who at weekends, when uniforms were not required, wore tight blue Levi's and bright Adidas training shoes. He hadn't got close enough to recognise him, but in the glances he had taken, he did resemble one of the older boys he had seen running up and down the school field chasing a rugby ball.

'How bloody stupid do you get?'

His mother's voice returned, and as it did, he glanced behind and judged the figure was still gaining on him. Geoffrey wondered whether his pursuer was the previous owner of the plant, who had hidden it in the car to give to his mother as a present today. That might explain the enthusiasm for the chase. Geoffrey had the plant pot tucked under his left arm as he continued to run. He turned from the road and into the narrow lane that formed a footpath through the estate. He felt the change of surface through the soles of his training shoes as he left the concrete of the road onto the loose gravel of the path. The turn and change of running surface slowed him down, and he could now sense there were just a few metres between him and his hunter. He felt his feet slide on the gravel as he raced down the narrow lane between the houses. He did not dare to glance behind him, as he feared even this small diversion could not be afforded. Geoffrey could now hear heavy breathing and was sure he could feel the threatening presence behind almost touching him. He heard a grunt, 'Come here!' He could sense an arm reaching out to grab his shoulder and felt it brush the back of his collar. As that happened, Geoffrey reached out with his free arm towards a dustbin that was standing near a gate and pulling it down behind him in one smooth single motion, continued with his sprinting. His lungs now felt as though they were on fire.

He heard a loud crash, then a thud, and a piercing shriek as the air was forced out of the chest of his falling pursuer. After a few seconds Geoffrey turned his head and saw the figure lying on the gravel, face down and groaning. Geoffrey stopped, and realising he was now safe, slowly returned a few paces. He could see a hand of the fallen figure slowly moving as the rest of the body remained still, stunned by the fall. He continued to watch as the figure lifted its head and for the first time he could see a face. A boy Geoffrey did not recognise, who he judged to be about a year older than himself. He was probably one of those kids with rich parents who went to a private school. This pleased Geoffrey as it meant the stranger was unlikely to be able to identify him. Geoffrey knew this sort always called the police for everything, even for little things like missing plants. The strange boy was obviously hurt and winced as he looked helplessly at Geoffrey. Instinctively Geoffrey knew what was required. Lifting his free hand he extended his middle and index fingers and waving the two fingers at the collapsed figure he shouted, 'Wankaaaaaaaa!' And then, after a few seconds of just waving his fingers in the V-sign, he again shouted, 'Wankaaaaaaaa!'

Triumphantly Geoffrey turned around and continued to run. Within fifteen minutes he was back to the safety of his own estate and his running, which had turned into a gentle trot after he had left the fallen pursuer, now became a walk. He felt a wave of relief after his narrow escape, especially for being spared the wrath of his mother, who would have been dragged to the police station to hang around for hours, as the police went through their long rituals of statements, interviews, fingerprints and photographs, before charging him to appear at the Juvenile Court again. After that, there would have been a visit from a social worker or, as his mother called them, 'those dozy prying bloody do-gooders.' The worst ones were those who tried to be friendly. The last one had made a remark about how difficult it was to raise children these days.

'How many children do you have?' his mother asked.

'None yet,' was the reply.

'Then how the hell do you know how hard it is?'

The conversation had been brief and intense after that, and all Geoffrey could recall was his mother calling the social worker a 'dozy bitch.'

Geoffrey's quick thinking with the dustbin had saved him from a whole load of grief, and also made him think about being a little more cautious in the future. Perhaps he would go back to the park and try for better luck than he had enjoyed on his last visit.

The plant had not fared well through its ordeal and now had only two remaining blooms. Geoffrey opened the back door of his house and was not surprised to see his mother, sitting at the small kitchen table with a burning cigarette between two fingers. Her elbow was resting on the table, her arm upright, with her hand in the air and falling back from the wrist, as if in a careless wave. Geoffrey placed the plant on the table in front of his mother.

'Happy Mother's Day.'

'I thought you had no money.'

'Managed to save a little up.'

'Geoffrey, that's smashing thanks. You're so thoughtful. I wondered where you'd got to.' She smiled broadly, 'Sit down and I'll make you some breakfast.'

Bacon was fried and then placed between slices of bread with lashings of tomato ketchup and, as it was being consumed by mother and son, the beleaguered-looking plant took pride of place on the Formica table, the overflowing ashtray having been pushed aside especially to accommodate it. Once the bacon sandwiches had been devoured two fresh cigarettes were lit and both sat back on the kitchen chairs, taking deep gratifying inhalations, and then blowing smoke in the direction of the plant as it was being admired. The thickness of the combination of smoke and bacon fumes went unnoticed.

Mrs Trent smiled as she looked at the remaining petals which had survived the plant's recent adventure.

'Geoffrey that was really thoughtful thanks.'

For a few seconds both gazed at the plant, as if they were expecting it to do something, but instead it just stood there slowly wilting.

It was his mother who broke the silence.

'Where did you get the plant from?'

'A shop in the toon.'

'Did you beat it up, or did you pay extra for them to do it?'

'Aye, sorry about that. I, er, dropped it on the way home.'

'Never mind son,' Mrs Trent placed her arm around Geoffrey, 'it's the thought that counts and I'm really grateful. You're a lovely lad. You love your mum don't you?'

Geoffrey winced as his mother planted a long kiss on the side of his head whilst she held him in a strange stranglehold.

Like her son, Mrs Trent did not know the plant was a chrysanthemum. The full, rounded, bright-yellow flowers of the 'butterball' variety had been in perfect bloom, forced unnaturally to do so at this time of year, by their grower's strict regime of darkness and light, to simulate the autumn days when the chrysanthemum would itself have chosen to display its natural beauty to the world.

Nor did they know the chain of events that had just been triggered by the theft of a pot plant. And, as mother and son sat together, blowing satisfying smoke into the air of their kitchen, they had not the slightest inkling that one of the consequences of that theft would be the premature and unnatural death of Geoffrey Trent.

Chapter two

Present day

'Bollocks!'

The phone rang in the large CID office at Newcastle Police Station and, as it did, Detective Constable Frank Whittle cursed. He looked at it and remained still, as the thought crossed his mind not to answer its high-pitched whining. After all, he was on his own, and no one would know whether he was there or not.

Working day shift on Sunday had its advantages and disadvantages; at least that's what he thought, as he sat at his desk just before 9.00am. The main advantage was the peace and quiet that came with the minimum number of staff required for this shift. At this moment he was the only person in the CID office, there was no bustle, and Frank enjoyed the way the station felt empty. It wasn't that he naturally disliked all the people he worked with, but he did like to keep a little distance between himself and others. It was a fact that he was not comfortable with some of the staff who inhabited his workplace; the world in which he lived was an ever changing one, and Frank was firmly of the opinion that not all change was for the better. It was also clear that not all of his colleagues were comfortable with him. Recently the thought had occurred to him that he was becoming something of an oddity. A detective constable for twenty-one years now, and at forty-three unlikely to be anything else. Not that Frank wanted to be anything else, he was content. But the source of his contentment was a mystery to others and sometimes even a reason for suspicion, as if the absence of the desire to be elsewhere was not normal. Not wanting more was an unnatural state of being.

The solitude of today also meant he could get on undisturbed with the mountain of paperwork that had been caused by recent cases. But he knew the phone's querulous tones would probably bring an example of the disadvantage of working on a Sunday morning: clearing up after Saturday night.

'Bollocks!' He repeated the curse and then snatched the phone in front of him. 'CID, DC Whittle.'

'Jet, it's Sharkie.' Having the same name as the inventor of the jet engine meant Frank had long ago accepted the nickname, and, as his given name was Francis Earnest Whittle, he'd been secretly quite pleased to accept it. 'Can you have a look at a job that's been in for a few hours now? Some of my lads are looking at it, but it's definitely a CID job.' The voice on the other end of the telephone was that of Sgt Sharkie from the uniform shift.

'I'm really busy Sarge; I need to get this file in for a case

I've got at court next week or I'll be right in the shit.'

'Sorry Jet; I had a word with the duty Detective Sergeant, Mark Groom, and he said Roger Freeman from your office should pick it up. But Roger's just rung in sick, which leaves you.' Sharkie continued. 'Man in his twenties is in intensive care, taken in overnight, looks like an assault, no witnesses, looks in a bad way.'

'Is there no one else Sarge? I've got to get the paperwork in for this burglar; it's at court on Wednesday.'

'Sorry Jet, you're it now according to the duty roster, unless there's anyone else in the office up there that can take it on?'

Jet looked around at the empty desks. He did not know whether anyone else was supposed to be at the office, but as Roger had gone sick, it looked like he had been left holding the baby. It crossed his mind that perhaps the young man in the hospital was not the only victim of Saturday night, and wondered if his absent colleague was nursing a Sunday morning hangover; it wouldn't be the first time.

'OK Sarge, who's at the hospital?'

'Ron Watson's speaking to the staff. Not much detail known yet though. They did recover a wallet from the victim, and someone's making enquiries at an address, but we don't have a result yet.'

'Tell Ron I'll be there soon.'

'Good man Jet.' Sharkie swiftly hung up the phone.

Twenty minutes later Jet was driving his car into

Newcastle Infirmary. The car park was tightly packed and presented its usual challenge of finding a space. He wondered where all the owners of these cars could possibly be. After all, it was Sunday morning and there was a distinct lack of activity or urgency in the hospital grounds, but still there were no spaces. After a fruitless search, Jet saw a police car parked on a road near the intensive care unit, far enough on the grass verge to allow other cars to pass. He parked his car behind the police car and walked into the nearby entrance. PC Ron Watson stood near the reception desk, close to a coffee machine, with a paper cup in his hand. He appeared to be chatting to the young woman who stood behind the broad counter and it struck Jet that neither of them seemed particularly dedicated to their chosen profession. Jet guessed that Watson was in his late twenties and thought he possessed a confidence beyond the few years of his service; it seemed to border on an arrogance that Jet couldn't understand. Dressed in full uniform, the tall constable no doubt thought he cut an imposing figure; a long baton hung menacingly from a utility belt which also played host to a rigid set of handcuffs and a small canister of CS gas. The officer's bright-white shirtsleeves were a direct contrast to the thick, black body armour, which covered the rest of his upper body. Jet couldn't help wondering what danger Watson thought lurked in a hospital corridor at nine thirty on a Sunday morning, to warrant all of this protective and offensive equipment. It was that sort of thought that

16

made others within his profession think Jet was quite odd. Jet knew he was a misfit and had learned to live with the position.

'Does that taste like coffee?' Watson had not been aware of Jet's approach and was taken slightly by surprise.

'It's supposed to be hot chocolate, and the best thing you can say is it's hot.'

'What's the story with the casualty?'

As Jet spoke, Watson moved away from the reception desk and both men stood at the side of the hospital corridor, in an attempt to conduct their conversation in confidence; trying to ignore the fact that people continued to pass them in the busy walkway.

Watson had his back to the wall as he answered. 'Brought in at about two thirty this morning with extensive injuries. Looks like he's taken a good beating, with a baseball bat or something like that.'

'Have you ever seen anyone playing baseball in Newcastle?'

'What?' Watson seemed taken aback by the question.

'You see them being sold in every sports shop, but you never see anyone playing with them. The only thing they get used for is beating people up. You should need a licence to buy one; what do you reckon?'

'Yeah, whatever.' Watson continued, 'He's got a broken leg and a broken arm and numerous bruises. The doctors are worried about his head injuries; he's obviously taken a number of blows, and they don't really know yet how bad it is. Doesn't look too good.'

'Any suspects?'

'No, nothing. He was found lying in the lane near the back of the Barking Dog pub in Carr Street. Couldn't have been there long, so the assault probably happened just before he was found lying, about two this morning. No one has seen anything.'

'Do we know who he is?'

'He had this wallet on him.'

Watson produced a small, black leather wallet, which he handed to Jet. Jet unfolded it and removed the contents; a driving licence and five-pound note. He replaced the cash and unfolded the driving licence, examining the details. He read the name and address out loud to Watson. 'Gerald Goodman, 23 Barmouth Avenue, Wallsend.' He looked away from the licence and at Watson. 'Do we know if that's him yet?'

'We think so. There's a car bringing his parents up; they should be here any minute.'

'Well, that's something to look forward to. Anything else I should know?'

'Apparently the parents haven't seen him for a while; he's been living with his mates somewhere in town.'

'Anything else?'

'Yeah, don't drink the chocolate: it looks and tastes like shite.'

'That's very helpful. I'll bear it in mind.'

Watson smiled and turned away from Jet towards the pretty face at the reception desk.

'See you soon Julie.'

The young woman smiled at Watson as he walked towards the exit.

After Watson had left the hospital, Jet decided to go in search of further information and entered the double doors that marked the entrance to the intensive care unit. Jet had visited this ward several times in the past and was more familiar with the place than he would have preferred; he always felt on edge here. Although there was something about people being on the brink of extinction that made him feel his problems were unimportant, it also reminded him of his own mortality. He felt uncomfortable and while he would not admit this to anyone, also intimidated. All the staff wore the same dark-blue uniform and seemed constantly engaged in urgent activity, which made informal conversation impossible. As a consequence, even though he did recognise the odd face, he did not feel familiarity with any of the staff, and felt a total stranger. There was also something about nurses wearing trousers that didn't sit well with Jet, and he thought their crumpled suits resembled pyjamas too closely for relaxed discussion. As he entered the ward corridor, he immediately felt like an intruder: a fully-clothed man in a huge private bedroom, harbouring germs in an environment that looked and smelled sterile, where he and his germs were not welcome. He approached a blue-suited woman who sat, reading medical notes, in a small room behind an open door. He produced his warrant card.

'Here to make enquiries about a young man brought in this morning. Possible assault.'

The woman looked up but seemed disinterested in Jet's identification.

'It seems pretty clear to us that he's taken a good battering.'

'Any update on his condition?'

'Stable for now, but there is so much swelling to his head that it's impossible to assess the damage at the moment. We're still awaiting the results of a scan.'

'Any chance of having a look at him?'

'If you think it's necessary. I only have a few minutes though – we're very busy.'

'I appreciate that; it would just help me to try and make some sense of what's happened.'

Jet followed the nurse through another set of double doors which led to the intensive care unit beds. Jet thought it was as sombre as ever. A dozen beds were spread evenly around the room, which felt warm and claustrophobic. Each bed was occupied by a patient connected to a variety of medical equipment. The staff busied themselves with their patients. Out of the corner of his eye, Jet caught sight of two visitors who gazed from the foot of one of the beds at its occupant. One, a woman, held a handkerchief covering her nose and mouth, whilst continually sniffling; she was being comforted by a man's arm. Parents, Jet thought. This was not a pleasant place.

The nurse indicated a bed, where a man's naked torso was visible above the low-folded sheets. Clear plastic tubes carried liquids between nearby stands to the unconscious body; two in his arm and one disappearing under the bedclothes. Another wider, cream-coloured tube ran from his mouth to a machine which loudly regulated his breathing. Wires ran from his chest to another machine which made regular, hostile bleeping noises. He was severely bruised all over the visible parts of his body. His face was so swollen and black with bruises that it was difficult to tell his age. Jet stared at him for a moment, trying to make some sense of this vision, as if it could ever make sense.

'Are there any marks on the body other than bruising? Cuts, stab wounds, that sort of thing.'

'No, it looks like the poor sod's been repeatedly kicked or hit with something.'

'Probably both,' Jet added, as they both stared at the young man.

The nurse then pointed to the battered man's arms. 'You might be interested in those track marks though.'

Jet looked hard at his arms and saw the scars around the fold on the inside of his elbow. 'Drug addict?'

'Looks like he's been injecting something regularly.'

The door of the ward opened carefully, and the head

of another nurse protruded through the gap. She fixed her stare directly at the nurse with Jet.

'Trish, the parents are here.'

The nurse turned to Jet, 'Excuse me will you?'

'Of course.'

'You can wait here if you like.' She quickly walked out into the corridor.

The feeling of intruder returned as Jet remained stationary, conscious of the activity of other medical staff in the room. He stared at the motionless body on the bed in front of him and considered the few facts now available. He had long since learned it did no good to ponder possible theories too deeply; it led to jumping to conclusions, which he knew wasn't helpful. He had seen some of his fellow officers make rash early judgements, which led them to try to get the unfolding facts, fit their theories. All he knew at this time was his victim had taken a severe beating, had probably been kicked a good many times, and possibly hit with a blunt instrument. He also knew that a wallet had been recovered, and therefore it seemed unlikely that robbery was the motive for the attack, which meant it was possible the victim knew his attacker. Jet did not yet know the man in the bed before him and it was obvious he was not going to give up his secrets in the near future. He felt a twinge of sadness at the sight, and thought it was as much evidence as anyone would need to prove the fragility of the human condition. Jet was always careful not to express his feelings to anyone, but another lesson his years of experience had taught him was emotions could not be eradicated; you had to learn to deal with them. On occasions, he heard some colleagues telling others they had seen it all before and nothing bothered them. He knew most of the time this was just rubbish, bravado perhaps – something he had no time for. Far more troubling though were the times when he actually believed them. Jet knew the day you stopped having feelings about things in this job was the day you should go home and not come back.

Jet was pulled from the internal world of his own thoughts by the sound of voices too emotional to belong to staff. Two people were being shown into the ward, and Jet thought they must be the young man's parents. Their actions quickly confirmed this assumption, and it was immediately obvious they recognised their son, despite his disfigurement. Mrs Goodman was generating sounds of anxiety and Mr Goodman followed silently a few paces behind. They had their eyes fixed on the bed, which contained their battered son, and were so focused on this horrific sight they seemed unaware of anything else in the room and oblivious to Jet's presence. As they approached the bed from the side, Jet, who had been at the foot of it, backed away a couple of steps.

'My God, Gerry! What have they done to you?' The sobs from Mrs Goodman took over from her words, as she grabbed a handful of the blanket covering her son, apparently as a substitute for his battered body, and squeezed; gently at first and then more intensely. Her husband put his arm around her shoulders and both parents stood staring at their son for a few seconds, then Mrs Goodman turned her face and nestled into her husband's chest. She quivered as her cries became louder. Mr Goodman's stare remained impassive as he held his wife and continued to look down at his son. Jet felt uncomfortable at the intimacy of this scene and, trying to put a little extra distance between him and the emotions on display, took a few more steps backwards. Neither Mr nor Mrs Goodman noticed as he slowly turned then made his way to the door and, slowly pushing it, disappeared into the corridor.

Outside the ward Jet pondered for a few seconds. He needed to speak to Mr and Mrs Goodman and find out whether they had information that would help. He needed to know when they had last seen their son and if they had any idea who had attacked him, or why the assault might have happened. He needed to know who Gerald Goodman had been staying with most recently and who else he had been associating with. But he concluded that, at the moment, their need was greater than his, and he would leave them to cope with their distress and return in a couple of hours to speak to them. For now, he would be content that he at least had a positive identification of the victim as Gerald Goodman. In the meantime, he would make some enquiries about Goodman and, if he had time, visit the Barking Dog public house and see what secrets the scene of the assault might share with him.

Outside the ward he saw another blue-suited nurse sitting in the same small room where he had found Trish, the first nurse he had spoken to, who was now trying to console the Goodmans.

'Excuse me, I wonder if you could do me a favour?' The nurse remained straight faced and Jet wondered whether she was waiting to see how big the favour was before committing herself to any expression that might obligate her to do something. Jet handed her a card, 'I'm with the police. I've just left Trish with Mr and Mrs Goodman; they're obviously distraught. I'll come back in a little while to talk to them. If anyone needs me, my mobile number's on there.'

The nurse stared at the card and then looked up at Jet. He did not detect any change in her face as she replied, 'I'll pass the message on.'

'That's very kind of you; I'll be back in a few hours.'

'We'll try to survive on our own until then.' The nurse remained poker-faced and Jet didn't know whether he'd been insulted or not, but after a seconds' thought, he decided it didn't matter. He summoned a false smile.

Jet turned and walked out of the intensive care unit into the hospital's main corridor and, as he did so, his steps became more purposeful. He passed the reception desk and was soon in the fresh air. He squinted as the sunlight hit his face, and he walked the short distance to his car. As he passed the space where the police car had been parked in front of his own, he noticed something odd about his red Ford Fiesta. A large piece of paper was lodged under the windscreen wipers. He looked around to see whether there was anyone about that may have been responsible for leaving him anonymous notes. Carefully, he unfolded the paper and read the few lines it contained. It told him his car had been clamped for parking in an unauthorised area.

'The bastards!' he said out loud to himself, crumpling the paper into a ball and putting it in his jacket pocket. The outside pockets of his jacket were well used and his wife, Julia, often complained they gaped open untidily, like hungry mouths. He looked around but could not see anyone in the vicinity, and after a few seconds of gazing in exasperation at the sky, he pulled the paper out from his jacket pocket and examined the details. He plucked his mobile phone from his pocket and rang the number on the notice. It was answered promptly.

'Hello.'

'Is that the person who's just clamped my car?'

'What make is it pal?'

'Red Ford Fiesta?'

'Parked outside the entrance to the intensive care unit?'

'Yes. I'm DC Whittle; I'm here on police business.'

'You got fifty quid?'

'Why?'

'Cos that's how much you need for me to come and take the clamp off pal, and I ain't wasting my time coming if you ain't got it.'

'I've got it.'

'Good. See you in ten minutes pal.'

Jet pressed the button on his phone to end the call and spoke out loud to himself as he did so. 'Bollocks!'

He placed the notice back into his gaping jacket pocket and wondered if things could get any worse. He did not know that the answer to his question was a very resounding 'yes'.

Chapter three

'Bollocks!' Jet cursed as he sat at his desk and thumbed his now empty wallet before replacing it in his inside jacket pocket. 'I've got even less than Gerald Goodman,' he muttered to himself and then returned his attention to the computer screen on his desk, and saw the photograph of Gerald Goodman looking back at him. The rest of Goodman's criminal record was as vague as he had expected from someone arrested only three times: twice for shoplifting and once for drug possession. For the first twenty-two years of his existence, Goodman had not come to the notice of the police; it was only in the last twelve months that he had racked up his tally of convictions, which had led to one official caution, and then a court appearance and a conditional discharge. Jet checked the details of Goodman's record and saw he'd been arrested for drug possession two months earlier at the Wooden Doll pub, which was not far from the Barking Dog. As he moved his fingers gently over the keyboard, Jet wondered what had happened to the pubs in the city. It seemed to him there was a contest to find the dreariest name. The computer screen told him the last time Goodman had been arrested he had been at the pub with another three people when it had been raided by the police.

The sound of the *William Tell Overture* alerted Jet to the fact that his mobile phone was ringing. 'Ju' appeared on the display. It was his wife Julia.

'Hi Ju.'

'Frankie, did you ring mother?'

'Not yet; I haven't had a chance. Do you think she'd mind if I just wished her happy birthday when I saw her tonight?'

'Well, if you can't be bothered Frank.'

Jet knew when Julia called him Frank he was being disapproved of.

'Ju, I'll do my best to ring her.'

'It'll mean a lot to her.'

'I'll do my best.'

'You know mother's always had a soft spot for you.'

'Yeah, a shallow grave on the Town Moor.'

'Now then Frankie, mother always speaks well of you. It was father who thought you were odd.'

'He thought you married beneath yourself.'

'He did have a point.'

'Thanks.'

'You won't be late tonight will you?'

'I'll do my best.'

'Heather said she'd be here for seven.'

'Oh joy.'

'Best behaviour tonight Frankie, for mother's birthday dinner.'

Jet didn't really mind Julia's sister Heather, but he thought if bragging were a martial art, her husband would easily have been a black belt. A car dealer who kept emphasising that he only dealt in 'quality' vehicles, he was always on the brink of some new advance or adventure which revolved around how wealthy he was.

'Heather's making a special effort; she's been off work all week with laryngitis.'

'I didn't know she'd taken up with a Greek bloke now. Mind you, he'd have to be more exciting than that dozy husband of hers.'

'You're not going to take the pee all night are you?'

'I promise I'll be on my best behaviour. I'll set my tongue to charming.'

'That'll be the day. Can you call into a shop on the way home and pick up a nice bottle of red wine?'

'There were three in the rack last night; you're not drinking it through the day now are you?'

'I was thinking that, as it's a celebration, we might go beyond the supermarket three ninety-nine range.'

'Are you questioning my taste?'

'Yes.'

'I'll have to go to the hole in the wall first and get some cash.'

'I thought you did that yesterday.'

'Just spent it getting my car unclamped at the hospital.'

'Why?'

'I parked it where I shouldn't have.'

'Don't the police pay for that?'

'Not likely, and if I asked I'd just end up with a lecture about parking the car in illegal places, as well as the fine.'

'Why were you at the hospital?'

'Just a job I'm dealing with.'

'Will you try and get home on time?'

'I'll do my best.'

'Goodbye Frankie, don't be late.'

The line went dead. Jet had been married to Julia for eighteen years and could not imagine life without her. His parents had been dead for many years and he knew that she was now the only person he could really depend on. Jet smiled as he replaced the phone in his jacket pocket and resolved to do his best not to be late tonight.

Jet's thoughts turned back to Gerald Goodman, and he decided that a walk to the second floor of the police station might be of help, to see whether there was anyone about in the office upstairs used by the drug squad. A few minutes later, he was again struck by the solitude of Sunday as he walked along the quiet corridor that led to the drug squad office. He poked his head into the large main office and saw it was empty. He walked further along the corridor and, in the smaller detective sergeant's office, saw Mark Groom sitting at one of the two desks.

Groom's huge frame seemed to dwarf the office furniture; his hobby of lifting heavy weights had added considerable muscle to his tall frame. He seemed absorbed with the documents on the desk in front of him and did not notice Jet standing in the doorway. Groom's thick forearms rested on the desk as he leaned forward. He wore a yellow short-sleeved shirt which contrasted with his tanned brown skin, the only blemish being a deep scar that ran for three inches in a straight line across his left elbow. Jet had often wondered whether steroids had played any part in Groom's muscle growth. To Jet's knowledge, Groom had been a detective sergeant on the drug squad for at least five years now, and worked in Newcastle for almost as long as Jet, in one position or another. Despite this, Jet did not know a great deal about him. They were very different people and Jet was comfortable with the distance that existed between them. He felt there was a strong air of conceit about Groom who often seemed impatient, bordering on aggressive, with people like Jet who were outside his circle of associates. Although this seemed to make him a popular figure with some, it was a club Jet was happy not to be a member of. Not that Groom had ever shown signs of wanting Jet to join. Groom had often referred to him as 'one of the drones downstairs', an indication of his contempt for those who did not aspire to the more elite world occupied by him and his drug squad cronies. After looking at Groom's intimidating muscular frame, Jet glanced down at himself and the slight paunch that pushed his shirt, causing it to hang over his trouser belt. Jet did not consider himself to be desperately unfit, but there was no doubt that he and Groom were very different people.

Jet smoothed the front of his shirt and, with the same hand, tucked his shirt into his trouser belt. He then broke the silence.

'Mind if I interrupt for a minute or two Sergeant?'

Groom looked up, and Jet thought he looked surprised to see him.

'Jet, how are things going?'

'Well, I've had better days, just spent half an hour and fifty quid getting my car unclamped at the hospital. Other than that things are about fair. I know you're the duty detective sergeant today; I just wanted to have a word about this lad in the hospital I'm dealing with.'

'Sounded like another Saturday night pub fallout to me.'

'He's called Gerald Goodman; taken into hospital this morning after a really good beating. He was arrested by your squad about two months ago at the Wooden Doll. I was wondering if you might have some information that wasn't on the computer that might help?'

'Can't say I've heard of him; do you know who dealt with him?'

'Ray Harris, according to the computer. He was arrested with three other people.'

'Ray should be in later; I'll ask him to ring you. Any idea who attacked him?'

'Not yet. He was found by the Barking Dog pub at about two this morning.'

'Is he going to come round soon?'

'We'll know in a while. It could be very serious; do you think I need to let the detective inspector know about it?'

'No need Jet. It's a straightforward Saturday night assault. Just make the usual enquiries, no need to panic; let me know how you get on. I'll make sure Ray gets in touch as soon as he gets in and we'll give you a hand if you can't do it on your own. Get the first team in if the reserves can't manage, eh?'

The two men looked at each other for a few seconds in silence and then Jet smiled, pretending that Groom's insult had not offended him. Groom remained silent and did not return the smile. Jet took the hint and turned to leave Groom's office. He made his way back to his own office and stayed only long enough to pick up his coat and keys. He made his way to his car and ten minutes later was back in the hospital car park. He waited in his car for another ten minutes, until he spotted someone leaving a parking space which he quickly moved into. Five minutes later, he was back in the uncomfortable surroundings of the intensive care unit and interrupted the nurse he recognised from his last visit as she walked purposefully along the corridor.

'Excuse me, Trish, I was wondering whether it was a good time to try and have a word with Mr and Mrs Goodman?'

The nurse smiled at Jet's familiar address. 'They're still at his bed; if you like you can use this room and I'll ask them to come and speak to you.'

She nodded towards a small office off the unit corridor,

and Jet smiled. 'I'm grateful. Thanks.'

Two minutes later, and moving death-march slow, Mr and Mrs Goodman entered the room. Mrs Goodman was sobbing and her husband's arm was still resting on her shoulders, in what appeared to Jet to be exactly the same pose they were in when he last saw them. It surprised Jet that it was Mrs Goodman who spoke first. 'Do you know who did this to him?'

'No, not yet. He was brought in earlier; he was found lying in the street and hasn't been conscious since.'

'Someone must have seen or heard something.'

'I can assure you that I'm going to do everything I can to find out what happened. It would help me if you could answer some questions for me?' Jet did not wait for a reply, 'When did you see him last?'

Mrs Goodman urgently rubbed her nose with her handkerchief and continued. 'He left home about six months ago, and we haven't seen him since.'

'Do you know where he's been staying?'

'No. Somewhere in Newcastle.'

Mr Goodman immediately added to his wife's reply. 'He got in with a bad lot and left home. About a year ago he started taking drugs, turned into someone we didn't know. Got himself into bother with the law. We tried our best, but he even stole from us to buy drugs. We couldn't cope with it. He used to be such a good boy, but he was out of his mind most of the time; he even hit Brenda here when she found him stealing from her handbag. After that he fled; we haven't seen him until today.'

'How do you know he was in Newcastle?'

Mrs Goodman gazed down at the floor, and she almost whispered, 'A friend of mine said she'd seen him in the town a few weeks ago, that's all.'

Jet, suspecting this might not be true, was silent for a few seconds as he looked at Mrs Goodman. He decided not to press the point and concluded that, if a mother's love was causing her to hide something, the chances were it was not vital for him to know this now; but any revelation could bring her and Mr Goodman further misery on a day when it was already in abundant supply. Jet continued. 'No idea who he was staying with?' Both parents shook their heads. A few seconds of silence followed, accompanied by an awkwardness that made them feel longer. 'OK, I'll do what I can; I'll keep in touch.'

'He's a good boy really, he didn't deserve this. Please find out who did it, it's not fair.'

'I promise, Mrs Goodman, I will do everything I can.'

Jet felt a weight lifting from him as he left the ward for the second time that day, and was also relieved to find his car intact when he reached the car park. He got into the driver's seat, flicked open his small black notebook and reviewed the day's scribbled notes.

'The Barking Dog,' he quietly said to himself and looking at his wristwatch, saw it was a few minutes before noon. 'Well, the regulars should be in there by now. That's if they ever leave.'

To Jet, the Barking Dog had two things in common with the intensive care unit: he was familiar with it, and he didn't particularly like the place.

He placed the notebook back into his jacket and started the engine of his car.

'Time to pay a visit to the place where nobody knows your name – or anybody else's for that matter.'

And as he sat in the confines of his Ford Fiesta driving towards the Barking Dog, pondering his routine enquiry, he did not know what an event that occurred long ago had triggered. He was totally unaware that, like a tsunami, it was silently tearing across the ocean towards him, and he was now very close to facing the devastating consequences.

Chapter four

'I'm sorry Shirley.' Mark Groom held the phone in his left hand and, as he did so, his right hand gently massaged the scar on his left elbow; it was an unconscious act. 'I didn't mean to shout at you this morning.'

'You're always saying sorry; it never means a thing.' Shirley's voice was angry. The argument she and her husband had before he left for work that morning was still weighing heavily. She was also feeling the effects of the wine that had flowed freely the night before.

'You could barely get out that taxi last night; I was worried.'

'Because I had a night out with my friends?'

'You're always out with your friends.'

'Not as much as you're in that gym.'

'I don't come home pissed.'

'Why shouldn't I go out with my friends?'

'What about the expense?'

'I manage on what you give me don't I?'

'We've a lot to fork out with the new house and all. We might have to cut back.'

'You mean you're going to cut the housekeeping so I can't afford to go out?'

'We've a lot to pay out every month that's all.'

'I can read you like a book; you're going to stop the only bit of pleasure I get. I'll be a prisoner in this house.'

'That's not it at all Shirley.' As Mark spoke, the figure of Ray Harris appeared at his office door. On seeing him, Mark summoned a weak smile and turned his head away to look out of the office window. 'Look, I'm busy at the moment, can we discuss this tonight?'

Harris walked into the office, oblivious to the clear signs that Mark Groom was having a private discussion. He sat down in the empty chair of the desk directly opposite Groom's; he leaned back and the sides of his open leather jacket fell onto the chair arms. He watched Groom as the telephone conversation continued.

'What time will you be in?' Shirley barked.

'About half seven.'

'After you've been to the gym I suppose?'

'I'll not be late.'

'Please yourself Mark,' Shirley said and abruptly hung up.

Mark replaced the phone receiver.

'Problems?' Harris smiled at the same time as making his enquiry.

'Nothing to worry about.'

Harris continued to smile. 'How's your daughter getting on these days?'

'Diane? Fine, settling into life at the high school.'

'Yeah, they grow up fast don't they?'

'Yeah,' was Groom's disinterested response, and he quickly changed the subject. 'Have you spoken to Jet today?'

'No, why?'

'He's got some assault on the go, and you dealt with the victim a while ago; he wanted to see if you had any info.'

'Do you know who it is?'

'Goodson or Goodman, something like that. He was given a good beating outside the Barking Dog. Can you ring Jet?'

'No problem. No doubt it'll be a waste of time.'

'Maybe, but speak to him in any case, yeah?' As Groom spoke, he stood up and lifted the light-blue cotton jacket that was on the back of the chair and pushed his left arm through the sleeve. 'I'm just going for a sandwich; won't be long.'

'Sure.' Harris raised himself from his chair.

'How did you get on last night?' Groom spoke as he was putting his right arm through the other sleeve.

'I met a few snouts but nothing of note. No one seems to know who's bringing in most of the gear at the moment.'

'Not sure I go along with the theory that there's some big organisation shipping all of the drugs into the North East. Seems unlikely to me.' Groom straightened his jacket as he spoke.

'I'll keep working the informants; someone's bound to turn up something.'

'Yeah. Keep me updated will you?'

'No problem.'

Groom walked out of the office and Harris followed. Groom moved quickly down the corridor and Harris headed in the direction of the drug squad detective constables' office, where his own desk was.

It was noon by the time Mark Groom was out of the office and walking up Newcastle's Northumberland Street. He felt at home as he walked in the fresh air of the street which was always busy, even on Sundays. But the argument he'd had with Shirley preyed on his mind. They had been married for seventeen years, and during that time they'd had their ups and downs, but he could not remember as many disagreements as had recently occurred. It all seemed to start when they moved house. He had thought that moving into their new home in Prudhoe would make her happy. They'd always talked about buying a house on one of the new estates and, as they had now achieved it, he was at a loss to understand why Shirley could not just settle down and enjoy her new home. It was a marked improvement on their last house and Groom had stretched himself to buy it. Then there were all of the things to buy for inside: carpets, fitted wardrobes, beds, and a new fireplace to name but a few; the list had seemed endless. Then there was finding Diane a new school and all the problems that brought. Leaving old friends and making new ones. Teenage girls could be difficult at the best of times. There was no doubt they had all taken a lot on recently. As he walked up Northumberland Street thinking about his problems, he came to the same conclusion that he had reached several times lately, things would settle down. Shirley's regular nights out with her friends were just her way of blowing off steam. They would discuss it tonight, and he would make her see sense. There was really no need for him to worry.

The walk up Northumberland Street was Mark's lunchtime habit. He was a man who liked routine and tried his best not to be disrupted from it. Once he had finished his shift today he would, as usual, call into the gym on the way home and spend the best part of two hours using the machines and lifting heavy weights. Carefully, he would go through his exercises, making sure all the muscle groups were covered; he enjoyed the burn as his muscles were being strained. He also liked the feeling of dominance that his physique gave him: even the criminals thought twice about taking the piss out of Mark Groom.

Now he was going for lunch and walked into Marks & Spencer on Northumberland Street, which was busy as usual, and went directly to the food hall. When they had first married Shirley had attempted to make him lunch to take to work, but there was something about carrying Tupperware containers that didn't sit well with him. She had quickly abandoned the attempts as the Tupperware box usually returned untouched, having got no further than lying on the rear seat of his car. He preferred his routine and found Marks & Spencer sandwiches were one of the few things he could truly depend on. There was something comforting about their clear, tightly-sealed plastic containers that assured him they were fresh and fit for his consumption. The store seemed particularly busy today and, after he had picked up a packet of his regular ham salad sandwiches, he moved to the checkout, joining what he judged to be the shortest queue. As soon as he did he started to feel impatient. The bleeping sound of the tills seemed far too loud to be fulfilling their obvious purpose, and he wondered whether there was some psychological trickery going on, to make the checkout staff work faster than their colleagues, as they heard the adjacent tills. He studied this for a few moments and realised, if this was the case, it was not working, as the queue seemed to be making very little progress. He looked around the store and found his eye drawn to the back of a person he had not noticed a few seconds earlier when he'd looked at the same spot. The large blue anorak with the hood pulled up was out of keeping with the warm July air. Groom continued to look as the coat flapped open and closed. As the furtive movements continued Groom quickly realised what was happening. The thought 'fucking amateurs' flickered across his mind as he continued to watch, and got closer to paying for his food.

The blue coat remained in the same place as Groom moved up the queue, and then, as he was being served. The checkout assistant slid the plastic sandwich container over the star-shaped light and, when there was no response, she examined the bar code and attempted to straighten it out. She ran the bar code over the light again, but the machine refused to make its familiar noise.

'Bloody thing.' Groom was not sure whether the sales assistant's remark was aimed at him or the bar code.

'Is it giving you hassle?'

The assistant didn't look at Groom as he enquired but remained fixed on the bar code. 'It only has to do one bloody thing.' She continued to wrestle with the bar code, then slid it past the light again, and cursed when there was still no noise. 'I'll have to type the whole bloody code in the till now, bloody thing.'

'That's modern technology for you.' Groom's smile was not returned as the assistant examined the wrapper and then typed the long sequence of numbers into the till. After what appeared to Groom to be a long and sustained effort from the assistant, she pressed a last button on the till.

'That's two pound sixty.'

'Hardly seemed worth all the effort,' Groom remarked as he handed over a five-pound note.

The assistant finally lifted her head to look at Groom. 'It's a hell of a carry-on when it doesn't work. Bloody thing.' She opened the till and, after a little period of rattling, handed Groom his change.

'Thanks, bye,' Groom said and, as he did so, he saw that

the blue anorak was still in the same place.

Groom walked away from the till and stood at one of the many exit doors. There were three steps up to the doors, which meant he now had a bird's-eye view of activity in the store. He could clearly see the back of the blue anorak hood turn as its wearer checked up and down the aisle. As this happened, the coat flapped open twice more. When the hood turned from side to side, Groom caught a glimpse of the face and saw that it was a man he guessed to be in his mid thirties. He looked small to Groom, not like the drug dealers and robbers he was used to dealing with, but it was evident he was a criminal all the same. Groom decided to remain at his vantage point and began to enjoy his observation of the man in the blue coat, thinking of it as a little playful lunchtime sport.

'Fucking amateurs.' This time it was quietly said under Groom's breath.

The man in the blue coat turned and pulled the zip up to his collar, walking straight past the checkout towards the exit door. The man looked startled when Groom took hold of his arm as he was about to step out of the store into the fresh air.

'I'm a police officer; I think you and I need to go and talk to a security officer and see what you've been putting inside your coat.'

Groom's vice-like grip on the arm of the blue coat was sufficient to persuade swift compliance.

Groom guided the blue coat towards a neatly-dressed uniformed security guard, who was standing like a sentry near one of the end exit doors.

The guard wore neatly-pressed, brown trousers, a pristine white shirt, brown tie and a brown cap, the shape of which reminded Groom of an old threepenny bit. Shirley had bought him a key ring with one of the old coins on it, and it still hung from the large bunch of keys that he permanently had in his possession.

'I'm a police officer; I think this man's been concealing the store's property inside his coat. Can we go somewhere?'

'Sure, follow me.'

Groom kept a tight hold of his prisoner, as they followed the guard into a private corridor and then into a windowless small office.

A wooden table and two wooden chairs stood in the otherwise empty room, but none of the three made any attempt to sit down. Groom let go of the arm of the blue coat. The stranger turned around in the small office to face Groom and the guard who were blocking the door.

'Open your coat.' Groom's request was calm but firm.

The man did not reply or move.

Groom's eyes widened as he moved his face close to that of the stranger. He knew the stranger would be able to feel his breath as he spoke again. 'What is your name?'

The stranger spoke softly. 'Jack.'

'I said open your coat, Jack.'

After a few seconds thought, Jack reached his hand up to the top of the zip and slowly pulled it down the bulky coat. There was a clink as the coat finally opened.

'Pull out what's inside the coat Jack.'

He put his hand inside the coat and produced a bottle of champagne.

'And the rest Jack.'

He put his hands back into the pockets three times and on each occasion pulled out a tin of salmon, placing it with the champagne on the table.

'Is that everything Jack?'

'Yes.' The reply was gentle, and Groom thought Jack had the expression of a startled rabbit caught in the headlights of a car on a lonely country lane.

Groom looked at the four articles on the table. 'Are you planning a party Jack?'

There was no response.

Groom turned towards the security guard. 'We've a real noisy one here; I'd better call the station, and we'll deal with him there.'

Ten minutes later, a police car pulled up outside the rear entrance of Marks & Spencer. Groom gripped the arm of the shoplifter and led him to the waiting vehicle where he quickly bundled him through the back door and pushed him along, climbing in the same door to share the back seat.

'What have we got here Sarge?' enquired the Panda car driver.

'Just a shoplifter. Let's get him to the station before he shits himself.'

The Panda driver smiled and drove from Marks & Spencer through the Haymarket and turned left. He ignored the 'no entry' sign and drove the Panda car through the bus-only street along Eldon Square, taking the most direct route to the police station.

Groom sat back in the car seat, feeling relaxed and confident. Like Jet, he did not know what had been triggered by an event long ago, and had no idea of the terrible consequences that were soon going to bring devastation to his life.

Chapter five

As Jet walked to the entrance of the Barking Dog, it struck him how different pubs seemed on Sunday afternoons compared to the electrically-charged weekend nights. No need for burly doormen to maintain their own brand of order at this time of day, which according to his wristwatch was twenty minutes past noon. The smell of stale ale hung outside the open front door in the still summer air, making it an uninviting place to Jet. He walked inside and all traces of summer quickly disappeared in the dark interior. The wooden floor, walls and ceiling had a consistent damp hostility about them, and harsh wooden chairs and tables added to the unloved atmosphere. It took Jet a few seconds for his eyes to adjust to the contrast of the new world he had just entered and, once they had, he immediately noticed that his presence had merited the stares of most of the dozen or so people who were inside. Those who did not look chose to stare at the glasses before them that bore dark-coloured liquids, and they seemed to be indifferent to activity outside that fluid domain.

Jet walked to the bar and saw behind it a middle-aged man whose stern face confirmed that Jet was an intruder. Jet produced the leather wallet that contained his police warrant card.

'Are you the licensee?'

The question did not provoke a verbal response but a nod of the head.

'I'm making enquiries about a young man who was found lying unconscious outside the back of this pub in the early hours of this morning, and wondered if you could help me?'

'How?'

Jet smiled at the barman, not because he considered the answer humorous, but because the response caused a random thought to dart into his head. A boyhood reminiscence – a television programme of that name, that he used to watch, which explained the little mysteries of the world. The name Fred Dineage came to mind, as well as the regular voice of an American Indian Chief who would loudly say the word 'how' between explanations of things, like perpetual motion and the reason it didn't actually exist. It briefly crossed Jet's mind to raise his hand, showing his palm to the barman, and repeat 'how' back to him. He decided against this as he was sure it would be misunderstood. Back to reality, Jet thought.

'Do you know a man called Gerald Goodman?'

'Not that I know of; a lot of people come in here.'

Jet absorbed this information and, whilst doing so, looked around the bar at the customers, none of whom looked as if they were actually enjoying their visit to the Barking Dog. Jet wondered whether their presence was more out of addiction to the brown fluid they were consuming or an absence of anywhere else to go. Either way, he did not think this was a place that attracted a great many strangers.

'That's the name of the young man found injured in the back lane behind here early this morning.'

'Doesn't ring any bells with me.'

'Was there any trouble in here last night?'

'No; if there had been, I would have rung you lot.'

'Did you notice any disturbances outside?'

'Nothing.'

'What time did you close?'

'The time I'm supposed to. The last customer left about half past eleven. Sophie will tell you, we were both serving here last night until closing time.'

The barman pointed to a petite girl at the end of the bar. Jet hadn't noticed her until now. She looked up at Jet and smiled. She looked clean and fresh and out of place in these surroundings. Jet guessed her to be about twenty.

'Sophie, did you see anything out of the ordinary last night?' The barman continued to look at Jet whilst he asked the question.

'No, nothing; just the usual busy Saturday night.'

Jet looked at Sophie and smiled. 'What time did you leave last night?'

The barman responded on her behalf, 'By the time we cleared up it was about midnight before we got away, wouldn't you say Sophie?'

'Yes, about then.' She nodded and smiled.

'When you left, did you see or hear anything suspicious?'

'This is Newcastle, the party city, at midnight it's still noisy and busy. Who can say what's going on? But we didn't notice anything out of the ordinary. Sorry we can't help you.'

'Thanks for your time anyway. I'm DC Whittle from the CID; if you hear anything that might be of use to me, I'd be grateful if you'd give me a call.'

'Sure.' The response had the sound of insincerity resonating through it, and Jet made a promise to himself to pay the Barking Dog another visit the next time he was on duty on a Saturday night. If it achieved nothing more than making the licensee feel uncomfortable, then it would be worth the effort and the expense of a glass of orange juice, which was the strongest thing he touched these days when he was at work. There had been a time when he enjoyed a beer or two, but that was a thing of the past. Julia had 'detoxed' him as soon as it became the fashion and forbade him to touch beer again. Not that it was something he had ever done to excess, but she had been convinced life was going to be more fulfilling without the aid of all the calories and poison contained in beer. Only a moderate amount of red wine was now allowed for the sake of a healthy mind and body. Jet always thought the path of least resistance was the safest with all matters Julia, and since she possessed a sense of smell better than any Alsatian the police dog section employed, that added up to no more beer.

The sunlight hit Jet's eyes as he moved back into the outside world making him squint, and he instinctively raised his hand to shield his face. He walked around the drab grey building to the back lane. The smell of refuse and rotting food invaded his nostrils as he slowly walked down it. He was not sure what he was looking for as he walked the seventy yards the lane ran behind the pub before it joined the main road, but nothing obvious appeared of interest. He had not expected to find blood, as it was apparent Goodman had not bled a great deal, but he would have felt better had he been able to identify a scene for the crime he was investigating. As he walked through the lane, he looked up at the surrounding buildings, hoping to identify a flat or house where someone may have looked out during the assault and be able to give him a clue to what had happened. But the few windows he did see over the high walls looked dirty, as if they had not been cleaned or looked through for years. This was a place people had not lived in for a long time. If you were so inclined, this was a good place to commit a crime.

Jet heard a clatter behind him and turned to see a scruffy-looking man pushing a battered supermarket shopping trolley. Jet saw that one of the front wheels was rattling from side to side as it was being pushed, and he guessed the wheel had become worn and trapped with age. This did not deter the old man from pushing the trolley across the cobbled back lane. The trolley was overflowing with old carrier bags laden with empty drinks cans and bottles, which Jet assumed the old man had collected from the streets and bins. This seemed to be an activity several people in Newcastle engaged in and Jet had seen them doing this quite regularly. He had also witnessed other people blaming them for the petty crime that occurred in the city, but he had never seen any evidence to back up that allegation.

Jet moved to the side of the lane and waited for the old man to get closer. Jet was struck by the long thick hair and beard that hung wildly around his head and face, the dark matted hair had not felt shampoo for a long time. The man wore a long fawn coat which was open and flapped behind him like a cape. Jet looked at the grubby face of the stranger and realised that the man was not as old as he had first thought. The man looked determined and consumed totally by his task of pushing the trolley; he looked straight ahead and Jet was conscious that at no time had he made eye contact. Jet had seen similarly dressed people roaming the streets at all times of the day and night, looking for items to collect and knew they often kept to the same routes. It was possible this man was Jet's first witness to what had happened here at around two o'clock that morning. As the man was pushing his trolley past him, Jet spoke. 'Excuse me, I'm from the police. There was an incident here last night, and I was wondering, were you in the area?'

The man continued to look straight ahead and his reply

was loud and had the qualities of a quick burst of gunfire. 'Fuck off cunt.'

The tramp did not miss a stride, and Jet could only see his back as he spoke again. 'Well, thanks for your cooperation. If I have any more questions, I'll just call back.'

'Fuck off cunt.' This Parthian shot had the same rhythm.

'Nice chatting; see you later.'

Jet did not know whether the tramp had heard his last comment above the loud noise of the trash-laden trolley as he rushed away down the lane and turned the corner out of sight. He thought it highly likely that anyone attempting conversation with him would receive the same three-word reply which, from the tramp's mouth, seemed to enjoy the quality of a well-used phrase.

Jet spoke to himself as the tramp disappeared. 'Good to see care in the community at work.'

Jet resigned himself to the fact that the back lane, just like the licensee of the Barking Dog, was not inclined to give up its secrets, if it had any. He circled the building again and then found his car and decided the best thing he could do now was to return to the station and speak to Ray Harris, to find out whether he had any information that would help. The engine of the Ford Fiesta rumbled for a few seconds as he turned the key before bursting into life. He left Carr Street and joined the busy traffic of the city centre back towards the police station. He did not know whether Ray Harris would be in his office, but he decided not to contact him by mobile phone and just take his chances. He felt an uneasiness about the fact he found the prospect of speaking to a fellow police officer so unpleasant. There was no doubt about it in his mind, Jet was a misfit.

Chapter six

The police car drove up to the rear of the police station and came to a halt directly outside the prisoner entrance of the cell block. As it stopped, Mark Groom spoke to his prisoner. 'Sit still Jack.'

Jack complied and Groom opened the car door, got out, and then leant back inside the car and took a firm grip of Jack's arm. 'Come on.'

Jack did not need Groom's verbal encouragement and shuffled across the back seat towards the door Groom had just exited. Groom did not loosen his grip as Jack stood up and was led towards the large dark-blue door. The door stood in a recess of the building, and on the wall to the right of the door was a chrome intercom. High above the door, a small CCTV camera pointed down towards the two men as they stood. Groom pushed the intercom and there was a squeal from the speaker next to the button. A tinny, slightly amplified voice spoke out. 'Yes?'

Groom pushed the button again and this time spoke into the intercom. 'DS Groom with a prisoner.'

There was a loud buzzing noise and the door lock popped. After it did, Groom pushed the door open with the timing and ease of a man who had performed this task many times before. Groom held firmly onto the arm of his prisoner and, having pushed the door, steered Jack ahead of him so that he entered the cell complex first. Once both men were inside the building, the door clicked firmly shut behind them. The inside of the door was smooth and contained no visible locking mechanism. Groom released his grip on the prisoner, secure in the knowledge that escape, as unlikely as it had been before, was now impossible.

They stood in a narrow corridor and Groom pointed ahead of him to another door. Jack walked towards it and then through into a large open space where the main charge room was dominated by a huge desk behind which stood the custody sergeant. The windowless environment was made no more attractive by its magnolia walls and bright fluorescent strip lights, that burned, warming the atmosphere. A thick smell hung in the air: a combination of microwave food, body odour and the stench of well-used toilets. This unique aroma, having no escape route, assaulted the senses of those who had not had time to acclimatise. Mark did not notice the change of surroundings as he walked from the daylight into the detention facility.

In front of the desk stood a young man, dressed in blue jeans and a green cotton short-sleeved shirt. He swayed as he stood facing the Sergeant, Bernard Sharkie. Beside the young man was a uniformed officer, and it was apparent to Groom this officer must have just arrested the drunken young man and brought him into the custody office, ahead of him and his prisoner. Groom turned and pointed to a long wooden bench which ran almost the entire length of the wall opposite the custody desk, ten metres away from it. 'We'll have to join the queue.'

They walked to the bench and Jack perched himself nervously on it. Once he was seated, Groom also lowered himself onto the bench and leant back, his legs stretching straight out in front of him. Both men watched as Sergeant Sharkie spoke to the drunk. 'Name?'

'Fuck you.'

'That's a nice name, you don't look Japanese.' Sharkie's tone was calm, like a man used to being the subject of verbal abuse. 'How do you spell it?'

'Fuck you.' The young man swayed gently from side to side. His speech was slurred and he spoke loudly and deliberately.

'Fuck you,' Sharkie said slowly as he typed on the computer keyboard and then he looked up at the young man. 'We seem to have got a lot of Japanese in here today, I think we've got your brother in, "fook you too".' Sharkie looked through an open door behind the custody desk and shouted to a jailer in the office behind him. 'Stan!'

'What?'

'Do we have "fook you too" in cell three?'

The elderly jailer looked tired, as if repeating a well-worn act. He looked back at Sharkie. 'Cell four.'

Sharkie turned back to the drunk. '"Fook you too" in four.'

The drunk man looked confused. 'Four what?'

'For what? I ask myself that all the time. What is it all for? It's a question that has troubled philosophers for generations. What do you think, fuck you? Or as we're friends now, should I just call you "fuck"?'

'You're fucken' mental you man.'

'That may be so, but I'll be home at five o'clock. Whereas you'll be in one of our cells.'

'Fuck off man, I'm gannin to the match.'

'I fear that Newcastle United versus Blackburn Rovers will have to struggle on today without your input young man. Tell you what, I'll just type "refused to give details" on this form, and we'll put you in a cell and you can sleep it off for a while.' Sharkie turned to the jailer again. 'Stan, can you put fook you here in cell three, next to his brother?'

The weary-looking jailer constable walked around the large desk fumbling with a bunch of keys. He had selected one from the bunch by the time he had reached the drunk and, without breaking stride, took hold of his arm. 'Come on bonny lad,' the jailer said smiling. The drunk complied without any further comment and was led down the cell corridor.

Sharkie turned to the young arresting officer who had not spoken a word since Groom's arrival. 'Do you know whose car he was jumping on when you arrested him?'

'Not yet; I've got the registration number.'

'They obviously got an early start on the drink today.'

'Yeah, apparently they started at the Blacksmiths Arms at eight this morning.'

'That's what I like to see, people taking the Government's policy seriously; twenty-four hour drinking is just what this country needed. I don't know how people used to manage when pubs were only open fifteen hours a day. Do you?'

'No Sarge.'

'And football matches on a Sunday; what strides mankind has taken.'

'Yes Sarge.'

'Well if you make your enquiries, he should be sober enough to talk to in about six hours.'

'Thanks Sarge.' The young officer turned and left the room.

Once the desk was clear, Groom stood up. 'Come on Jack, our turn.'

Groom's prisoner followed him to the custody desk. 'Bernie.' Groom spoke to the custody sergeant. 'I thought Superintendent York told you not to wind the prisoners up any more after the last carry-on?'

'What carry-on?'

'You know, after that solicitor complained you told his client the Police and Criminal Evidence Act said before a prisoner could speak to a solicitor, he had to do a decent chicken impression.'

'That allegation was never substantiated.'

'We all know you had him clucking down here for ten minutes.'

'Teaching prisoners new skills is Government policy as well you know; it's all about rehabilitation.' Sharkie had on his face the broad grin of a man who enjoyed his work. He nodded towards Groom's prisoner. 'Any case, what we got here?'

'I was in Marks & Spencer buying a sandwich when I saw this man take goods from the display and place them inside his coat. He then left the store without paying.'

'Jesus wept Groomie, can't you even go out for a sandwich without collaring someone? It's no wonder your lass doesn't like taking you out shopping.'

Sharkie turned to the prisoner. 'What's your name?'

'Wagstaff, Jack Wagstaff,' was the quietly spoken reply.

'Take your coat off and put it there.' Sharkie pointed to indicate a space on the custody desk which was directly in front of the prisoner.

Wagstaff did not speak but took his coat off and laid it across the desk as instructed.

'Turn you pockets out pal. Put your stuff on there.' This time Sharkie indicated a space next to the coat. Wagstaff obeyed in silence.

Sharkie was typing details on the computer keyboard and focused on the screen in front of him, only occasionally looking at the prisoner to ensure he was complying. Wagstaff put his hands in his trouser pockets and brought out a fistful of coins which he placed on the counter.

Groom did not know why the name Jack Wagstaff

seemed vaguely familiar to him, even though he was certain he had never seen the face before. Sharkie nodded towards the large blue coat which lay on the counter. 'Check the coat pockets Groomie.'

Gently Groom put his hands in each pocket and from one pulled out a plain envelope. It was not sealed, and Mark pulled out three photographs from it and placed them on the desk. He spread the pictures with his thick fingers and, as he did so, he immediately recognised the schoolgirl who filled the full frame of the middle picture. Groom, as usual, reacted swiftly and decisively, his large hand grabbing the loose collar of his prisoner and twisting it tightly, pushed him violently against the shiny magnolia wall. 'Where the fuck did you get those from?'

Wagstaff could not speak at the same time as being choked by Groom's far more powerful figure. Sharkie moved urgently around the desk and grabbed the arm that Groom was using to prevent Wagstaff from breathing. 'What's the matter man? Stop it now Mark.' Sharkie struggled against the superior strength of Groom, 'Stop it man!'

The mist that had so quickly risen subsided slightly, and Groom released his grip as Sharkie continued with his pleas.

As soon as the two men were separated, Sharkie gently held the shoulder of the prisoner, who seemed to be recovering his breath. 'Are you all right?' Sharkie said to the prisoner.

Wagstaff nodded but did not speak.

'Come here Groomie.' Sharkie had turned his attention to Groom and, holding the sleeve of his jacket, he pulled him. Within a few seconds he had ushered him out of the main charge room and pushed him into a small interview room. 'Sit down Groomie, I'll be back in a second.' Sharkie's tone had lost all its previous flippancy. He returned to the custody desk, this time on the same side as Jack Wagstaff stood. Wagstaff looked shaken by his experience.

'Where did you get those photographs from?' Sharkie's enquiry was earnest.

'From a friend, just a friend: I'm thinking of buying his camera and he gave them to me just to see the quality. It's digital. I'm a 35 mil man myself.'

Sharkie picked up the photographs from the custody desk to see why they might have caused such a furore. Two were of a vehicle-filled residential street, and one appeared to be the same place, but occupying the centre of the picture was a schoolgirl in uniform, walking down the street. She did not appear to be posing for the photograph and simply looked like she was walking to or from school, unaware of anything else.

'Who's the girl?'

'I don't know.'

'Where were they taken?'

'Don't know; I wasn't there. I got them from this lad I know. He's selling his camera.'

'OK, let's sit you down in a cell for the moment.' Sharkie

shouted down the corridor. 'Stan!'

'Yeah?'

'Can you bag this prisoner's property? I'll put him in cell seven.'

Sharkie led the prisoner to the cell and closed the door behind him as Wagstaff sat on the wooden bench inside it.

Sharkie walked back to the desk, picked up the photos and then went into the small interview room, which Groom's huge frame dominated. Groom was sitting on one of the two chairs in the room; his elbows were on the round table and he rested his head in his hands. He lifted his head to look at Sharkie as he entered.

'Do you want to tell me what that was about?' enquired Sharkie.

'The girl in the picture is Diane, my daughter. What's a shoplifter got that on him for?'

Sharkie spread the pictures out on the small wooden table. 'Are you sure? Have a good look.'

Mark did not need another look to recognise one of the few things in his life he considered truly precious, but he looked again in any case. There could be no mistake; it was Diane. Mark's composure began to return, and he looked closely at all three photographs. He turned them over to look at the back of them and saw pencilled at the bottom of each 'G Trent'. Everything inside Mark's body went into overdrive, yet, although he could have lifted an elephant above his head, he could not talk. Sharkie looked at the

67

name. 'Where do I know that name from?'

Mark did not answer but just shook his head.

'Look, he's just a shoplifter. He says he got the photos because he's thinking of buying someone's camera. I think it's best if we just leave things for the moment. Don't you?'

Groom remained silent.

'The superintendent doesn't like us trying to strangle the prisoners in the charge office. He doesn't look injured, but if he makes a complaint there could be trouble.' Groom looked at the photographs which still lay on the table as Sharkie spoke. 'I'll get someone to sort the shoplifting thing out, and we'll ask him about the photographs. Don't panic, we'll do a good check on him; we'll find out if there's anything to worry about.'

Mark Groom had listened but used the time only to calm down and do some thinking of his own.

He nodded his head and stood up. 'Thanks Bernie, just got a shock. I'll leave it to you; let me know what you find out.'

'I don't think there's anything to worry about Mark; it's just a photo and he's just a shoplifter. Just a strange coincidence, that's all.' Sharkie gave a broad smile as he looked at the huge figure of Groom. 'Divvent worry man,' Sharkie said, almost singing the familiar, reassuring Geordie phrase.

Groom smiled at Sharkie, but he was not reassured. He knew he had been sent a message, a threat, to be taken very seriously. Not the sort of threat he could take to his senior officers. This was something that could only be sorted out by him, alone. These things he instinctively knew. What he did not know was life for Detective Sergeant Mark Groom was just about to end.

Chapter seven

Jet returned to his desk and looking at the papers he was supposed to have completed for the burglar he had in court on Wednesday, cursed his luck.

He picked up the phone on his desk, rang the number of the hospital and, after a short wait, was put through to the intensive care unit.

'ICU.' The female voice was quick and sounded efficient.

'This is DC Whittle. I'm making enquiries about a Gerald Goodman. You were waiting the result of a scan on his head, and I was wondering if you had an update?'

'Yeah, just hold the line.' After a few seconds of unexplained silence, the nurse returned. 'He's still critical and is being taken to the neurological department. The scan showed some internal bleeding to the brain and he needs to be operated on to stop it. He will come back here once it's done.'

'How serious is his condition?'

'It didn't look like a major bleed, but it needs to be resolved as soon as possible. He's in good hands, and he'll receive the best of treatment.'

'Thank you very much. When is there likely to be more news on his condition?'

'You could try ringing later on this evening; they'll have operated on him by that time.'

'Are his parents still with him?'

'Yes, they're bearing up well. They know he is young and in good hands.'

Jet thanked the nurse and put down the phone. He thought for a while about contacting Groom and telling him what the hospital had said, but recalling his remark about the first team being called in when the reserves couldn't cope, he thought better of it. Jet was happier conducting enquiries on his own at the moment, and in any case couldn't think what anyone else could do to help.

Although he did not feel like speaking to Ray Harris, Jet thought he should go and see whether he was in the building and find out what he knew about Goodman and any associates. Jet believed Harris had assumed the role of sidekick to Groom – Robin to his Batman, and as such had taken on a lot of Groom's less pleasant attributes. When the two of them were together, they oozed a mutual smugness he could barely stomach. Jet hoped that Groom might be somewhere else, so he could be spared the joint ribbing the visit to their office was bound to provoke. Nevertheless, he made his way to the next floor up in the building and, to his slight relief, saw the figure of Ray Harris sitting on his own, writing in a notebook. Harris was a tall and slim man who looked in his early thirties. He wore a light-blue, open-necked shirt, which exposed more deeply-tanned skin than

Jet thought necessary. Harris's hair was swept neatly back, and he looked immaculately groomed. The gel on his hair gave it a wet appearance, holding each strand in its correct place and looked like the result of considerable time and effort. Harris's dark-brown leather jacket hung on the back of the chair he was sitting on. Jet could not help but think that Harris would not have been out of place in an old episode of *Miami Vice*, and wasn't sure whether his efforts to look unlike a police officer had in fact been counterproductive. Jet had been around the bars and clubs of Newcastle long enough to know this type of fastidious appearance was shared mainly by the criminals and undercover cops. The irony being, that as all the criminals knew each other, it was not hard for them to work out who the cops were. Jet sometimes wondered whether people like Harris actually worked to reduce crime or to live out some sort of strange lifestyle they had fantasised about. Perhaps Harris as a child had been brought up on programmes like *Miami Vice* and was now living out his childhood imaginings. It all seemed a little odd to Jet.

On seeing Jet enter the office, Harris stopped writing and closed the cover of his book and placed it in the desk drawer to his right-hand side.

'Ray, did Mark Groom speak to you about a job I'm dealing with today: a man called Gerald Goodman?'

'He mentioned something about it earlier; said he's had a slapping outside a bar or something.'

'Bit more than a slapping; he's in intensive care. They're

taking him into surgery this afternoon.'

'I wouldn't worry about it Jet; if he's a criminal he'll recover. It's the innocent people who don't.'

'Suppose so. You locked him up a few months ago with three other people; I was wondering if you had any information that might help? I can't find out who he was knocking about with or where he was staying. I checked his records and he gave his parent's address when he was arrested, but it's clear that he hasn't lived there for well over six months.'

'Not much to tell you Jet. He was arrested when we raided the Wooden Doll with a drugs warrant. He's a small-time drug pusher as far as I remember. Had a small amount of cocaine on him, I don't think there was even enough to charge him with more than possession. Small fish Jet, barely worth throwing back.'

'What about the people he was arrested with?'

More small-time dealers, nothing exciting.'

'Were they working together?'

'Not that I recall; can't remember who they were now but I think they were all just little independent dealers, selling bits to the pond life in the pub when we got there. The main dealer we were after wasn't there when we did the raid. I think we just missed him. The ones we arrested were just mugs who were in the wrong place at the wrong time.'

'Did they have anything interesting to say to you after they'd been arrested?'

Apparently realising that the question Jet was really

asking was whether they had given any information about other drug dealers, Harris laughed in a tone Jet thought was meant to be patronising. Jet had dealt with enough drug dealers to know they were not honourable characters and people like Harris exploited that trait. For a little bit of cash, they would grass up their own mothers. It all seemed far too seedy to Jet, as well as self-defeating. Giving sums of money to people who were more than likely going to spend it on buying more drugs or, at the very best, paying off their fines. It just didn't seem right and, in Jet's problem-solving-orientated thought process, just plain illogical. After Harris had completed his short, hollow laugh, he replied to Jet's question. 'They didn't interest me in the slightest. I charged them all with possession, and I haven't seen them since. It was a waste of my time and a good warrant. Not even sure if they've been dealt with by the court yet.'

'Goodman has: he got a conditional discharge. Don't know what happened to the others; can you remember their names?'

'No chance Jet. The custody office will have all of the details, but I'm telling you they'll be of little use to you: all insignificant low life. Don't think they'll be of any use to you at all.'

'Thanks for your help; it's always worth checking up on these things.'

'No problem Jet, always pleased to be of assistance to one of my colleagues.'

Jet left and made his way down to his own office. The encounter had not raised Jet's opinion of Harris and had taken him no further forward.

Back at his desk, Jet entered his password into the computer terminal, typed in the name 'Gerald Goodman' and waited for his record to come onto the screen. He looked at the date of his last arrest and then retrieved the list of people he had been arrested with. A check of their records confirmed the assessment of Harris: another three small fish.

Jet sat forward in his chair, his right elbow resting on his desk as his right hand stroked his chin in deep thought. His concentration was interrupted by the loud ring of the office phone. The line being shared by a number of extensions meant a chorus of phones was activated in the office by one single incoming call. It was an unattractive howling which cried to be put out of its misery at the earliest opportunity. Jet lifted the phone receiver on his desk, silencing the noise, and spoke his name into the mouthpiece.

'Are you the policeman who was at the Barking Dog today?' The voice sounded soft, more a girl's than a woman's.

'Yes, who's this?'

'Never mind, I just wanted you to know that what happened to Gerry was wrong. They came in the pub and got him outside and just kept on hitting him and kicking him; he never had a chance.'

'Who took him out of the pub?'

'I don't know them all, but John Metcalf was the leader. He was like a mad dog, out of his mind on something; dragged Gerry out into the back lane. It was terrible.'

'What time was this?'

'About two this morning.'

'Were there many people in the pub at that time?'

'About the same number of people that's normally in for a lock-in on a Saturday night: about twenty.'

'What was the fight about?'

'Don't know; but they were going ballistic, screaming and shouting.'

'Sophie, is that you?'

The line went dead, and Jet immediately regretted asking the question as early as he had. During the brief conversation, he had picked up a pen from a holder on his desk and scribbled the name 'John Metcalf' on a piece of notepaper. He looked at the name, which for some reason seemed familiar, and searched his memory, looking for the reason why that should be. As he did his eyes glanced at the computer screen in front of him. The names of the three people arrested at the Wooden Doll still remained on it. He cursed his own stupidity when he realised that the middle name on the list was John Metcalf.

Without realising it he whispered to himself under his breath, 'Well what do you know Jet, things are looking up.'

Chapter eight

'Eddie, do me a favour and sort me a permit for a visit to Geoffrey Trent in Durham nick; he's on remand there awaiting trial. The boss wants me to see him today as a matter of urgency. Something has cropped up about the drug-dealing job we nicked him for. I need to see him.'

Mark Groom was in the small office on the ground floor of the police station which constituted the local intelligence officer's working space. He spoke to the middle-aged man who was sitting behind the small desk surrounded by bundles of documents that were, without exception, enclosed in green file covers. Every one of the files was stamped in bold type with the word 'confidential'.

'I thought you had him charged with a watertight case. When you arrested him he had two kilos of cocaine and a sawn-off shotgun. Sweet job that Mark, but I would have thought the last person he would want to speak to in prison would be the man who's putting him away for a long stretch.'

'I know, but the boss wants me just to talk to him, to clear up a couple of matters, I just need to see his reaction when we put a few other names to him, possible accomplices; we still haven't got the people he was dealing with.'

'Wouldn't have thought he'd be dealing with anyone else; I thought he'd just employ some low life to do the running around for him. You don't think he could lead you to the main dealer in the North East do you?'

'What do you mean?'

'You know as well as I do that all of the intelligence we've got points to the bulk of the drugs coming into the North being arranged by one organisation. You don't think Trent could lead you to the people behind that do you?'

This question did not provoke any response from Groom, but this did not prevent the questioner from pursuing the thought further and continuing with his own line of enquiry. 'You don't think that Trent is our mysterious "Mr Big" of the drugs business do you?'

'I don't know that Eddie, but what I do know is I'm never going to find out by standing here talking to you. Now for fuck's sake get me the pass into the prison to see Trent.'

Groom's comment, coupled with the cold stare of his ocean-blue eyes, was sufficient to stop Eddie's interrogation in its tracks. He had been the local intelligence officer at the station for enough years to know it was not wise to annoy Mark Groom.

'Mark, keep your hair on. I'll sort it out; give me ten minutes.'

'Thanks Eddie; I'll be back in ten minutes.'

Groom looked at his watch and saw it was now one

thirty. He left the office without any clear destination in mind and found himself nervously pacing the corridor, before walking out of the front door of the police station.

He took his mobile phone out of his jacket pocket, scrolled through the list of numbers and stopping at the name 'Shirl' he pressed the dial button.

'Hello?'

'Shirl, it's Mark.'

'Checking up to see if I've spent any more of your money?'

'I said we'd talk about that tonight. Where's Diane?'

'She's upstairs with one of her friends. Why?'

'It's nothing. One of the lads here had an anonymous threat that someone was going to put his house windows out and I was just being cautious, making sure that you and Diane are OK.'

'We're fine.'

'You haven't noticed anyone strange knocking about? Has Diane said anything?'

'No. You're worrying me. What's the matter?'

'Nothing to worry about. I'm just being overcautious.'

'If someone throws a brick through the window, I'll let you know.'

'Yeah, thanks, I'm sure it's nothing to worry about – just checking. I'll see you tonight. Bye Shirl.'

'Bye.'

Groom pressed the 'end call' button on his phone and

put it back in his pocket. He looked at his watch again and decided to go back and see Eddie.

By the time he walked back into Eddie's office, the minute hand of Mark's watch was not quite touching the eight. 'Got that permit sorted Eddie?'

'I rang the prison and they're expecting you. I've done the form for your visit.' Eddie handed Groom an envelope in which the standard letter was contained. 'Just show this with your warrant card, and that'll get you in to see him.'

'Thanks Eddie.'

Groom folded the envelope, put it in his trouser pocket and left the office. He walked to his two-seater Mazda sports car, and within a few seconds he was driving towards Durham Prison. He raced through the gears of his car, determined to make a thirty-minute journey last no more than twenty-five. He succeeded and pulled into the car park outside the prison. As he closed the driver's door behind him, he looked at the huge brick walls and could see that for good measure the tops were fortified with spirals of barbed wire.

At the reception desk, Mark explained the appointment that had been made for him with Geoffrey Trent. After the letter Eddie had prepared and his warrant card were examined, he was asked to wait for a few seconds. Two minutes later, a uniformed warden approached him. 'You the policeman got an appointment with an inmate?'

'Yeah.' Mark produced his warrant card which the warden briefly glanced at.

'OK, follow me.'

The warden removed from his pocket a bunch of keys, which was attached by a long chain to the belt of his trousers. With a swift motion, he opened the lock of a heavy door, and they walked down another long, narrow corridor. The corridor was lit by strip lights sunken into the ceiling and, being narrow and windowless, it had a claustrophobic feel about it. Groom followed the warden through a door leading to a large waiting area, which he assumed was used as a gathering area for relatives of inmates.

'We need to go through the metal detector; it's procedure I'm afraid.'

'No problem.' Groom replied.

'Can you turn your pockets out, and put the contents in this container?'

The exercise reminded Groom of his recent holiday to Ibiza, when he stood in the airport queue with Diane and Shirley, listening to his wife's constant complaints about long waits and inefficient service. Groom placed the coins from his pockets and his warrant card in the small plastic container.

'Will I need to take my belt off?' Mark indicated to the large, silver buckle, of the belt that circled the top of his black denim trousers.

'Would be best.'

Mark complied and then walked through the doorway of the large metal detector. It did not make a sound as he did so.

'Thanks; you can have these back.'

The warden pushed the plastic container along the counter beside the metal detector, and Groom put the coins back into his pocket and replaced his belt.

'This way,' the warden said to Groom and, without any further comment, he led him through three more locked doors. Groom felt he was getting close to the heart of the prison.

'You been a policeman long?'

'Eighteen years or so; feels longer.'

'Know what you mean.' The warden did not look at Groom when he spoke, but looked straight ahead down the corridor. 'I tried to join myself.'

'Really?'

'Yeah but I failed the medical. Joined this job instead.'

'Looks an interesting job.'

'Yeah it's all right, but I really wanted to join the force after my old man was killed.'

'Killed?'

'He'd always carried a photo of my mum around with him; she'd given him it, when he went off to fight in the war. When some thief nicked it, he gave chase, and poor old soul had a heart attack.'

'Tragic.'

'Yeah, they never found out who stole it but if I found out…'

'Not fair is it?'

'You can say that again; he was just an old man playing bowls in a park.'

The warden turned the door handle of a plain door and, opening it, said to Groom, 'Just in here.'

Groom could see two chairs and a table in an otherwise empty small room. He walked in and sat in the chair on the opposite side of the table to the door. The warden closed the door and left Mark watching the back of it in the silence of the room.

Mark continued watching the door. His arms were crossed, and his right hand gently stroked the scar on his left elbow. It was an unconscious act.

After a five-minute wait, which to Groom felt like an hour, the room door opened, and the small figure of Geoffrey Trent was almost pushed in by a warden who was not, to Mark's surprise, the same person that had shown him in. This warden was not wearing the same dark-blue sweater as the previous one but had on a white shirt so bright it was dazzling. Like most people, the warden dwarfed Trent. Trent was ushered to the vacant chair and sat on it. The warden spoke to Mark. 'How long do you need?'

'Not long, thanks.'

At that the warden turned around and, leaving the room, said, 'I'll not be far. Just ring the buzzer when you finish.' He nodded towards a red button on the wall next to the door.

Trent looked wearily at Mark. 'A bent copper. Standards

must have dropped: they'll let anyone in here now.'

'Good to see you too. Are they treating you well?'

'What's it to you?'

'No need to be like that Geoffrey. I've gone to a lot of trouble to come and see you.'

'Only my mother calls me Geoffrey, and you aren't her. What do you want?'

'Nice lady your mother. I was talking to her the other day at home; you should remember that I know where she lives. I like to keep in touch.'

'Very considerate. If she needs the drains unblocking whilst I'm in here, I'm sure she'll give you a call.'

'I ran into a friend of yours today, Jack Wagstaff. He had some photographs belonging to you.'

'Never heard of him. Now why don't you just fuck off?'

'Don't you want to tell me about the photographs you sent me?'

'What photos?'

'The ones you had delivered to me.'

'Now why would I send you photos?'

'That's why I came to see you, to ask you in person.'

Trent looked at Groom and smiled, oozing a confident smugness Groom thought designed solely to irritate him. Trent leaned back in the chair he was sitting on, making the front two legs rise from the ground as he slowly extended his legs.

'They weren't the photos of your lass and the pit pony

shagging were they? You can have them; never was one for cruelty to animals myself. Poor animal spends all its life in darkness, and as soon as it gets in the fresh air, some old boiler takes advantage of it being blind.'

Groom's body became rigid as he lifted himself slightly in his wooden chair, but he managed to control the anger that was rising like a piston inside him.

'You know what I'm talking about you little weasel! You've gone to a lot of trouble to send me a photograph of my daughter. Did you really think, in that perverted mind of yours, you could frighten me off just like that?'

Fear was one of the many emotions that Trent had difficulty experiencing, and, in his prison environment, even the large angry figure of Mark Groom could not shake his confidence. His mother had often told him it would be his undoing. He smiled and continued to lean back in his chair.

'Groom, you seem upset about something. Having trouble at home? Don't tell me that your daughter's turning out to be as ugly as your lass? Most parents like to have photographs of their kids, even if they have a face like a bag of hammers. Look at the bright side: at least you're not going to have to worry about the boys trying to shag her.'

The piston rose inside Groom again, and this time it was beyond his control. He jumped up and pushed the table over on its side, then swiftly put his huge hands around Trent's slim throat. Trent was taken totally by surprise and did not react as Groom lunged towards him. Groom's powerful arms locked Trent against the wall. It was no match. Groom looked at Trent's startled face and watched as he squeezed the life out of it. Trent's arms thrashed in frenzy, but without purpose, and even this effort quickly relented. Groom felt relief, almost joy, as the shocked face stared at him helplessly. He had absolute power now over the person who had been so irreverent just seconds before, and he was not going to resign this power until he had neutralised the threat Trent presented to him.

'Not so cocky now,' Mark whispered to the now deep-crimson face. Trent could not make a sound and spent the final conscious moments of his life experiencing fear for the first time.

Chapter nine

Jet stood up from his desk and picked up his jacket. He had read what little information the police computer had on John Metcalf and thought that, although he didn't have enough evidence to arrest him, a little chat couldn't hurt. Who knows, he may even get lucky. Experience had taught him that people sometimes do the strangest things, and even if Metcalf did not want to tell him what he had been doing at two o'clock this morning, there may be other things to be learned. Jet liked to see the whites of their eyes: he could learn a lot from people's reactions.

He looked at his watch, saw that it was almost four o'clock in the afternoon and wondered where the day had gone. He walked to the car park and ten minutes later was driving in Newcastle's West End. Jet saw the sign for Rochester Road and turned his car into it, following the even numbers on the right-hand side of the terraced street, until he found number twenty-six, then parked. The terrace was constructed of dark-red brick, which looked soiled with the stains of years of urban pollution. The dirty white paint flaking from the window frames added to the air of neglect. The street may have seen better days, but as Jet surveyed the harsh environment, he thought they had long been forgotten. The number of doors lent weight to Jet's assumption that most of the houses had been converted into flats, and he soon found the door with the number he was looking for. Jet pushed the doorbell but did not hear any sound and, on closer inspection, drew the conclusion that it had not worked for years. He knocked hard on the door and then stepped back to see whether there was any life evident at the window. A moment passed and nothing happened. After another knock there was again nothing. Jet opened the letter box and looked in. An interior door stood ajar which appeared to lead to a passage in a ground floor flat. He moved closer to the door and shouted through the letter box, 'Jonny, Jonny open the door mate it's me, Geordie. Howay man, I need to see you about something. Jonny, Jonny are you in there man?'

Jet heard the inside door move as it rustled against some discarded newspapers lying on the hallway floor. The front door opened a few inches and a bleary face appeared in the small gap.

'Who's that?'

Jet placed his foot on the bottom of the door to prevent it from being shut.

'John Metcalf, I would just like a few words with you. I'm DC Whittle from the CID.'

'What?'

'Just need to ask you a few questions. It's all right if I come in isn't it?' Jet was gently pushing the door as he spoke. Metcalf still seemed groggy, as if he had just woken from a deep sleep, and did not resist. Jet moved into the hallway and then Metcalf turned and walked through the internal door which led to the main room of the flat. Jet followed, and he could see that inside was as untidy and as grubby as outside. The curtains were closed, which made the room gloomy, but the thinness of the material meant that everything was still clearly visible.

'What do you want?' Metcalf repeated his question. He wore tracksuit bottoms, which were pulled high up his leg, revealing most of his calves and all of his bare feet. His checked shirt was unbuttoned, and it looked as if he had just pulled it on.

'Do you know a man called Gerald Goodman?'

'No, why?'

'He was assaulted last night and I was wondering if you knew anything about it.'

'Why should I?'

'Where were you last night?'

'Out with some of me mates for a drink.'

'Which mates? Who are they?'

'Don't remember: just a few of them I met round the town. Had a heavy night, don't remember much about it.'

'Are you still dealing in drugs?'

'What you talking about?'

'You were arrested for dealing drugs with Gerald Goodman two months ago at the Wooden Doll. Don't you remember that either?'

'Told you, don't know anyone called Gerald Goodman. I was arrested and I've been at court for that; don't know about anyone else. I've done nowt wrong.'

'Is that right? Are you sure about that? A couple of minutes ago you were telling me that you couldn't remember what you did last night. How do you know you haven't done anything wrong?'

'Just had a drink with me mates and come home, that's all.'

Metcalf was fully awake now, and Jet thought he appeared a little more confident. Jet's eyes circled the room, and he found it difficult to see beyond the mess it contained. Papers, pizza boxes, socks and assorted clothes were amongst the many items that lay in a disorderly fashion over the elderly sofa and the worn nylon carpet.

'Do you play baseball?'

'No.'

'So you don't have a baseball bat?'

'No.'

'Where are the clothes you had on last night?'

'Don't remember what I had on.'

'Let's have a look and see what's in your bedroom.'

'Don't you need a warrant for this shit?'

'Not for you. You said you didn't do anything; why would I need a warrant? Not feeling a bit guilty there are you? Do you want to tell me something?'

'I've done nowt.'

'Good lad; is this the room?'

Jet pushed open the only other door in the room and found it led to a small hallway which contained two other doors. He walked the short distance to the first door, pushed it open and realised by sight and smell that it was a small and bare bathroom. After a cursory look, he walked to the second door, pushed it and saw a small, unmade bed, the covers strewn half on the bed and half on the floor. A small pile of clothes lay on a wooden chair. He lifted the items on the pile hoping he might find a bloodstain but could not see anything of interest. Beside the bed was a pair of black training shoes.

'These look like your best shoes.'

'Aye, what of it?'

'Did you have them on last night?'

'Don't remember.'

'You won't mind if I borrow them for a bit will you?'

'What do you want me shoes for?'

'Just to check them and corroborate what you told me: that you had nothing to do with the assault that happened last night.'

'Fuck off. You can't have me shoes!'

'Just for a while; I'll get them straight back to you.'

'What am I going to wear? They're the only pair I've got.'

'You said a minute ago you couldn't remember if you had them on last night or not. How could that be if these are your only ones?'

'Me others are a bit knackered, that's all.'

'It's within your interests to get this sorted. I'm sure you'll manage for a couple of days, while I sort this out for you.'

Jet held both shoes away from Metcalf and smiled a big false smile at him. He walked out of the bedroom and back into the untidy living room.

'Where is the last place you remember being last night?'

'The Bigg Market with me mates.'

'Did you go to the Barking Dog last night?'

'No. Just went around some of the pubs in the Bigg Market. Don't remember much about it.'

'OK John, that's all for now. I'll pop back and see you soon, to give you your shoes back.'

Jet swiftly left and closed the door behind him, leaving a stunned Metcalf standing in the hallway of his flat, trying to collect his thoughts.

Jet went to the boot of his car, opened out a clean plastic bag and carefully placed one of the shoes in it and then did the same with the second shoe. He looked at the window of the flat and saw the edge of the curtain being pulled inwards as Metcalf looked out into the street at him. Jet waved and then got into his car and drove off.

Jet parked his Ford Fiesta in the yard of the police station, went to the boot of his car and removed Metcalf's shoes. By the time he was at his desk, it was five o'clock. To send the shoes for forensic examination, he needed to fill in two lengthy forms, and his heart sank as he looked at the blank documents in front of him. There seemed to him to be a lot of unnecessary detail required just to get the shoes examined, to see whether there were any signs of blood or fibres belonging to Gerald Goodman on them, but he knew he had no choice. He also knew it would be more than worth the effort if there were traces on the shoes, as he would have something serious to talk to Metcalf about. He remembered the days when he would have just arrested him, taken him to the station and left him overnight in a cell to be spoken to the next day. This used to give criminals time to think and loosened their tongues. These days, prisoners were told their rights and given the services of a solicitor straight away and free of charge. Solicitors invariably told their clients to say nothing and demanded to have all of the evidence disclosed to them before they would consider anything else. Once the evidence was known to them they worked out a story with their clients to suit their needs. The rules had changed, and Jet had amended his tactics to do the best he could, but it was getting harder and harder. When he saw criminals walking away scot-free, he found that very hard to stomach.

It was close to six o'clock by the time Jet got the paperwork finished for the day and the shoes submitted for examination. He quickly left the office, knowing he needed to call into the hospital on his way home, to tell Mr and Mrs Goodman he was still trying to find out what had happened to their son, and to make arrangements to speak to them again the following day. As he walked across the police station car park his mobile phone sang its tune again, and he saw Julia's name flash on its screen.

'Hello Ju.'

'Have you called in and got the wine for tonight?'

'No not yet, but I will soon,'

'Shit!' was the thought that occurred to him, as he was reminded he had an evening of Julia's sister and her husband to look forward to. The last thing he really wanted to do tonight was listen to more talk from Heather and her precious husband Craig about how they were living the high life: upwardly mobile with plans for another holiday no doubt. It sometimes left Julia in an odd mood. He preferred the days when he went home to fish fingers and they pissed themselves laughing as Jet told her about his latest attempts to fight for truth, justice and the Newcastle way.

'They'll be here soon. Please don't be late.'

'Almost home love – be about thirty minutes.'

Julia had heard that sort of optimistic estimate before.

'Don't let me down Frank.' The line went dead. '*Frank*' Jet thought; I am in the shit!

Chapter ten

'Is it raining out there?'

Jet had not expected the enquiry from Jean the cleaner, as he walked up the first-floor stairs of the police station, even though he knew she did have a habit of breaking into sudden conversation.

'No, it looks like it's going to stay dry.'

'Thank Gawd for that,' she said. As she spoke she continued to rub the metal stair rail for a reason Jet could not fathom. Her large blue overall covered red trousers and a tee shirt that were the uniform of her trade.

'Did you leave the washing out?'

'Nah, Billy's cutting the bloody hedge doon; daft bugger cut the electric cord last time. Divvent want it raining cos he'll be up in a blue flash in nee time, daft bugger.'

'Well, it looks dry enough.'

'Thank Gawd. It's not even our bloody hedge-trimmer, daft bugger. I said stop off the ladder, but he'll be up the ladder now, daft bugger.'

Jet continued to walk up the stairs, and Jean remained where she was, continuing to rub the rail. As he walked away from the stair landing, Jet wondered how many other weather reports she would solicit as people arrived for work.

It was eight fifteen on Monday morning by the time Jet sat at his desk. He always came in early on weekdays to enable himself to get sorted out, and be at his desk while the rest of the office sprung to life around him. It meant he didn't have to become entangled with rituals of tea making, gossip and accounts of out of work activity. It was the kind of detachment he preferred. It was especially comforting today because he had not had a weekend that he wanted to relive in any detail. Particularly last night. Mrs Goodman had taken a lot of time to reassure at the hospital, and by the time he had got home Heather and Craig were already there having brought the guest of honour, Julia's mother, with them. His late arrival had not been well received by Julia at all. Then the evening consisted almost entirely of listening to Craig's stories of their house-hunting exploits, in search of a second property in the country, which they were intending to let to others and occasionally holiday in themselves. This was punctuated by detailed descriptions of their new car.

'How much detail does a person need to know about the engine of their car for Christ's sake?' Jet had later asked Julia, as they were getting ready to go to bed, but she was not of the same mind. In truth, Jet thought, the worst of the evening had been Julia's incessant nodding and admiration at every painstaking detail. Her squeals of appreciation were equal in measure to her looks of disappointment at Jet and his lack of earthly possessions. When they had finally gone Julia had accused him of being rude because he had been quiet for most of the night.

'I'm just tired; I've been at work all day,' he'd protested.

'Looked like sour grapes to me,' she'd replied. 'You even took the mick out of his number plate.'

'It was just a joke.'

'Craig spent a fortune getting plates with his name on.'

'Well it's ridiculous: all that money to have half his name on his car.'

'And then telling them that you'd changed your name by deed poll to "R425XTN". You knew they wouldn't think it was funny.'

'Not my fault he doesn't have a sense of humour.'

'It wasn't funny.'

'It was a joke.'

'It was rude.'

The atmosphere had remained cool, and Jet's attempt to thaw it had not worked. He'd just put out the bedside light, and as he lay next to her he spoke quietly, '435.'

'What?'

'The car.'

'What?'

'You said R425XTN. It's 435.'

'Does it really matter? It's a heap of junk anyway. Go to sleep.'

They had not spoken much when they got up this morning, and he wondered whether he would get a frosty reception tonight.

As soon as he sat at his desk Jet picked up the phone and dialled the number of the intensive care unit. It was answered with the usual brief introduction.

'Hello, I'm DC Whittle. I'm ringing to get an update on Gerald Goodman.'

'He's had a comfortable night.'

'Any sign of him regaining consciousness?'

'There's no change in his condition.'

'Are his parents still with him?'

'They've never left his bedside all night.'

'Could you tell them I rang and I'll be in touch with them later today?'

'I'll let them know.'

'Thanks.'

As he replaced the telephone, he opened the top drawer of his desk and lifted a file from it. He decided the next few hours were going to be dedicated to getting the paperwork completed for the burglar he had in court the day after tomorrow. Opening the file, he spread the papers in front of him and tried to recall where he had been when he last left it. The fog in his mind was just clearing, when his concentration was diverted by someone shouting there was a telephone call for him. He picked up the receiver on the desk phone. 'Hello? DC Whittle.'

'Superintendent York here Whittle; come up to see me straight away please.' The phone was hung up before Jet had uttered 'yes' and he made his way straight to the third floor. On his way up, Jet searched his memory banks for a legitimate reason for this request – this mainly revolved around wondering why he might be in trouble, but nothing obvious came to mind. It did not seem likely that Metcalf would already have made a complaint about him taking his shoes yesterday, and even if he had, a personal visit to see Superintendent York seemed a little too severe.

Jet knocked on the door and quickly found himself following an instruction to sit down. The first thing he noticed was the large black swivel chair York was sitting on behind his desk. Standing quietly behind the superintendent's leather throne, was a figure Jet recognised as Detective Chief Inspector Anderson. This made him feel even more anxious about this unexpected meeting.

Jet also could not help noticing the superintendent's desk was much bigger and newer than his own, and a lot tidier! He wondered whether someone else was employed to do his paperwork.

'Whittle, when was the last time you spoke to Mark Groom?'

'Yesterday morning sometime: he gave me an assault to look at.'

'How do you get on with him?' This question seemed even odder than the first to Jet and he was feeling a little confused.

'All right. Like me, he's been here a long time.'

'Are you close?'

'No, just work colleagues.' Jet hesitated. 'Can I ask what this is about?'

York's eyes had been fixed on a document in front of him on his desk, but now he lifted his head and stared directly at Jet. He did not look too pleased at the enquiry. He was silent for a second, as if his train of thought had been interrupted, and then spoke. 'Groom was arrested for murder yesterday afternoon in Durham Prison.' York was silent again, as if allowing time for the news to sink in, and perhaps looking at what reaction it might produce. Jet stared at York and said nothing. After a few seconds, York continued, 'Do you know a Geoffrey Trent?'

'Most of us that have been here for any time know him. A prolific criminal, petty mostly, until a little while ago when the drug squad nicked him for major dealing. He must have shifted up a league or two. He's been a pain for a long time.'

'Not any more he isn't. Groom killed him yesterday. Did Groom tell you why he was going to see him?'

'There's no reason why he'd tell me anything.' There was another pause and this time it was Jet who spoke. 'What's this got to do with me?'

York held Jet in an icy stare for a few seconds then spoke. 'Groom has asked to see you.'

'Me? Why?'

'I was hoping you might tell us.'

'Haven't a clue.'

There was another silence as York's eyes remained fixed on Jet, then he spoke. 'We want you to go and speak to Groom.'

Jet had not expected this and it made his mind whirl. He wondered why they would want him to go and speak to Groom and whether there was some catch he needed to look out for.

'Are Durham Constabulary investigating this murder?'

'Of course.' Jet could see the impertinence of the question had touched a nerve with York. 'It happened in Durham, who else would be dealing with it?'

'Do the investigators at Durham want me to speak to Groom?'

'They've no objections. It's pretty straightforward. Groom was the only person in the room when Trent was murdered; there's no doubt about who did it. He'll be charged with murder this afternoon.' There was another silence and the superintendent looked at Jet and then, for the first time, there was a trace of a smile on his face. 'Look Whittle, I can see it's a lot to take in. Have a think about it and come back in an hour, and let us know what you think.'

'OK.' Jet got up and walked towards the door, and as he did so York spoke again. 'It goes without saying that this is strictly confidential. You must not say a word about this to anyone.'

'Without saying.' Jet left the office and closed the door behind him, leaving York looking slightly confused.

Jet's body was on automatic pilot, and he found himself back at his desk with his mind racing. This had not been the start he had expected to his Monday.

He had known that he was going to agree to see Groom as soon as the question had been asked of him but was pleased he had not volunteered this immediately, as he needed to collect his thoughts. It was not at all clear to him why Groom would want to see him, and it seemed strange that York would be so interested in him going. He looked at the case papers on his desk and felt the urgency of Wednesday's court hearing had waned. He had fifty minutes to do some thinking, and the first decision he made was to take a walk outside so he would not be interrupted.

As he stepped out into the street, the freshness of the air struck him, and the bright sunlight was a welcome change from the lack of elements in the cellular office. He walked onto Northumberland Street and, not for the first time, marvelled at the large number of people who were also walking along it. Conforming to the unwritten convention of the city centre, he walked in zigzags, to avoid the occasional strutting scavenging pigeon and oncoming walkers, consciously never making eye contact. He walked through the Haymarket and passed people of all descriptions forming careless queues at the many stops in the bus station. He continued with his stroll and turned left towards Old Eldon Square. There, on the grass surrounding the war memorial, he saw small groups of people who looked like students, enjoying each other's company and the sun's friendly efforts to warm them. A little further on he found himself at the foot of Grey's Monument. The tall stone structure towered over its surroundings – a tribute to the politician Charles Spenser Grey who had lived well over a hundred years ago, and whose name was associated with some of the grand buildings in the city. These buildings still stood proudly, embarrassing those more recently constructed, which Jet thought resembled delinquent children: dressed in drab colours, unloved, some even looking unplanned. It seemed a strange sign of the city's progress that the Monument was now known as the place where the winos met. He stood for a while unnoticed by those who walked past him, as well as the two winos who shared a bottle of cider and a hostile-looking bench. In the tidy part of his mind he reviewed the facts as he knew them and the possible conclusions this led him to. He then found himself occupying the untidy part of his mind and thought of Geoffrey Trent's mother, who he had met many times. He knew only too well that she doted on her sole offspring. He also thought of Groom's wife and the daughter he knew they had.

Thirty minutes later, Jet found himself knocking on Superintendent York's office door for the second time that day. On command, he walked in and then spoke first. 'When do you want me to go and see Mark Groom?'

'He is keen to see you as soon as possible.' York's tone

had changed: it was gentle, and Jet thought he could almost detect a trace of compassion.

'OK. I'll go now.'

'Thank you Frank.' It came as no surprise to Jet that York knew his first name, but he was surprised he had chosen to use it. Julia was the only person who called him Frank these days, and when she did it usually meant he was in trouble. He wondered whether the same rules applied here.

York continued, 'I've made arrangements for you to call into the technical unit first. I think you need to be protected. They're going to fit you with a covert recording device. Once you've had the meeting, come straight back here, and I'll take the tape from you. Don't talk to anyone else about this.'

Jet was taken aback by York's words but tried not to betray this through his expression. He found it hard to believe that a secret recording was motivated by the desire to protect him. After a few seconds of thought he decided not to object to wearing a wire, as he did not feel there was anything he was going to say or do that needed to be kept secret from York. He was not confident York was sharing his secrets, if he had any, but he thought that no reason to be difficult now.

'OK.'

'DCI Anderson will meet you at the technical unit in twenty minutes. Just listen to what Groom has to say, that's all you need to do and we'll work out what needs to be done after that.'

Jet walked out of the office. Before he went to the technical unit, he decided to make one call of his own. He would have to be quick.

Chapter eleven

Jet rushed into the technical unit which was a separate building at the back of the police station, isolated in a way befitting the secrecy of its operation. Jet thought DCI Anderson cut a grim figure when he saw him waiting inside, and his expression remained unaltered as he ushered Jet briskly into a small office. The tall technician inside the office remained expressionless and uttered few words, other than the occasional 'lift your arm' as he fitted the small tape recorder and a minute microphone to Jet. The microphone was threaded through his shirt into the back of his tie, and the small recording device was fastened to his leg and concealed above his ankle under his trousers. The whole experience seemed to happen very quickly, and Jet complied without any great thought. Even when he was asked to loosen his trousers, so the wire could be concealed down his leg, he dutifully obeyed. In truth, his mind was elsewhere. He was given brief instructions on how to operate this spying equipment and confirmed, when asked to do so, that he understood what he needed to do, to turn the tape on and off. He was insulted by the question, but did not share this emotion with the company present.

Jet left the building with Anderson and felt uncomfortable

when he followed the instruction to get into the front seat of Anderson's car. It was a BMW which was several years old, but unlike Jet's Fiesta, very clean and cared for more than Jet thought strictly necessary for a machine required simply to get you from A to B. Jet sat up still and straight in the black leather seat and, after pulling the seat belt over him, he placed his hands carefully on his knees to avoid the chance of contact with any of the buttons on the dashboard.

Anderson started the engine, and Jet was struck by how quiet and smooth it sounded, compared to the din he was used to from his own car. Within a few minutes they were on Newcastle's central motorway and heading towards the A1, which would take them to Durham.

Anderson seemed totally consumed by the task of driving and indifferent to Jet's presence. Jet decided to break the uncomfortable silence. 'Last thing I'd have imagined doing today was being driven to Durham by a detective chief inspector.'

'Suppose.' Anderson remained fixed on the road ahead.

'Strange Mark would have asked for me.'

'Strange all right.'

Jet waited a few seconds expecting Anderson to add to his reply, but it became evident that there was no more to come. Silence then dominated and Jet felt relieved when they pulled into the car park of Durham Police Station.

As Anderson pulled on the handbrake he spoke to Jet. 'You know what to do, don't you?' Anderson's question was unnecessary, and Jet simply nodded. 'No need for anyone to know about the wire except you, me, and Mr York.'

Jet realised this was a statement, not a question, and again nodded.

Once inside the station, Jet seemed to spend a long time hanging around in empty offices on his own, as Anderson spoke to his counterparts from Durham Constabulary. He felt the same uncomfortable feeling of being an intruder as he had in the intensive care unit the previous day. After a while, Anderson poked his head around the door. He did not speak but jerked his head backwards, which Jet understood as a command for him to come to heel, as if he were some sort of performing animal; a seal perhaps. Jet obeyed and followed him to the custody office where three other plain-clothes officers stood. He assumed they were senior detectives with Durham Constabulary. One spoke to him in a rolling Durham accent and although the words were familiar enough, the inflections rose and fell so much more than Jet's own Geordie tone, that it was hard to believe they were only twenty miles from their own station.

'Groom's asked to see you. He's been cooperative, and we see no reason why he shouldn't be granted his request. Don't ask him questions about the murder he's charged with; tell him you can't talk about it if he asks you. You'll need to tell us if there is anything he says which you think is relevant to our enquiry.'

Jet nodded as this man spoke to him. At the same time

he was deep in thought, and his mind puzzled over why the detectives from Durham shouldn't know about the tape recorder.

He was led to a cell by a uniformed officer and waited the few seconds it took for the large keys to clumsily unlock the heavy metal door. He entered the cell. Groom remained seated on the wooden bench, and Jet thought he seemed a good deal more pleased to see him than he had at their last encounter.

'Thanks for coming Jet; I thought you would.'

'How are you being treated?'

'As well as could be expected. I feel better for seeing you. I need your help.'

'What can I do?'

'There was a shoplifter yesterday. He had on him a photograph of my daughter Diane. I think it was stage-managed by Trent to frighten me, to get me to ease the pressure with his case.'

'It obviously didn't work.'

'No, but I could well have made it worse. Once Trent's people find out what I've done, they could get me back by hurting Diane or Shirley. I don't know what happened with that shoplifter yesterday, but Trent obviously has more friends and connections than I gave him credit for. Will you make sure they're all right? Ask around, visit the shoplifter and make sure he knows you're on to him, and if my girls get hurt, he'll be for it. Warn them off. Look after the girls, please Jet.' He had never seen Groom this way before; he was emotional and, despite his large muscular frame looked helpless, even pathetic. Jet was touched by this plea.

'Why don't you ask the force to do this? You're still a serving officer, it's a reasonable request.'

'They're not witnesses, no one's going to protect them. You know what will happen, an alarm installed in the house until the trial is over, that's as much as they'll get. No one's going to watch them or look out for them.'

'Why me Mark? I thought I was just one of the reserves,' Groom stared at Jet as he continued, 'why not someone you work with, who you know better?'

Groom looked him straight in the eye. 'I know you. You'll keep your promise, and you'll not forget. I've seen you following cases, most of them lost causes, still going like a dog with a bone when most people would've given up ages before. You've always had two big weaknesses Jet: you're honest, and you care. Help me please; don't let them hurt the girls.'

Jet was not expecting this remark and for a few seconds stood considering it, looking solemnly at Groom. Then he slowly nodded his head. 'OK, I'll do what I can.'

'You're a good man Jet.'

'What do you know about the shoplifter?'

'Nothing. I've been chasing Trent for years, and I'd never seen him before. He must have widened his circle of friends or paid him. I really don't know.'

'I'll see what I can find out. Is there anything you want me to tell your wife?'

'Tell Shirley I'm sorry. Tell her I'm OK, and I'll work something out.'

'Is there anything else I can do?'

'Just look after the girls.'

'OK, I'll do what I can.'

'Thanks. Can you come back and see me soon?'

'If you want. I'll have to speak to Superintendent York.'

'OK.'

Jet turned to the cell door and pushed the big red button which sat in a silver-coloured metal surround. A loud buzzer sounded, and after a few seconds the sound of a key could be heard turning in the heavy door lock.

Jet left the cell, and as he walked along the passageway he thought about what he had just heard and wondered exactly how Groom thought he was going to work something out. A long prison sentence was certain. A police officer murdering someone in prison was an act the courts were going to frown upon whatever the circumstances. In Jet's experience courts had never been good at dealing with criminals. In fact, they relied on them coming back to keep the system going. That's why the sentences were always so poor. But someone like Groom, a one-off, was going to get everything thrown at him.

After another silent journey with Anderson back to Newcastle, Jet found himself in York's office again. He handed the tape to the superintendent.

'He asked me to do what I could to look after his family. He's frightened that Trent's associates will hurt them.'

'What did you tell him?'

'I said I would do what I could. Seems to me he's got a point. I'll visit them and do what I can to reassure them both. He mentioned a shoplifter that he nicked yesterday – said he had a photo of his daughter on him.'

'Looks like we messed up there. He was cautioned as a first-time offender but, when we went to look for him again, turns out all the details he gave were false. So we don't know who he is or where he is.' York looked annoyed as he said this, and Jet could understand how this must have looked like real incompetence when he was trying to explain it to his counterparts in Durham. Groom's reason for murdering someone and he had been allowed to walk out of the police station with a caution. We didn't even have his real name and address. The press were going to have a field day with this once the trial was held. York continued, 'Keep me updated. If you want to go and see Groom again, come back and see me first.'

'OK,' Jet paused, 'and the shoplifter?'

'What?'

'You don't mind if I make some enquiries about the mysterious shoplifter?'

York again looked stunned at Jet's impertinence. 'I don't care what you do about that, but I have people looking at it. Just don't get in the way. But if we can't find him, I don't see what chance you have.'

'No harm trying though.' Jet's smile was not returned, and he left the office feeling like a chastised schoolboy leaving the headmaster's study.

After Jet had left, Anderson walked to the office door and closed it. He turned to York, who remained sitting at his desk. 'Do you still think he's involved?'

'Why else would Groom want to see him?'

'A bit obvious though.'

'What choice does Groom have? He's in for murder.'

'Seems a bit of a risk letting Whittle make contact.'

'Let's just wait and see. Maybe if we give them enough rope…'

Chapter twelve

It had only been forty-five minutes since Jet had taken his leave from York's office, and already he found himself pulling up outside Groom's home in Prudhoe, a town to the west of Newcastle. He parked his car on the street of the Castlefields Estate and walked up the drive which led to the detached house. The estate was new and, as he looked at the neatly-mown lawns on the open-fronted gardens, it occurred to him that this was the sort of house Julia would give her right arm to live in.

The brass doorbell stood proudly on the pristine white door frame, and the door opened only a few seconds after he had pressed it. The door abruptly stopped moving after opening ten inches. A woman's face appeared in the gap at an uncomfortable angle. The skin around her eyes looked unnaturally dark and traces of mascara were running down her cheeks.

'Mrs Groom?'

'Yes.'

'I'm DC Whittle from Newcastle. Your husband has asked me to come and see you.'

The door closed slightly for a few seconds whilst the door chain rattled, and then it opened fully. Mrs Groom turned and walked in silence down the hall. Jet followed after closing the front door behind him. The inside of the house was as immaculate as the outside. Jet's feet sank into the thick pile of the carpet, and he felt as if he should have taken his shoes off before he entered. Jet followed Shirley Groom into the front room which had as its focal point a large, ornate, white fireplace.

'I saw Mark today at Durham.'

'You spoke to him?'

'Yes, he's worried about you and Diane.'

'Does he want me to go and see him?'

'We didn't talk about that. He'll be at court tomorrow morning and then we could make arrangements after that.'

Shirley Groom looked tired; she did not look at Jet but stared into the lifeless fireplace. 'What's the daft bugger got himself into now?'

'I'm not sure Shirley. How are you holding up?'

'I don't know what to do. They told me he murdered some criminal. He's always been a hothead, but murder?'

'You need to look after yourself and Diane, that's the most important thing. It's also the best thing you can do for Mark at the moment.' Shirley sat staring at the fireplace, shaking her head as Jet spoke, 'Shirley, where's Diane?'

Shirley's response was sluggish, 'Upstairs in her room. She was here last night when Superintendent York came to tell us what had happened. I don't think she really knows what to expect; she just knows her dad's away for a while.'

'Mark mentioned some photographs that someone had of Diane, and he didn't know how they came to have them. Do you know about anyone taking photographs of Diane?'

'No, is it important?'

'It might be. Can I talk to her?'

Shirley walked to the open door leading to the hall and shouted her daughter's name loudly up the stairs. Soon the sound of footsteps could be heard; they quickly got louder, and Diane appeared in the front room. Jet guessed she was about thirteen.

'This is a man who works with daddy; he wants to know if anyone has been taking your photograph lately.'

'No.'

'Are you sure Diane?' Jet smiled. 'It's very important.'

'I'm sure.'

'What about any strangers? Have you noticed anyone hanging around here, or your school perhaps, acting in an unusual way?'

'What's this about?'

Jet sensed Diane had an independence that was not going to be satisfied with a smile or a pat on the head.

'A stranger was arrested yesterday, by your dad, and he had on him a photograph of you. There's no need for you to be worried, but I've promised your dad that I would try to find out who took it. If I find out, it might help him. Do you know a man called Geoffrey Trent?'

Shirley Groom interrupted. 'No she doesn't know

Geoffrey Trent. What's he got to do with this?'

Jet was startled by this response, and he turned his head away from Diane to look directly at Shirley.

'Do you know Geoffrey Trent?'

'Long time ago; what's he got to do with Diane?'

'Didn't York tell you about Trent last night?'

'No, why? What's he got to do with this?'

'Trent is the prisoner that Mark is accused of attacking last night.'

Shirley shook at the information and sat down in the large, cream leather chair close to the fireplace. It looked to Jet as if she had lost control of her legs.

'Mum, are you all right?' Diane said as she moved towards her, anxious at seeing her mother's distress.

'I'm fine. It's just been a difficult day. Could you do me a favour and run me a bath? That might help me to feel better. I need to speak to…' She stopped in mid sentence and looked at Jet.

'Frank.' He said, helping her.

'Could you be a dear and do that for me please?'

Diane hesitated for a few seconds as her mother and Jet looked at her. 'Yes,' she said slowly and Jet thought it was more a submission than anything else. She reluctantly left the room, closing the door behind her. Shirley remained silent, listening to the footsteps going up the stairs.

'Is Geoffrey Trent dead?'

'Yes. It looks like Mark killed him in Durham Prison

yesterday. Have you seen Trent recently?'

'No, not for years. Do you know why Mark did it?'

'The photograph of Diane; it had the name "Geoffrey Trent" written on it. It looks like Mark visited Trent in prison to find out what was going on and they fought.'

Shirley's distant look returned as she sat staring at the fireplace.

'Did Mark talk to you about Trent? He's been an active criminal for years. Mark's team arrested him a while ago; he was in prison waiting to go on trial.'

'No, Mark didn't talk to me much about work.' There was a slight pause as Shirley turned her head to Jet. 'With Mark's work and the gym, we didn't get much time to talk about anything really.'

'How do you know Trent?'

'I wouldn't say I really know him. Years ago, I worked behind the bar at a pub in Newcastle, where all the trendy people used to go. He was a regular there, always showing off, a bit of a Jack The Lad – you know the type – always had a fistful of cash.'

'How long ago was that?'

'I worked there for a few years after we got married, to help make ends meet.'

'Have you seen him recently?'

'No, not for years.'

'Is Mark aware that you know Trent?'

'I don't suppose so. No reason why he should. He was

just a punter from the place I worked, one of many.' Shirley looked agitated at the question. 'Look, I know you're trying to help, but I really can't take this now.'

'I understand, but there's just one thing that I need to talk to you about before I go. Mark is really worried that someone from Trent's family might try to hurt you or Diane because of what's happened.'

'I told your superintendent last night that I'm not leaving my home. I haven't done anything to anyone.'

'I know that, but I just think it would be wise to be careful.'

'We'll be fine. That superintendent had some sort of alarm put in last night, and we'll keep the doors locked.'

'As long as you're sure.'

'Home's the best place for us now. I don't think anyone's going to hurt us. Please don't worry about it.'

Jet was not certain whether Shirley's confidence was justified, but he did not want to add to the distress that the last twenty-four hours had brought her. He took his wallet from his inside jacket pocket, removed a card and handed it to her. 'My mobile number's on that. Please ring me if you need anything, or if you see anything suspicious at all. I'll call back and see you tomorrow, if that's all right.'

Shirley nodded. 'Thank you, you're very kind. But I'm sure we're safe from harm. I don't see why anyone would want to hurt us. '

Jet smiled and then walked out of the room, leaving

Shirley staring at the fireplace. As he left, it struck him, not for the first time, how ostentatious the fireplace was; the sort of thing Julia dreamed of and he dreaded. He walked out along the passage, past all of the bright new possessions that Mr and Mrs Groom had accumulated, and he thought how they had come a long way, in the time since she had worked as a barmaid to help make ends meet. As he walked down the driveway of the house, he passed the same silver four-wheel drive that he had on the way in, and assumed it was Shirley's runabout. He knew it was not Mark Groom's, as he had seen him driving in and out of the police station yard in something that looked a little sportier, and in keeping with his image. For a second, he stood at the driver's door of his own Ford Fiesta and looked at the Grooms' home and the trappings of their accumulated wealth. Then another thought occurred to him, but he decided to push it out of his head for the moment.

'Getting too suspicious for your own good in your old age Frank,' he quietly murmured to himself. Then he got into his car and drove.

Chapter thirteen

It had already felt like a long day, but Jet had more things he needed to do. He looked at his watch and knew if he were quick he would be able to catch Sgt Sharkie before he finished his shift. As he drove, his mind was fully occupied with the events of the day, and the details of his journey were entirely secondary. The twenty-five minute journey had seemed much shorter to him, as he parked his car in the police station yard, and made his way to the custody office. He entered the small room which masqueraded as a sergeant's office and there, at the single desk it contained, he saw Bernard Sharkie, writing with the determination that only came towards the end of a shift and the promise of home.

Sharkie lifted his head as he sensed Jet's presence. 'Jet, how you doing?'

'OK I think. Have you heard about Mark Groom?'

'Who hasn't? This isn't a place to keep secrets. Sounds like he's done it big style this time.'

'He brought a prisoner in yesterday, and I was wondering what you could remember about him?'

'What's that to do with you Jet?'

'I saw Mark Groom in prison today; he's asked me to see

what I can do to help him out.'

'I'm right in it over this one Jet. York is determined to have my guts. I cautioned him for a first-time offence, and it turns out all the details were false. That's what I'm writing here, my statement for York.'

'Have you any idea who he might be?'

'Not a clue. I've been around criminals for years, and I would've staked my pension on him being some first-time loser. He was crapping himself. I checked his details on the voters register, the name and the address checked out. So I let him go with a caution. Bastard was either very lucky or the best actor I've ever seen.'

Jet realised that York's enquiry team would already have visited the person who really owned the name given by the mystery shoplifter, but he wrote the details down in his own notebook in case he decided to pay him a visit.

'Did York take the videotape from the station CCTV?'

'Yeah, he took the original.'

'Do you still keep copies?'

'Yes. I ran a few off for here in case we needed them for any other prisoners.'

'Do you think I could have a copy? York's quite happy that I'm helping out.'

'Don't see a problem Jet.'

Sharkie handed him the videotape and Jet smiled. 'I hope it goes well.'

'Yeah thanks Jet; this is just my luck. How's Mark?'

'You know Mark Groom: still thinks he'll be able to work something out.'

'He's a character that's for sure. Good luck Jet.'

Jet turned and left. Within a few minutes he was sitting at his own desk again. On the desk he saw a message informing him that Mrs Goodman had rung, not for the first time, and would like to speak to him. He cursed himself that the events of the day had caused him to neglect speaking to her. He rang her home telephone number, but was not surprised there was no reply and no answering machine on which to leave a message. Knowing the Goodmans would be at their son's bedside he followed his instinct and within a few minutes was driving towards the hospital.

He saw Mrs Goodman in the corridor near the entrance of the intensive care ward; she held a plastic cup in her right hand and a handkerchief in the other. She looked distant and remote from the hospital activities going on around her. She did not notice Jet's approach.

'I'm not sure if the coffee here would pass the trading standards test.'

Mrs Goodman's reaction was slow, as she drifted from her own thoughts to the conscious world around her. 'Oh, officer, sorry. I've been trying to speak to you. Have you caught the people who attacked Gerry yet?'

'Not yet I'm afraid, but I'm doing my best. How's his condition?'

'They say he might have brain damage.'

A few seconds passed, as if neither knew what else to say. Then Jet changed the subject. 'Do you know someone called John Metcalf?'

'No I don't think so; who is he?'

'Someone I think Gerry knew. I spoke to him yesterday about the attack, but he denied knowing anything. I was hoping you might know him or have seen him with Gerry, or know something about him that might help. I know he was arrested with Gerry two months ago, but he said it was just coincidence.'

'I haven't seen Gerry for months so if he'd just met him, I wouldn't know.'

Jet made an obvious show of looking up and down the corridor, and Mr Goodman was nowhere to be seen. He lowered his voice. 'I can't imagine how hard it must have been for you when your son left. I can see that you were obviously a close family. Are you sure you didn't see him after he left home?'

Mrs Goodman's head nodded as she began to sob. She lifted her well-used handkerchief to her face, but it was unable to contain the sound.

After a few seconds, she tried hard to compose herself. 'Please don't tell Phillip.' Her voice became stronger, 'He took it really hard when Gerry went off the rails: thought it was his fault, like he had failed somehow. When Gerry hit me, it was the last straw, and Phillip said he wanted nothing else to do with him; he'd go mad if he knew I'd seen him.'

It seemed to Jet that with her last words Mrs Goodman's tone resembled that of a pleading little girl, not wanting her parents to discover some naughty deed.

'Don't worry, I won't say anything.'

'I met him a few times and gave him money and food. I was so worried about him. He's a good boy really.'

'I know that,' Jet said as he reached into his pocket. 'It would be really helpful if you'd have a look at this photograph, and just tell me if you ever saw this man with Gerry at any time.'

Mrs Goodman examined the photo, which was a print from Metcalf's police record. Metcalf's expressionless face looked out at Mrs Goodman as she scrutinised it. 'Sorry, I've never seen him before. When I saw Gerry he was always on his own. We would meet in McDonald's and I would buy him a burger, just like when he was a kid.' Mrs Goodman started to cry uncontrollably. Jet felt helpless and without thinking lifted his hand and moved it towards the top of her shoulder. His hand got to within an inch and it stopped. There was an intimacy barrier Jet did not feel comfortable breaching. His hand yo-yoed slightly and then he put it in his pocket. Mrs Goodman was oblivious to the activities of Jet's hand.

He spoke. 'Is there anything I can get you?'

'No I'll be all right. Phillip's just gone for some fresh air, he'll be back soon.'

'I'll not wait for him if you don't mind. I'll let you

tell him I've been, and I'll keep you informed of what's happening. I hope Gerry comes round soon, and maybe he'll tell us all what happened.'

Mrs Goodman nodded gently, and Jet turned and walked out of the hospital.

As he walked towards his car, he knew the next two things he needed to do were, to check the videotape to find the image of the mysterious shoplifter, and to go and see Mrs Trent. He had encountered Mrs Trent many times in the past and seemed to recall her last direct comment to him had been, 'Why don't you and your ugly fucken' face, go and fuck off?'

He was not looking forward to speaking to Geoffrey Trent's mother, so he decided to do that first.

Chapter fourteen

If Geoffrey Trent had made a successful living from being a criminal, then the fruits of that success were not reflected in the home of his adoring mother. Jet had visited the house for professional reasons several times in the past, to either speak to or arrest Geoffrey Trent. As he now looked at the front of the terraced council house he thought how it had barely changed over the years he had known it. It just seemed to look a little more weary with each visit. It had taken Jet a familiar fifteen-minute drive to get from the hospital to the house Mrs Trent had lived in with Geoffrey since he was a boy. It was in Cowgate, an estate on the northern edge of Newcastle. There had never been a Mr Trent that Jet was aware of. But over the years it had occurred to Jet that Geoffrey must have had claims on the world record for the most uncles.

Jet opened the gate and walked up the short path through the small neglected garden which was covered with cracked paving. The front door was ajar. He gently pushed the door but could see no sign of life. He rang the doorbell, and after a few minutes the door was eased back by a figure he instantly recognised as Mrs Trent. Mrs Trent also recognised her visitor. 'What do you bastards want now?'

In Jet's experience, this was as affectionate as Mrs Trent got towards any police officer. 'Hello, Mrs Trent. I was hoping you might spare me a few moments. I know it's a difficult time, but it's important.'

'You murdered him, what else do you want?'

'I just want to do what I can to stop anyone else getting hurt.'

Mrs Trent stared at Jet for a few seconds and, as she did, he could see her squeezing the edge of the door with such pressure that it caused her hand to tremor, making her knuckles taut and white. Then her hand pulled the door open wide, and she released her grip and walked away up the narrow hallway. Jet had a sense of déjà vu, thinking of his visit to Shirley Groom. He followed Mrs Trent through the hall into the kitchen. It was small, cluttered, and dominated by a square table, which had one side pushed against a wall and three chairs around the other sides. A large ashtray full of folded cigarette stubs was located in the centre of the table. At least one of the stubs was still smouldering, ejecting a stream of smoke which climbed in a straight line to the ceiling. Mrs Trent sat down at the table, lifted a new cigarette from an open packet, placed it between her lips and lit it with a green plastic lighter, which she then threw carelessly back onto the table. 'Well, what do you want?'

'I know how close you and your son were Mrs Trent. I'm sorry for your loss, I really am.'

'Don't give me that shit. You weren't sorry when you

were around here hassling the poor lad. He never had a chance: every time something happened, you lot were here accusing him. Aren't you happy now you've murdered him?'

Jet was silent for a few seconds and looked her directly in the eye. He responded slowly. 'No Mrs Trent, I'm not happy that your son's dead. He didn't deserve to die.'

Mrs Trent returned Jet's stare as she listened to him and after a few seconds of silent thought she spoke. 'So what do you want?'

'What do you know about the crime that Geoffrey was awaiting trial for?'

'I know he didn't do it. Fitted up by that bastard Groom and the rest of you lot.'

'Did Geoffrey tell you that?'

'He didn't need to tell me, I was his mother. You must have known he wasn't a drug dealer for Christ's sake. He never touched drugs – wouldn't know what they were, let alone buy and sell them.'

'Why would anyone want to frame him for a crime he didn't commit?'

'You were always picking on him every chance you got; he got the blame for everything, and that evil bastard Groom always had it in for him. He said he'd get him and he fucken' well did, didn't he? Wasn't even satisfied with sending him to prison for something he didn't do, had to murder him. I hope he rots in hell.'

'Geoffrey and Groom fought about something; do you

know why they would be fighting?'

'The last lot of coppers who were here said that Groom had gone to see Geoffrey and attacked him.'

'Groom told me that Geoffrey had threatened his family, to hurt his daughter. Is there a reason why Groom might have thought that?'

'Don't be ridiculous, Geoffrey wasn't a threat to anyone. You nicked him plenty, were you frightened of him?' Mrs Trent looked directly at Jet and was speaking quickly; her tone was aggressive but earnest.

'No.'

'Course not. Whatever Groom did was because he's an evil bastard.'

'Did Geoffrey have a camera?'

'What are you talking about?'

'Groom received some photographs of his daughter and they had Geoffrey's name on them. They were taken with a digital camera, I think. Did Geoffrey have a digital camera, or know anyone who had a camera?'

'Geoffrey with a camera, are you joking?'

'Was Geoffrey living here when he was arrested?'

'Of course, this was his home.'

'Could I have a look in his room?'

Mrs Trent was silent, her face stern. Jet thought he had pushed her too far with this request and feared she was using the silence to think of a suitable insult before showing him the door. She plunged her cigarette into the mound of butts in the ashtray and then looked up at Jet. 'Oh why not? Come on, I'll show you how a fucken' big-time drug dealer lives.'

Mrs Trent rose to her feet and marched out of the kitchen into the hall and then up the stairs. At the top of the stairs the landing was small, and she pulled the handle of the first door and opened it. 'There you go.'

Jet stepped past Mrs Trent, who remained in the doorway, and watched him as he looked around. The room was small. The single bed neatly made up and pushed tight against a side wall. A white bedside cabinet stood next to the bed and also in the room was a white wardrobe and a white chest of drawers. Jet was not sure why he was surprised at how tidy the room was, but he was. He was also struck by the lack of personal items. The room looked bare, the walls were clean with no posters or pictures but simply the vivid stripes of the wallpaper. Jet opened the wardrobe door and lightly fingered the shirts, jackets, and trousers, which hung in a neat row. One by one he opened the drawers of the chest, then of the bedside cabinet and closed each of them quickly, being satisfied none contained anything more sinister than folded sweaters and other items of Geoffrey Trent's clothing.

'Happy now?' Mrs Trent was still standing in the doorway.

'Yes, thank you.' Jet replied.

He looked around the room again, and it occurred to

him this was not a place Geoffrey Trent had spent a great deal of his time, other than to sleep. 'Did Geoffrey have a job?'

'No never. You bastards saw to that; with his record he was never going to be given a chance by anyone, was he?'

'How did he support himself?'

'Support himself!' Mrs Trent scoffed. 'He had benefits and earned a little here and there where he could.'

'What did he do with himself in his spare time?'

'Spending what money he did have in the bookies.' Her tone changed as if, from somewhere within, she had found warmth from a recollection. 'He usually lost everything, but you should have seen his face when he won. He was like a schoolboy. He'd take me out and spend his winnings on me; we'd go to the pub and have something to eat. He bought me this necklace the last time he had money.' She held a small diamond pendant, which she moved back and forth along a fine gold chain around her neck. 'He was a good boy. He looked after me the best way he could. Yes, he wasn't perfect, but he was a loving boy; he wouldn't hurt a fly.'

'Did he ever deal drugs?'

'Never. He was never into anything like that. I know what he was you know; he was a petty criminal, but always small-time. You know why he wasn't very good at being a criminal?'

Jet shook his head.

'Because he couldn't hurt anyone that's why. He was just a big softie deep down inside. He was a lovely boy. He couldn't deal drugs because he wasn't that sort of boy. He could nick a car or take a car stereo, but he was strictly small-time. Look at what he had, this is everything.' Her speech faltered and Jet thought he could detect another change in her. This time it was a return to sadness but without the anger he had seen earlier. 'Not much to show for a lifetime is it?' Her eyes filled with tears, and they quickly ran down her cheeks. She wiped her face with her hands and breathed deeply. Jet did not know how to respond to her question. The honest answer would have been no, there was not much to show for a lifetime. He looked around the room once again, and more questions rushed through his mind. He now shared Shirley Groom's confidence that she and her daughter were not at any risk from Trent or his associates, if he had any. But he seemed no closer to understanding what was happening than when he'd been speaking to Groom in his cell at Durham Police Station. If Trent had nothing to do with the photographs, then who did and to what end? It just didn't add up. Jet's thoughts returned to Mrs Trent whose mind also seemed to have drifted. He was confident she was not thinking of problems with photographs, but of her son, who would never be back to give her gifts bought from the proceeds of his good luck at the bookmakers, or to lie in the neatly arranged bed, which Jet was sure she would have lovingly made up every day of her son's existence.

Jet smiled at Mrs Trent and whispered, 'Thank you,' as he walked past her and out of the bedroom, feeling uncomfortable and now a little guilty at the intrusion he had made. He walked down the stairs and straight to the front door where he reached for the Yale lock and turned it to open the door.

'Do you know why Groom murdered my son?'

Mrs Trent was a few steps behind Jet and he was not sure whether this was another of her rhetorical questions, but part of him hoped that it was. 'No, I don't.'

'Will you try to find out?'

'Yes.'

'Will you tell me the reason if you do?'

'Yes.'

'Good.' And with that reply she closed the door behind Jet, and he found himself standing on the paved garden.

He walked back towards his car and, as he did, he wondered whether it were possible Geoffrey Trent had another house, another home and existence, which his mother did not know about; another life in which he was a ruthless drug baron with hidden wealth. As he reached his car Jet looked at the house he had just visited and, for some reason, thought it looked smaller than it had previously. Looking at the house he also knew that all Geoffrey Trent had been was on display there, and he knew he could never have kept such a secret from his mother.

Jet drove back to the station, trying to separate the things he knew as fact from those things that instinct was telling him were likely. He knew the photographs had existed, as did the mysterious shoplifter, but they seemed to make less sense than before. He wondered how close York's men were to identifying the shoplifter, realising they had a huge advantage over him in the quest to find him. However, he did not think there was anything to be lost by having a look at him. As he drove in the direction of the station, Jet thought about the people who would be there and wondered how easy it was going to be to look at three hours of videotape in peace and quiet, especially given the interest there was bound to be in his current task. He pondered his options and realised he was not that far away from the video recorder he had at home. Jet decided he would use this and so he turned his car towards Station Road in Wallsend and his own semi-detached house.

Chapter fifteen

Jet parked his car on the small driveway of his home and once he got out of it stood for a second and looked around the garden. Julia had never worked full-time during their eighteen years of marriage, but she was never still. Jet knew she had been influenced by her middle class parents. Her father was the breadwinner and her mother the homemaker. Her father had worked abroad for long periods of time in the engineering business and had provided a comfortable existence for his wife and two daughters. Jet had often felt inferior to his father-in-law when he was alive, and on occasion had felt inferior to his memory since his death. Economic factors had led to Julia working part-time as a receptionist at a local dental surgery. She seemed to enjoy the job, but it sometimes made Jet feel that he was somehow failing.

The garden was neat. The grass was short and looked as if it had been combed with every blade standing to attention, perfectly vertical. The narrow borders which surrounded the lawn were full of regiments of small flowering plants, which added attractive bands of colour. Jet smiled at this display, and he knew that, even if he had been interested in gardening, he would never have been allowed to interfere. In reality, he was quite happy that this fell into Julia's domain and he felt warmth from the pleasure she clearly derived from the order she brought to both of their lives.

'Ju, just me!'

Jet shouted as soon as he turned the lock of the front door and was opening it. He did not know why, but he instinctively knew when Julia was in the house; it felt empty when she was not there. He could not describe how he knew, he just did. He knew that she was in at this moment, but he did not know what reception he would get following yesterday evening's birthday dinner and the disagreement that had followed between the two of them.

Jet walked down the hall and into the living room before he heard any acknowledgement of his greeting. He was in the process of inserting the tape into the front of the video recorder when Julia appeared from the kitchen. 'Frankie, you didn't tell me you were coming home early.'

'Frankie,' Jet thought, not 'Frank.' He felt relieved. Julia's tone was bright and breezy, and he decided not to mention last night, or to attempt an apology for not being enthusiastic enough about Heather and Craig's most recent acquisitions. 'Sorry pet, I'm just passing through. I need to have a look at this videotape and this was the only quiet place I could think of.'

'Oh, is it something exciting? Let's have a look. Is it an armed robbery or a car chase or something? How much blood is there about?'

Julia was like a schoolgirl straining her neck to get close to the television set to see what was on.

'I'm afraid it's not very exciting at all. It's just a video of the police station cameras. It flicks between the cameras in the car park, the prisoner entrance and the front desk where the public come in. I just want to see if I can recognise a shoplifter that was brought in.'

'So no blood then?'

Jet looked at Julia and slightly twisted his face in disapproval of her desire to witness something unpleasant. 'No. No blood.'

'Never mind; put it on and let's see what's happening.'

Jet pressed 'play' on the recorder, and a black and white picture flickered onto the screen. Both he and Julia knelt on the rug in front of the television and watched it from a few feet away. The tape gave quick bursts of activity in each of the three areas where the cameras were located in the police station. After a few minutes of joint concentration, Julia spoke. 'Couldn't you get a tape with just the camera you're interested in?'

'No. There's only one recorder and it tapes from all three cameras in turn – there's no way of separating the images.'

'Not very exciting is it?'

'I did say it wasn't.'

They both returned to silence and stared at the screen as the images flickered on and off. After a few more minutes, Julia broke the silence again. 'Do you know what time the person you want to see is on the tape?'

'Yes, about one o'clock in the afternoon.'

'Then why don't you turn it to that time?'

'Because there's no time on the screen. The tape records in time delay for the entire day so this covers twelve hours of activity at the station. I know this tape covers the time I want to see, but it doesn't show the time on the tape, so the only way to be sure is to watch the whole tape.'

'That's not a very good system is it Frankie? You'd have thought the time would be on the tape wouldn't you?'

'Yes, you would, but it's not, so I just need to be patient and watch the whole tape, so I don't miss anything.' Julia was oblivious to Jet's tone, which was growing a little impatient with her enquiries. Silence returned as they both stared at the screen. After a few minutes Julia spoke again. 'There are a lot of people going back and forth aren't there?'

'Yes, it's a police station; lots of people go back and forth.'

'What day was this?'

'Yesterday, Sunday.'

'That would explain it.'

'Explain what?'

'The people. There's a market on at the Quayside: a lot of people go to that.'

Jet took his eyes off the screen and looked at Julia. 'How could the market a mile away on the Quayside, have anything to do with the number of people in the police station?'

'It's very popular that market. You get some really good bargains there.'

Jet's eyes returned to the screen, and he decided he would not pursue Julia's course of logic any further. Quiet returned for a few seconds and then Julia spoke. 'Everyone I know goes to that market.' She paused for a second. 'Except us.'

'Julia, this is very important.'

'It's very boring.'

'Detective work often is; you need to be patient.'

Both sets of eyes returned to the screen and the silence returned for a short time.

'You said you'd take me to the market months ago, but you never did.'

Jet did not respond.

'It's very popular.'

'What is?'

'The market – you can see on this tape how popular it is.'

'Julia this is the police station; it has nothing to do with the market.'

'Why else would they be there on a Sunday?'

'Because those coming through the back door have been arrested, and those coming in the front door need help of some sort.'

'Why would they need help?'

'All sorts of reasons. They might need directions, or have lost a purse or something.'

'Probably want directions to the market. You get some good bargains at that market, or so I'm told. I never get there myself.'

'Julia, I promise on my next weekend off we'll go to the market on the Quayside.'

Julia smiled and they both returned to watching the tape. After a few minutes Julia spoke. 'It's nice having you home during the day.'

'Hmmm.' Jet was trying to concentrate as much as he could on the video and he fast-forwarded the tape to speed up the process, being certain that even with the disjointed way the frames were being thrown up, he would immediately recognise the distinctive figure of Mark Groom.

'I was reading an article in a magazine the other day which said it was good for relationships to do things out of routine.'

'Hmmm.'

'To be more imaginative.'

'Hmmm.'

Jet stared at the images on the screen. The thought 'bloody magazines' crossed his mind, but he did not say it. They watched the screen for a few seconds and Julia spoke again. 'You know my husband would get angry, if he knew I'd let a stranger I'd just met at the carnival into the house, when I'm all on my own.'

Jet looked away from the television and directly at Julia again. 'Would he? What carnival?'

'He'd get really jealous if he thought I was mixing with strangers.'

'I should think so.'

Julia turned towards Jet and placed her hand gently on his elbow, slowly moving it along his arm towards his shoulder. 'I don't know what he'd do, if he came in now, and caught us here together, alone.'

'I've heard he's strong and athletic?'

'I hope you didn't pay for that information.'

'What do you mean? I heard he did the Great North Run.'

'He started it once and got as far as an ice cream van in Gateshead.'

'It's a long way to Gateshead.'

'Let's not talk about him; let's concentrate on us.'

Julia's right hand was now cupped behind Jet's neck, and she used it to slowly pull herself close to him, until her face was so near to his that he could feel her warm breath on his lips – it was fresh, familiar, and he thought, strangely reassuring.

'I'm really busy at the moment.'

'My husband gets really jealous.'

'I'm not surprised, you're very beautiful.'

'He works a lot and I get lonely.'

'I'm sure he doesn't mean to neglect you.'

'Are you sure?'

'I am sure he loves you.'

Julia's left hand moved towards the top button of her blouse, and as she looked at Jet, she gently unfastened it. It sprung softly open and Jet felt his heart accelerate.

'I don't think my husband will be home for a while yet.'

'Good.' Jet's voice was soft and he moved his lips onto Julia's, and they fell slowly onto the rug as they kissed. He was a hooked fish. He could not resist. He had never been able to resist her, right from the very start. Twenty years he had known her, and he still could not resist her. He knew in his heart he never would. 'You should be careful with us carnival people,' he whispered as he unbuttoned the rest of her blouse, and for a while he forgot about the intensive care unit, Durham Police Station and the videotape which flickered over them as they locked themselves together in a world only they shared.

Julia came into the room from the kitchen. She carried a tray on which two cups of coffee and a small plate rested. On the plate was a neatly-cut sandwich. She placed the tray on a small table near the sofa and then sat next to Jet. It was now over an hour since Jet had returned home to watch the videotape, and he sat on the sofa watching his television.

'Thought you might need some sustenance, Frankie.'

'Yes thanks pet. I find I do use more energy, since I got that job with the carnival.' He smiled at Julia and then his eyes returned to the screen. 'Any case Ju, now I come to think of it, how long is it, since a carnival came to Newcastle? And anyway isn't that an American thing? I thought we had funfairs here in England.'

'Oh Frankie you're such a stickler for detail. I was just reading about a carnival in *Time Magazine*. You weren't worried about it a little while ago.'

'No I wasn't. Don't get me wrong, I enjoyed being from the carnival but I just wondered if, next time, for the sake of realism, I shouldn't be from a funfair.'

'Frankie you're so common. Carnival is so much more romantic. Here's me imagining some rugged hunk who tames lions, and you want to be some seedy bloke from the dodgems.'

'Well I didn't have the advantage of your posh education. I'm a commoner.'

Julia smiled. 'Yes I know, but I'll keep trying.'

'Can't make a silk purse out of a sow's ear.'

'That's what father said to me after he first met you.'

'I know, you told me.'

'He liked you really.'

'He thought you should've married the Duke of Northumberland or someone like that.'

'And live in some big dusty castle? Bad enough keeping this place tidy.'

'I don't think the duchess will spend much time hoovering the castle.'

'Wooden floors, Frankie: she'll just need to run a mop over it once a week, which is what I'd do if we had parquet flooring.' Julia ran her eyes over the carpet. 'It would look really nice.'

'Ju, I'll get round to it. It's not cheap you know, and it'll take a bit of putting down.'

'If you say so,' Julia replied as she looked at the television screen, which was still showing flashing images of pictures taken from the different CCTV cameras at the police station. As only every eighth frame from the cameras was recorded on the tape, the pictures jerked. The people on it appeared to take great leaps every time the picture moved. Julia turned to Jet who was concentrating on the images. 'Is that not hurting your eyes yet?'

'Yes. Worst part of it is I can see the light outside is dimming, so it's getting to evening time, and I still haven't found Groom and his shoplifter. I don't understand. They should've been on by now.'

'You don't think you could have missed them?'

'I don't think so. I have fast-forwarded a lot of it, but I'm sure I'd have seen Groom bringing a prisoner in. He's hard to miss, even in these time-lapsed images.'

Jet had been perched on the front edge of the sofa but now moved back so that he leaned against the backrest. He was frustrated at the lack of progress with the tape.

'Never mind Frankie. The last few hours haven't been a complete waste of time, have they?'

Jet smiled. 'No, definitely not.'

'I don't know why you like doing this sort of work

anyway. You know, if you put your mind to it, you'd be in charge of that station.'

'Not sure I want to be in charge, if the truth's known.'

'I don't know what's wrong with you Frankie. You're as clever as any of the people down there. I don't see why you want to keep on dealing with criminals all of the time.'

'It's just what I do Julia. I like it.'

'I don't know how you can actually enjoy dealing with criminals Frankie and, judging by that video, even the people who come for help don't look too savoury.' Julia looked at the screen and wrinkled her nose up at the picture of a young man at the enquiry office.

Jet looked at the screen and realised he had seen the face before. 'Hold on a second,' his mind puzzled, 'what's he doing there?'

'He looks the type that should be coming through the back door to me, not the front.'

Jet thought Julia's observation very astute. 'Yes I think you're right there, but this still doesn't make sense to me.'

'Why not? Who is he?'

Jet looked at the image of John Metcalf on the screen but did not reply directly to Julia's question. 'I took his shoes from him yesterday.'

'Why on earth would you want to do that Frankie? I hope you didn't put them on.'

'Of course I didn't put them on. I took them because he's a suspect for an assault I'm investigating.'

'Maybe he's come to ask for his shoes back.'

'Maybe.' Jet said, but did not believe this to be true.

They continued to watch the screen as it hopped from one camera to another. As it came back to the front enquiry desk, they could see John Metcalf standing waiting. Then the back of someone's head appeared, coming from inside the station into the public area and spoke to Metcalf. This person directed Metcalf into a small interview room, which was adjacent to the public enquiry area, and both disappeared into the room. Julia and Jet continued to stare at the screen.

'Is this more interesting Frankie?'

'Yes Ju, this is more interesting.'

'Good. As long as we're enjoying it.'

The picture continued to flicker backwards and forwards. After a few seconds Metcalf and the other man came back onto the screen, as they emerged from the interview room. Metcalf walked away towards the exit of the station, and the other man headed towards the enquiry desk, walking back into the police station. Just before the man disappeared he lifted his head up and looked straight at the camera. Jet paused the tape and again recognised the face he was looking at on the television screen.

'Is that another criminal Frankie?'

'That's a detective, Ju.'

'Is he a friend of yours?'

'No I wouldn't say that. He's not what I would describe as my type.'

'What do you mean not your type?'

'He works on the drug squad. His name is Ray Harris.'

'What's he doing?'

'That's a really good question.'

'Why isn't he your type?'

'You know, Hawaiian shirt, leather jacket, hair gel.'

'Fashionable.'

'What do you mean? I'm fashionable.' Jet smoothed the front of his light-green shirt and then tucked the baggy parts of it into the top of the trousers of his dark-grey suit.

'Of course Francis.'

'He's a ponce: false smile, false tan, reeks of aftershave.'

'Yes Francis, definitely not your type.'

Chapter sixteen

'Why the hell would Metcalf and Harris be meeting at the nick yesterday?' Jet had a habit of talking to himself, especially when he was driving. He had just left home and was now driving back to the station, still puzzling over the images he had seen on the tape. It did not make sense that Metcalf would be talking to Harris at any time yesterday. It had been quite late when Jet had been at Metcalf's house and taken his shoes. As well as that, Harris said he'd not had anything to do with Metcalf since his arrest two months ago. Jet knew that the work of the drug squad depended a great deal on information given to them by criminals, but Harris had been adamant he had not seen him and was not interested in him. Why would he lie about that?

Jet wondered whether Metcalf had gone to see Harris after he had taken his shoes; there might just have been time for him to do this. But, if that was the case, why would Harris not have made contact and told him what had happened? Jet made a mental note to confirm with the lab that they had received Metcalf's shoes for the examination he wanted them to conduct, and then cursed himself for suspecting any detective, even someone like Harris, would be stupid or bent enough to tamper with evidence.

Even if Metcalf was in a position to be passing valuable information about drug dealing suspects to Harris, it would surely be madness for Harris to do anything that would be considered to be perverting the course of justice. No, this could not be the case – not least because Jet knew Metcalf's lifestyle was not that of someone who was doing well out of his criminal activities. Jet had looked around his flat just yesterday, and his possessions were those of someone well down the criminal food chain, if indeed he was being fed by any criminal profit. It did not make sense. The other great puzzle was why Groom and his shoplifter were not on the tape.

By the time Jet had returned to the station, it was well after five o'clock, and the building lacked the bustle it had when he'd last left it. He looked at his desk and saw a number of handwritten telephone messages which had been left for his attention. He thumbed through them. One message was from the forensic lab, asking him to return their call about the shoes he had submitted for examination. 'Well there's one less worry,' he said to himself as he realised the shoes had made it to the lab. Another message was from the detective inspector also asking to speak to him about the shoes. Jet had put them through to the lab as an urgent submission and the lab would charge a handsome fee for the pleasure of examining them. No doubt Jet would get a good reprimand and a lecture reminding him of the correct protocol for lab submissions. The detective inspector had his budget to worry about. Since the labs had been privatised Jet had enjoyed many such reprimands. Two of the messages were from Mrs Goodman asking him to contact her, and the last was from the Crown Prosecution Service asking the whereabouts of the court file for a burglar due to appear on Wednesday.

Jet picked up the phone and rang the number left by Mrs Goodman, which he recognised as the Goodmans' home number. As he suspected, there was no answer, and he expected they would still be carrying out their vigil at the intensive care unit. The Goodmans did not strike him as people who would ever carry a mobile phone, not that a mobile phone would serve them well in the intensive care unit. Jet had used his mobile phone in the hospital corridor only once and had secured the wrath of a young-looking member of medical staff who had pointed out a sign on the wall that prohibited their use. She seemed to derive joy from sternly explaining that people's lives depended on the accuracy of the medical machinery to which they were attached. He had apologised and in retrospect thought he had been more contrite than the circumstances strictly required. Who the hell pays any attention to posters on walls in any case?

The Goodmans' phone rang for a while and, remembering that they did not have an answering machine, he replaced his receiver and resolved to call into the hospital again to see them before the evening was over.

Jet looked at the videotape he still had in his hand and decided to go to Sgt Sharkie's office, just on the off chance there was something he had overlooked. The office was as untidy as ever. Jet opened the door of a metal cabinet and saw a large number of videotapes stacked on top of each other. He thumbed through them but could not determine any particular system. Jet looked at his watch and saw it was now after six o'clock. He picked up the phone in Sgt Sharkie's office and after a few seconds of conversation with the local control room, he had Sharkie's mobile telephone. He called the number and Sharkie responded quickly.

'Sharkie. Jet here. Listen, I'm sorry to bother you but I'm having a problem with this tape you gave me: it doesn't make sense to me. I can't find any sign of Mark Groom on it and yet I know he brought a prisoner in yesterday. I'm in your office at the moment, to see if I could find another copy of the tape just to check, but I can't follow your system. Can you help?'

'Have you looked through the whole tape?'

'Yes.'

'Are you sure? You know that CCTV system is as old as the hills; it's a real pain. I've been on at them for long enough to replace it; you would think in this day and age they'd have one with the time and the date on it. But no, they say it's not a priority. They reckon it's not worth spending the money on it, as it never gets used very much anyway. I said to York, if it doesn't get used, why do I have to change and file away the tapes every bloody day then? But no one listens.'

'Yeah Sharkie, that does seem unreasonable,' said Jet, summoning as much diplomacy as he could.

'Is there a label on the tape you have?'

'Yeah.'

'Is there a number on the label?'

'Yeah.'

'There is a big black register on my desk. Have a look at it and check the number on the tape against the numbers in the register.'

Jet opened the thick book. The cover was leather bound and worn with age. He doubted that its original purpose would have been to record videotapes, but it looked suited to the job. The pages were held together between the covers by two large metal fasteners which looked as if they had not been unfastened for years. Holding the videotape in his left hand Jet placed the index finger of his right hand on the page at the most recent entry. He looked at the date in the left-hand column of the register and went to the 23rd July, Sunday's date, and then had a look at the serial number recorded for it. It was not the same as the number he had on the tape in his hand. In fact, it looked nothing like it. He began to run his finger up the register and immediately realised the serial numbers appeared to be random.

'Jesus Sharkie.' Jet spoke into the phone, which was now nestling awkwardly between his shoulder and chin.

'Isn't there a system in here? Why don't you put them in numerical order or something?'

'It's my system Jet, and I put the numbers in any way I bloody well like.'

As Sharkie spoke, Jet realised the number matched that of two entries further up in the register. He looked at the date. 'Sharkie, this serial number corresponds to the tape marked in the register as number one tape, on the 22nd July. What does that mean?'

'It just means that it's the first tape of the day. We record two every day which last for twelve hours each. The tapes are changed at 10.00 am and 10.00 pm.'

'So this tape covers ten in the morning on Saturday until ten at night?'

'Yeah, sorry Jet, I must have given you the wrong tape. When York's team of people came in for that tape they had the place in turmoil. Sorry pal.'

'Will there be a copy of Sunday's tape about?'

'There should be. I keep the loose copies in the bottom drawer of the filing cabinet before I file them away. If you look at the serial number in the register for the tape you want on Sunday, then you want the tape with that number on it.'

'Thanks Sharkie. Sorry to have bothered you,' Jet said, placing the phone receiver back on its plastic cradle.

Jet looked at the tape he had in his hand for a few seconds, as he thought about the information he had just received. He was not sure whether it made more or less sense that the tape he had just watched was from Saturday rather than Sunday. He snapped himself out of this inconclusive pondering and moved towards the bottom drawer of the filing cabinet. He pawed his way through the disorganised collection of videotapes until he found the one with the serial number he was looking for and lifted it from the drawer. He checked in the register that it was the correct number and again breathed deeply at the total non-uniformity of the system administered by Sgt Sharkie. In all matters professional Jet liked order, and where documentation or evidence was concerned he actually enjoyed putting things in a logical sequence. Creating order out of disorder was one of Jet's few vices and one even Julia would have difficulty depriving him of. Confident he now had Sunday's tape as well as Saturday's, Jet made his way back to his office.

Sitting at his desk, Jet was absorbed in his thoughts. This had been a very unusual day, but he knew there were still many things he needed to do. He looked at his watch and then picked up the telephone receiver on his desk and keyed in the extension number for Superintendent York. He was not sure whether he would still be in his office but was not too surprised when the phone was answered and York barked his surname.

'Sir, it's DC Whittle. I saw Mrs Groom today and wondered if you could give me the OK to go and see Mark Groom again tomorrow?'

'Did she have much to say?'

'Not really – she seemed unconcerned about any retaliation against her.'

'I arranged for one of our alarms to be installed in her house, just in case.'

'She was obviously very upset when I spoke to her.'

'Quite natural I suppose. Do you want to see Groom for any particular reason?'

'No. I just want to reassure him that there's nothing for him to worry about, that's all. I promised him I'd speak to Shirley and let him know what happened.'

'OK, I'll see what I can do. Speak to me tomorrow.'

'Thanks for that Sir. One last thing, do you have any idea when Mrs Groom will be able to go herself and see him?'

'Does she want to?'

York's question seemed odd to Jet at first, then he realised it was something he had just assumed she would want to do, but it had not been discussed between them. It then triggered a whole series of other thoughts in Jet's mind which he decided to terminate for the moment. 'I'm not sure whether she wants to or not Sir, but just in case.'

'He's been charged with murder and will appear at court in the morning. I imagine he'll be remanded in custody. I think under the circumstances they won't do the usual and send him to Durham Prison on remand, so we'll have to see what they come up with; another prison further afield

I would have thought. I don't think anyone will object to him seeing his wife once that's done.'

'Thank you Sir. I'll speak to you tomorrow.'

Jet held the phone long enough to hear the connection to his senior officer terminated. Jet always referred to higher-ranking officers as senior and never superior. When people, usually irate criminals or their relatives, were protesting bitterly at Jet's actions and asked who his superior officer was, so they could complain, he always replied that he wasn't aware of having anyone superior to him, but he did have plenty of senior officers. Often the distinction was lost on them, but it was important to him. He had seen many examples of colleagues jumping on the promotion ladder long before they were really competent coppers, and if they played the game they could surrender independent thought for stripes on their arms or even pips on their shoulders. Not that Jet was an anarchist – he knew there needed to be a hierarchy to ensure the organisation operated at least partway efficiently – it was just that it was not a perfect world, and every day of his service he saw the evidence of that imperfection. The best coppers Jet knew weren't those who craved insignia, but those who worked to satisfy the craving in their gut, which told them the difference between right and wrong, and who wanted to put things right. It was true, Jet was a misfit, and with every passing year this seemed to him to be becoming more and more obvious.

Jet unlocked the bottom drawer of his desk and in it

placed the two videotapes before locking it again. He stood up and made his way to the drug squad office, in the hope that he would find Ray Harris there. As he walked up the corridor to the office, he saw Harris walk out with another detective from the drug squad. For a reason that he could not explain, the drug squad officers seemed instantly recognisable to him: they had a uniform quality that he could detect without conscious effort. Perhaps it was the jeans and tee shirts and too much effort not to look like police officers that made them stand out.

'Ray, just the man I was hoping to see,' Jet said, hoping he might get a cordial response and some cooperation on the questions that were to follow.

'Really Jet? What can I do for you?'

'You mentioned to me that you'd not seen John Metcalf since you arrested him at the Wooden Doll.'

'Yeah, what of it?'

'I was wondering if you'd had a chance to think any more about it. Are you sure you haven't seen him since?'

'I told you, I haven't seen him Jet. What are you getting at?'

'I was checking a videotape on the station CCTV, and I saw you talking to him on Saturday in the front office.'

Harris was silent for a few seconds and seemed taken by surprise. 'I don't know what you're talking about Jet. Let me think.' Harris continued to look at Jet, staring intensely into his eyes. 'Saturday. Let me think.' The stare continued.

'Now I come to think about it, there was someone who I spoke to in the front office on Saturday afternoon. Mark Groom asked me to speak to him. Was that John Metcalf? I didn't pay much attention to him. Mark said he'd turned up asking to see someone from the drug squad and he asked me to speak to him. Was that John Metcalf? I didn't recognise him.'

'Didn't he tell you who he was?'

'He might have Jet; it didn't ring a bell if he did say his name. He said he wanted to pass on some information and wanted money. It was obvious he was wasting my time so I gave him the bum's rush.'

'And you didn't recognise him from his arrest at the Wooden Doll?'

'I barely had anything to do with him. They were all small fish Jet – they didn't interest me. I told you that. What's it to you?'

'I was just curious. I was looking at the videotape as a favour to Mark Groom. I saw you and Metcalf and wondered if he'd told you something that might help me. He's a suspect for an offence that happened after you saw him.'

'Yeah, I remember you telling me. But as it happened after I saw him, it's not very likely that I could help you with it, is it?'

'Suppose not,' Jet said and thought Harris, no matter how distasteful he was, did have a point.

Harris changed the subject. 'Did you say you were doing a favour for Mark Groom?'

'Yes. You've heard what's happened to him?'

'Not many secrets in this place. Why are you doing him favours Jet? I didn't realise you two were pals.'

'No, me neither. He just asked to speak to me.'

'Have you spoken to him today?

'Yes.'

Harris seemed surprised and given that he had worked closely with Groom in recent years, Jet could understand why he would be. Harris continued. 'How's he doing? Did he have much to say?'

'He's doing as well as could be expected.' Jet purposely answered only the first question Harris had asked.

Harris remained silent, apparently waiting for more information from Jet, but when it became apparent nothing more was going to be offered he spoke. 'You've been a busy boy. Let me know if there's anything I can do to help won't you? As far as I can see he's done the world a favour by getting rid of that scum Trent. Tragic to see a good cop going to waste over a low life like that.'

'As you say, tragic.'

'Are you going to see him again soon?'

'Yes, tomorrow. I'm just helping him out with some things.'

Both men stared at each other for a few seconds more and then Harris broke the silence. 'Well, must dash.' At that he walked quickly past Jet, apparently trying to catch up with his colleague, who had continued to walk up the corridor during the exchange of words and had now disappeared through the door towards the exit.

Jet remained stationary in the corridor for a moment, both considering the conversation he'd just had, and also allowing time for Harris to leave the building, as he wanted to avoid any further awkwardness. Jet knew Harris had a thick skin, but even he would feel hurt at the thought that Groom, who he had worked closely with, would turn to somebody else at a time of crisis. Jet thought it would be particularly galling to Harris, that it was him Groom had turned to. As Jet had said to Julia, Harris was not his type – a fact he was certain Harris would be equally pleased about.

Jet walked back to his office, unlocked the desk drawer and removed the two tapes from it. He was going to pay a visit to the hospital to speak to Mr and Mrs Goodman and do his best to reassure them he was pursuing his enquiries as well as he could. As no one had contacted him with an update on Gerald Goodman's condition, he was confident this meant there had been no change. After that, he was going to take his video of Sunday home with him and see whether he could find the picture of Groom with his mysterious shoplifter, to see what benefit that might bring him. And, who knows, if he was lucky, he might find Julia welcoming when he told her the carnival was back in town.

Chapter seventeen

It was well after 4.00 am on Tuesday and Mr and Mrs Goodman were in bed. Mr Goodman was lying on his back snoring slowly and deeply. They had stayed at the bedside of their son since Sunday morning and had arrived home exhausted after eleven o'clock the previous night on the advice of the hospital sister who no doubt could plainly see their fatigue. They had not wanted to leave.

'Why don't you go home and get some rest? It's been a long couple of days for you both. There's nothing you can do here tonight. You must look after yourselves as well. After a good night's rest you can come back feeling much fresher in the morning.'

The advice had seemed sensible. After they had made themselves a cup of tea and a sandwich, they had gone to bed together at a few minutes after midnight, much later than they normally did, but these were not normal times. Mrs Goodman did not sleep as soundly as her husband of thirty-one years, but drifted into a fitful slumber due to exhaustion, waking regularly. With the return of consciousness, immediately came the image of her only son lying in the intensive care unit. With that thought, returned the pain which felt like a knife had been plunged into her chest; tightening her body and making breathing a greater effort than she could ever recall. Every movement was a challenge, and there had been moments when she thought that if she stopped and surrendered herself, then her breathing would stop and she would just drift away into nothingness. Perhaps if she ceased to exist, the pain and the problems would simply disappear. But she knew that she was needed, that she had to carry on for Gerry and for Phillip. She knew if there was going to be any hope of them being a family again, a proper family, then she would be the one who would have to make it happen.

One question returned to her time and time again, the same question that had haunted her these last twelve months: where had it all gone so wrong? It tormented her. She could see Gerry's face clearly in her mind. She could see the baby Gerry and then the toddler Gerry with the plump, round, smiling face. He was always smiling, she remembered. She recalled his first day at school, him tightly gripping her hand as they had arrived. He had not wanted to let go and in truth neither had she. But she tried to convince him that he would have a good time with his new classmates and that his mum would be back in a few short hours to take him home for a special treat: his favourite tea for being such a good boy. Always sausages – 'squashages' he called them – always squashages for little Gerry, and he had been very brave on his first day at school and he had earned his squashages.

Where had it all gone so wrong? What could they have done to prevent him from falling prey to the drugs that had gripped him and taken over his life so comprehensively? She had not noticed at first. He was a young man enjoying himself with his friends, nice friends she thought – never any trouble. Then a new girlfriend came along and new friends, maybe not as nice as his old friends from school. But he was a young man, a good-looking young man, and his mother had seen many girls come and go. Then his moods changed and he became irritable, even angry sometimes. After that he lost his job at the DIY shop where he had worked for nearly three years. They said he had become unreliable, turning up late for work at first and then not turning up at all. Who knows, she thought to herself, perhaps this assault might be a blessing in disguise? Maybe this could be a turning point, the thing he needed to get back onto the straight and narrow, to make him realise that the road he was on was one of self-destruction and he had been given a last chance to get off it. A chance he surely would not let go of now? He could return when he was well enough, to the home he grew up in. His room had been left bare when he had gone. He had taken away his hi-fi and the other electrical equipment, sneaked them out, sold them she thought, most likely to buy drugs. But they could be replaced, and she would replace them when he was back home. With all of her heart she wished he was now home safely tucked up in his bed. Yes, this could just be the turning point she had dreamed of, back to a time that brought a smile to her face when she remembered it.

A distant noise interrupted her thoughts. It hummed between her husband's snores, quietly but nevertheless she could hear it. So gentle was the sound that she wondered whether it had been going on for a long time and she had not noticed, being locked in her own world of introspection. She concentrated on the noise and heard it clearly now. The telephone had been in the hall at the bottom of the stairs for years, and although Gerry had brought up the subject of putting additional phones around the house – his room had been specifically mentioned – there never seemed any pressing reason to go to the expense of changing it. They had never been great ones for technological changes. She had seen adverts for cordless this and hands-free that, but could never see the need. The phone at the bottom of the stairs was quite adequate. Why would they need another phone in the bedroom? Who was going to call them at night? Since Gerry had got his own mobile phone, the landline in the hall rarely got used at all, and when it had rung it had usually been Gerry to say where he was and why he was going to be late. But even these calls had ceased, and now the phone did not often ring. It was ringing now though.

Phillip Goodman snored as he had done for more hours than his wife could remember, and there was no sign that the ringing was going to disturb him. She thought of waking him but dismissed this. Even if Gerry was his mummy's boy, recent events had hit Phillip and hit him hard, more than he was ever going to admit, she knew that. He appeared a tough, even remote man from the outside, and this had sometimes not helped communications with Gerry. However she knew that this shell sheltered a very soft interior, more sensitive than anyone really knew.

She raised herself gently from the bed and turned and placed her legs over the edge, then put her feet onto the floor, finding the well-worn slippers she had left there whilst carrying out the reverse manoeuvre some long hours ago. The night was warm and as her nightdress hem unrolled itself down over her knees she made her way in the dark towards the bedroom door. There was no need for the dressing gown that hung on its chrome hook on the back of the bedroom door. A turn of the handle and the volume of the ringing increased as the door opened, but still Phillip's nasal sounds were not disturbed from their regular pattern. After shutting the door behind her she fumbled a little to find the landing light switch. She closed her eyes and slowly opened them as she became accustomed to the harsh brilliance of the one hundred watt bulb. It was always one hundred watts, Phillip would have no variation. She placed her hand on the stair rail and accelerated slightly after the first two steps, as she made her way down the staircase towards the phone which was still ringing, and had been now for some unknown number of minutes. She let go of the rail as she stepped off the last stair and with a smooth natural swing of her arm, placed her hand on the receiver. As she did the phone abruptly stopped in the middle of one of its rings. She left her hand on the receiver and stroked it in a gentle caress.

She let her hand remain there for a moment, convinced the caller would ring again – she did not know why. The receiver felt warm, familiar, and she felt strangely reassured and comforted by its touch. After a while, she picked up the receiver and dialled the number 1471, which Gerry had taught her would give her the caller's number. She waited and listened to the automated voice, female for some reason, as it spoke to her. 'You were called today at 4.37am. We do not have the caller's number to return the call. Please hang up.'

It was 6.35am. when Jet walked through the doors which led to the intensive care unit. There had been no difficulty parking the Fiesta so early in the morning. After entering the corridor of the unit, he saw a nurse sitting in the small staffroom which seemed positioned to guard the comings and goings of the unit. He approached the nurse and produced his police warrant card. 'I got a call to say there'd been a change in the condition of Gerald Goodman.'

'Yes. His parents have just arrived. They're with him now. Perhaps if you'd just like to take a seat? I'll get the sister to come and talk to you.'

The nurse disappeared and a short while later another nurse arrived, who Jet thought must be in her late thirties. She had a pretty face and forced a sympathetic smile which looked to him well practised within the confines of the ward. Jet could see from the dark colour of the skin underneath her eyes that she was tired. He could sympathise with that. It had been after eight o'clock by the time he had got home the previous night, and after something to eat, he had spent nearly three hours watching the second CCTV videotape from the station, the black and white picture on his television showing the events captured by the three cameras on Sunday. His patience had paid off and after much fast-forwarding and occasional rewinding; he had found a picture which gave a good full-front shot of Mark Groom and his shoplifter. He had not recognised the shoplifter but it was something to go on. Julia had been patient with him as he monopolised the television, spending her time thumbing through magazines he thought she had already looked at several times before and then turned her attention to *Frankenstein* by Mary Shelley. It was one of her favourite books and she had often tried to interest him in reading it. But it had never appealed to him. He was familiar enough with the story or at least the movie's interpretation of it, and he really didn't want to invest any more time in it, no matter how often Julia tried to convince him that it was a Gothic classic which needed to be read.

As he and Julia had turned out the lights they had not pretended Jet was some stranger from the carnival, but were themselves, when they again disappeared into a world where they were consumed solely with each other. He had put his tiredness out of his mind and wholeheartedly escaped into that place where videos and victims were distant thoughts. He did not know what time he had drifted to sleep, but it had seemed just minutes before he was disturbed by the bedside telephone. During the phone call from the night shift sergeant he had learned the hospital had been in touch to say Gerald Goodman had taken a turn for the worse. A turn very much for the worse. So here he was.

'We were always concerned the patient had shown no signs of improvement despite his treatment.' The sister was speaking whilst looking at the documents in her hand. They were securely fastened on a clipboard, which Jet guessed had been the records normally kept at the end of a patient's bed. 'Suddenly this morning he apparently suffered some sort of major episode. All of the medical equipment attached to him just went wild for a few minutes and then suddenly it silenced.'

'What sort of major episode?'

'I don't know. I've never seen anything like it before. It was as if he was making some great effort, like he was trying to call out. It was really strange.'

'What's his condition now?'

'He's alive only because he's connected to our equipment. The initial tests show that he's brain dead. Looks like he suffered a huge brain haemorrhage. We'll run another test in four hours to be absolutely certain, but it's most likely that we'll be turning off the machines this afternoon.'

The news stunned Jet, and for a moment he was silent,

thinking about the implications of what he had heard. However, his thoughts did not immediately turn to his investigation, a trait he knew was his professional weakness. 'How are his parents doing?'

'As you'd expect. Mrs Goodman seems particularly distressed.'

Jet thought for a few more seconds and then his mind returned to his professional considerations. 'I'll need to arrange for a pathologist to do the necessary. It would be best if he could have a look at him before the machines are turned off. Perhaps we could make arrangements once I've made some calls and we've talked to Mr and Mrs Goodman?'

'I think they need time to be at the bedside. We should leave them alone for a while.'

'Thank you Sister, that's only right.'

Jet summoned a false grin for the tired-looking sister who lowered the clipboard and politely returned a gentle smile. Jet began to turn away, knowing he needed to speak to the station to make arrangements. Then he realised he had forgotten one important point. 'Oh Sister, one last thing please. What time did Gerald have the episode when the machines went berserk?'

The nurse looked at the clipboard again. 'The time recorded here is 4.37am.'

Chapter eighteen

'Why the fuck didn't you tell me about this on Sunday?' Detective Inspector Ormond's voice was loud and angry.

'I ran it past the duty sergeant, and he said I didn't need to.'

'Who was that?'

'Mark Groom.'

'Fucking marvellous!'

Ormond shook his head vigorously as if in disbelief. In the main CID office, Jet was sitting at his desk as Ormond perched himself on the corner of an adjoining desk. Jet had called Ormond after he had been told of Goodman's turn for the worse. He had just explained all the details of the assault and how it was now likely to become a murder investigation. Ormond had seemed to get more and more agitated as Jet explained the details.

'York's going to go mental when I tell him about this.'

Jet watched and thought Ormond was going for the world head-shaking record. But he remained silent.

'I'll have to go up now and tell him that there's been a man in intensive care for two days, who, barring a miracle, is a fucking murder victim, and I knew fuck all about it.' Ormond kept sighing and shaking his head. 'Two fucking days Jet!'

'I'm sorry boss. I did ask Groom, but he said it wasn't necessary.'

'Well I'll go and face the music with York. You don't leave here until I speak to you.' Ormond stood up from the desk and walked to the door. He spoke as he walked away. 'Two fucking days. We could have had it all sorted by now for fuck's sake.'

Jet sat at his desk trying to occupy himself but could not concentrate. He pulled out the file for the burglar he had at court. The case was now due to be heard tomorrow, but he could not focus on it. He pushed the papers around for nearly half an hour and then the office phone rang. He lifted the receiver and had barely announced his name when Ormond's voice interrupted. 'Come up to Superintendent York's office now.'

He realised, as Ormond had not simply referred to him as 'York', that the superintendent must actually be present and Jet made his way straight there.

As he walked up the stairs, he thought how York's office had become a far too familiar place in recent days; far more familiar than he would have preferred. It was now after 9.00am and once again the police station was well populated. There was a lot of activity in the corridors, and Jet passed several people he did not recognise.

He knocked on the closed office door and quickly found himself sitting in York's office.

'DI Ormond has briefed me about the Goodman case.

I've asked him to lead the enquiry now that it looks likely to become a murder, and he'll set up a team to assist. I understand you've spoken to the family a number of times already, so, it seems sensible to leave you on the enquiry as family liaison officer.'

Jet nodded, offering no verbal response. After a brief pause, York spoke again. 'You have a suspect I believe?' Jet was relieved that York seemed quite relaxed and was certainly a lot calmer than Ormond had been when he had left him half an hour earlier.

'Yes Sir, a man called Metcalf. There are no witnesses as yet and not enough evidence to bring him in, but I did fancy him as a good bet when I spoke to him.'

'No need to dash into arresting him now, we'll gather the evidence first. As it's now a murder, we might find people more talkative. We'll get to him in good time.' York smiled at Jet. 'I understand that you took the shoes he was wearing. A little unorthodox.'

'It seemed like an opportunity to get a lead on him, and there didn't seem anything to lose in the circumstances.'

'Yes, well, let's hope if they do come back with traces of Goodman's blood on them, that the court accepts them as evidence. They can get funny about things like that you know.'

Jet was not sure whether he was being chastised or not and decided not to add further comment in his defence. Jet had realised when he took the shoes that they alone would not be enough to charge Metcalf with the assault, even if they had blood all over them, but it would be a good starting point. No doubt after a discussion with a solicitor paid for by the taxpayer, Metcalf would come up with some story – probably that he had lent them to some strange person whose name he could not recall. A man he had met in a bar who needed some kind assistance and that he had offered him his humane support to ease the suffering of an unfortunate soul. No doubt his solicitor would claim Metcalf deserved commendation rather than interrogation. No, the shoes were a starting point and, without a confession, more evidence was needed. Perhaps the customers of the Barking Dog would help now. It seemed unlikely that Metcalf had acted by himself, and therefore accomplices might hold the key. If they played a minor part in the incident maybe there was potential in coming to some arrangement with them about what they would be charged with, in return for their full account and testimony in court. Although Jet found plea-bargaining with criminals a very distasteful activity, he could understand the practicalities involved.

'Are you going to use the major incident room?' York looked directly at Ormond as he made the enquiry, which was more a direction than a question.

'Makes sense.'

'Good, thanks. I just need a quick word with DC Whittle.'

'Of course.' Ormond rose from his seat and walked

quickly from the room closing the door behind him.

'I've arranged for you to see Mark Groom at eleven. You need to call into the technical unit first. Make sure you bring the tape back to me when you're done.' York's sudden change of subject caught Jet off guard for a second.

'Yes, thanks.' Jet almost stuttered, being more convinced now that the wearing of hidden equipment to record his conversation had a deeper and perhaps more sinister purpose than simply protecting him from any allegation that might be made later. It crossed his mind just to ask York whether there was anything else going on he should know about, but that seemed pointless. York would undoubtedly tell him if there was anything he needed to know, he would have said. Jet was feeling more and more that he was playing a small part in a bigger production. Perhaps the wisest thing he could do was to look after himself and do his best to help anyone else in need. At the moment that looked like Mrs Groom and her daughter. Jet decided for now he should content himself with that.

York remained silent and maintained a fixed gaze on Jet, as if wondering whether there was any further enquiry which required his clarification. Jet would have liked to say something to York along the lines of, 'Sir, we seem to be dancing around things here, can you tell me what the hell is going on?' But he knew there was no chance of York laying his cards on the table, if, in fact, he had any cards. With a false smile, Jet left York's office without further comment.

Jet knew York operated in a 'need to know' world. The more you told people, the more risk you ran of your secrets becoming known to the wrong people. Information was a currency, and the more people who had it, the less valuable it was. It was in that same spirit of 'need to know' that Jet had not told anyone about the visit Metcalf had made to see DC Harris at the police station on Saturday afternoon. There did not seem to be any reason to bring this into the equation. Harris had spoken to Metcalf at Groom's request before the assault had actually taken place, so Jet thought it irrelevant in any case. Anyway, York had people checking the tapes for him and if they were doing their job properly he would probably already know.

But something did trouble Jet about the meeting he stumbled upon while watching a videotape he had not intended to watch. He just didn't know why.

Chapter nineteen

'Unfasten your trouser belt.'

'What?' Jet's mind had drifted as he stood in the small fitting room in the technical unit.

'We need to run the wire down your trousers.'

'Yeah, I see.'

Jet felt uncomfortable as he unbuckled his belt and unbuttoned the top of his trousers. The technician had a thin wire between his finger and thumb and held it out in front of Jet.

'Run that down your trousers.'

Jet felt the cold metal connector at the end of the wire touch the flesh on his warm leg as it ran inside his trousers. As it appeared at the bottom of his trouser leg, the technician grabbed it and plugged it into a small tape recorder and set about attaching the recorder around his ankle with a small Velcro strap. It was now just after ten o'clock, and Jet stood uncomfortably attempting to look down at the activity taking place around his shoe. He could feel his neck stretch as he peered at an odd angle, but all he could see was the top of the technician's head. He saw the head bobbing backwards and forwards and wondered whether he was aware that his hair was thinning. There was a two-inch circle around the back of his head where his hair was clearly failing in its attempt to cover the pale scalp.

The technician pulled Jet's sock up over the small tape recorder and then pulled the edge of his trouser leg down, concealing the recorder, and stood up. 'You need to run this end up your shirt so I can attach the microphone to your tie.'

Jet fumbled a little with the wire as he led it through his shirt and then pulled the end through a gap between the buttons in the centre of his chest. The technician took hold of the wire and connected it to a small plug leading to a minute microphone which he began to fasten to the back of Jet's tie. 'OK.' The technician's comment clearly indicated that the adjusting of clothes was over. Jet tucked his shirt into the top of his trousers and buckled his belt. 'This is the same as the unit on your leg.' The technician held a small recorder in his hand.

'Yes, you fitted one to me yesterday.'

'To operate it you press this 'record' button and to turn it off you press this button. Before your meeting, you must press this button.'

The instruction had been unnecessary, and Jet simply nodded.

'When you turn the tape on, remember to make sure it's concealed under your trouser leg.' Jet felt insulted by the instruction.

'What about all of these remote-controlled radio devices

you see on American cop programmes?' Jet idly enquired. 'You know, the ones where the other detectives are sitting listening to the conversation outside on an earpiece, getting ready to swoop when Mr Big finally incriminates himself.'

'Strictly Hollywood, Detective, not Newcastle. They're too unreliable, and, because they work on radio waves, the reception can be a problem and you can lose contact.' The quietly spoken technician was clearly an authority on the subject. 'And one of the least attractive qualities of the ones I've seen is that they start whistling sometimes when they go wrong. A bit of a giveaway really. These tape recorders are simple and reliable, and it's just not worth taking chances when all you need to do is record a conversation.'

Jet had been surprised by the technical officer calling him 'Detective': it had a remoteness that even Jet thought strange. He also realised for the first time that this person was not a police officer. No, this was obviously a technical expert, a civilian recruited for his specialist skills and knowledge. Jet wondered where an individual like this would get this experience – MI5 or the military perhaps. It occurred to him to ask this man, who he estimated to be in his early forties, how he had found himself in this line of work. But the thin, phlegmatic technical officer, who at no time had offered a name, did not look like someone who was going to offer up explanations or anecdotes easily, so Jet did not pursue his line of thought by questioning him any further.

'That tape will be good for an hour,' the quietly efficient anonymous technician added.

'Can't remember M telling James Bond that when he was getting fitted with his gadgets.'

The technician's face remained impassive. 'Q, Detective.'

'Sorry?'

'It was Q who fitted James Bond with his gadgets. M was his boss.'

'Never was much of a fan of that spy stuff – all seemed a little too far-fetched.'

'As you say, far-fetched.' The technician's face remained expressionless. 'The tape will be good for an hour,' he added unnecessarily, but returning the conversation to matters in hand and Jet wondered whether this was part of a conscious strategy to remain detached for some professional reason. Or maybe, he thought, the technician was just a miserable bastard.

It occurred to Jet that perhaps this was how he himself was seen by his colleagues. A remote character who adopted similar tactics as he preferred not to get too close to those around him in the workplace. It was thirty years since Jet the boy had seen his best friend hit by a speeding car, as the two of them fooled about on their bicycles on their council estate. Jet had challenged Brian to a race and they both tore off along the Tarmac road, vying for the inside track as they began to take the left-hand bend in the road. Jet edged himself into the lead as they began to lean slightly on their bikes to negotiate the turn. Brian got close and, fearing a collision, Jet held out his right arm and touched his friend's shoulder. Brian's bike wobbled and then straightened up and went across to the other side of the road – the wrong side of the road. Jet knew when he saw the Ford Cortina hit thirteen-year-old Brian Edwards that he could not possibly have survived. He vividly remembered the car bumping up and down as the front and then the back wheels ran over Brian's head and body. After the car left the body lying on the road, Jet ran to him and knelt beside his mangled friend. In the panic that swept through him he could hear himself calling out Brian's name, as if it was someone else calling out. Above all he remembered the blood, the thick, slow-running crimson fluid oozing from Brian's mouth and even his ears. It lay on the road in congealed pools. Jet had not known what to do. The rest was like a distant nightmare. He knew he had been there, but it was as if he had seen it through a telescope, helplessly watching it all in slow motion – the blood, the distorted bike and then the people. It seemed as if there were crowds of people, all offering their conflicting advice. A blanket appeared from somewhere which was put over Brian's legs and chest, and Jet remembered some adults discussing whether they should put something under his head. 'He's not asleep in bed, he was hit by a car!' Jet wanted to scream at them as they uttered their trivial comments, but he said nothing.

Then Brian's parents came from their nearby home,

having been told of the accident by someone desperate to do something. Mrs Edwards screamed at the sight of Brian and stood watching, but afraid to touch her son's mangled body. Her husband knelt and held his hand. 'Brian.' He repeated, 'Brian.' But Brian did not respond, he just lay there leaking fluids, and no one present possessed the power to stem the flow.

Eventually an ambulance arrived. The wailing of the siren was loud as it speedily entered the estate, and Jet remembered someone saying, 'Here comes the ambulance,' as if it required their special talents to spot it.

'Can no one help him?' Jet wanted to scream. 'Please someone help him. He's dying, can't you see?'

But in those moments before the ambulance arrived, which felt like a lifetime, no one had been able to help him.

A uniformed man jumped out of the ambulance and looked at Brian as the driver reversed closer. Within a few seconds, the driver joined his colleague and pulled a stretcher from the back doors which Brian was quickly placed upon and then put in the vehicle. Brian's parents went in the back of the ambulance and within a moment of it arriving, it sped out of the estate. The crowd hung around after it left, like stragglers from a party, not wanting to go home.

'Didn't look good.' The man held his blanket in his hand as he spoke.

'Didn't look good!' Jet wanted to shout. 'How could it

ever have looked good?' But he hadn't been able to shout, all he had been able to do was feel useless and then, after that, all he could feel was blame. No one had ever said it was his fault but he knew that it was.

Then there'd been the funeral. His mum said, 'It's best if you don't go, it would be too upsetting for you and it's a time for Mr and Mrs Edwards to grieve in private.'

Jet hadn't understood the reason then, in truth he still didn't. He looked out of his bedroom window at his friend's house, watched the hearse pull away and felt empty and alone. But most of all he felt blame, for the death of his friend and the world of unbelievable grief this brought to his family. Worst of all, he had not been able to tell his friend he was sorry, or been able to say goodbye.

Jet could remember telling his story at the inquest. It had only taken him a few minutes to tell the coroner what happened – not long he thought given the consequences of what had taken place that day. The room full of people listened in stony silence and as he spoke, Jet could also hear himself talking. He heard his words circle the room and come back to his own ears. He felt the pain of every word hit him; the race, the push, the wobbly bike, it all came back, as it had many times before the inquest, and as it would many times afterwards. For a long time Jet felt an aching in his stomach, as if a red-hot poker had been pushed into his gut and left there. It had taken some time to leave him, and even now, these thirty years later, it returned when his thoughts went back to that day. Sometimes it happened when something he saw reminded him of it – a young boy on a bike perhaps. Sometimes it happened for no reason – the thought just flashed into his brain, and he felt the pain in his gut.

Jet did not really know whether that single incident was responsible for shaping the way he chose to conduct future relationships with his fellow man and woman, but he knew the guilt weighed heavily. His mother had taken him to see his GP as the nightmares continued to wake him up, but when the doctor suggested the services of a psychiatrist it was immediately rejected. 'Oh no Doctor, I don't think that's necessary. I just thought something to help him sleep.' He remembered what his mother said to the doctor. He also remembered what he overheard her saying to his father after they'd returned home, and he had been sent upstairs to wash. 'That's all we need, people thinking he's mental as well. Told him no thanks, he's just a boy, he'll get over it.'

The devastation of that day always stayed with Jet. He gradually learned to lock the pain away in a place deep inside himself and even the nightmares became less frequent. He had found a way to deal with these things on his own, but even now when his thoughts returned to Brian the pain came back as well. He did not know whether the way he had dealt with these emotions was the most effective, but he did know that he had coped. He survived. Survived with his guilt.

'Thanks' was the only other word exchanged between Jet and the technician. A few minutes later and Jet was back in his Fiesta, heading towards Durham and another meeting he was not looking forward to. This time he was going to ask questions he knew Groom would not like, but he knew that if he was going to make sense of the puzzles around him he needed answers.

Chapter twenty

It was 10.55am when Jet left his car in the car park of Durham Police Station. He walked into the front office and told the young fresh-faced woman who greeted him, that Detective Inspector Steven Lambert was expecting him. Within a few moments, the detective inspector greeted him with a firm handshake and more warmth than Jet expected. Jet thought the detective inspector was in his early thirties and had the air of a high-flyer. He was unlike the crusty Detective Inspector Nigel Ormond, who, with over thirty years service, was a career detective, with little time for people who were not of the same ilk. Ormond would doubtless have had something to say about this interloper, who was using the position to prepare himself for something else, rather than treating it as the vocation that Ormond was convinced it should rightly be. Jet knew Ormond to be a dedicated and committed detective but thought his view of things tended to be very narrow.

Jet followed as Lambert walked down the station's narrow corridors, occasionally stopping to use his key to open a security door as they moved further into the building. The last door Lambert unlocked led them inside the cell block. They walked up the first length of the narrow, magnolia passage and then Lambert pushed open the door of a small interview room. He walked around the table which was bolted to the floor in the centre of the room. Through necessity the surface of the circular table was minute and Jet thought it looked comically small. Lambert sat down on one of two thin metal chairs. Jet sat down on the chair opposite and felt cramped.

'He appeared at court this morning charged with murder. They remanded him in custody.' Lambert's explanation took Jet slightly by surprise; it was not the information that surprised him but the fact that Lambert was taking time to explain it. Had this been Ormond, then the odd grunt on the way in would have been the maximum interaction. Ormond was another devotee of the 'need to know' principle and did not like wasting his time on conversation with underlings. Jet knew it as the mushroom syndrome: he was usually kept in the dark and then shit on from time-to-time.

'Normally prisoners would be remanded to Durham Prison, but as that was the scene of the crime it wasn't appropriate.' Lambert continued, 'The only thing we could come up with was to keep him here until something else is worked out.'

Jet nodded. The interview room was claustrophobic and he felt uncomfortable at the close range of this encounter. Lambert leaned forward as he spoke, carefully resting his arms on the diminutive table. His fingers were interlocked as he clasped his hands together and Jet could see each of his perfectly manicured fingernails. Jet caught a subtle whiff of aftershave and as Lambert smiled and spoke he felt uneasy at the intimacy. He realised Lambert was trying to be as helpful as he could, but Jet could not avoid the feeling of dislike that had formed in him over the last few moments.

'Got the prison service in a right pickle,' Lambert said and Jet could well appreciate their dilemma. 'The upshot is,' he continued, 'that I don't think Groom will be going anywhere quickly. It seems very likely he'll stay here until his next court appearance in a week.' Lambert was well spoken, and Jet could not detect an accent in the voice which would not have been out of place on BBC's *Radio Four*. It was very unlike the rolling Durham accents he had heard on his last visit, which seemed very different to him than the inflections possessed by him and his fellow Geordies. The truth was there was something about the Durham accent Jet just did not like, but he could not put his finger on the reason why.

'Well, that's about all I can tell you.' Lambert said.

Jet uttered his first word of the meeting, 'Thanks.'

Lambert rose and Jet followed him back into the windowless corridor of the cell complex. As they approached the large custody desk, Lambert spoke to the custody sergeant standing behind it, who in turn eyed Jet briefly, before making an entry in the custody record and issuing instructions to a junior officer to take Jet to Groom's cell. The young jailer emerged from an office behind the custody desk and was carrying what appeared to Jet to be a collection of keys that must have held claim to be the biggest bunch in the world. The large black cell-door keys were individually so big that they were each numbered. The numbers were white and punched onto a thick red-plastic tape. As they walked into the corridor Jet was a few paces behind the young officer and shouted, 'Hang on a second pal.'

Jet bent down and took hold of his shoe and the jailer needed no explanation to realise that Jet wanted to be excused for a second whilst he fastened his lace. The jailer paid little attention as Jet pressed the 'record' button, which kicked his covert device into action. Jet remained on one knee for a few seconds longer and, as he did, fumbled with his laces. The jailer also paid no attention when Jet tugged the wire on his hidden tape recorder which led to the microphone, so it became dislocated. Jet took a deep breath and wondered if York would believe him when he told him the microphone must have become detached by accident on the drive to Durham. Jet preferred not to tell lies, but he felt this was one of those rare occasions when it was necessary. Jet rose to his feet.

'OK, thanks.'

He smiled at the young jailer who selected the appropriately numbered key and inserted it into the lock. The heavy lock mechanism turned and then he pulled the cumbersome outward opening door. Groom was sitting on the bleak-looking fixed bench which was the only thing in the cell that could be described as furniture. He smiled when he saw Jet. The jailer asked Jet to press the cell buzzer when he wanted to leave and then closed the door, leaving the two alone in the small cell. The feeling of claustrophobia visited Jet again as he heard the metal thud of the door close, locking him in.

'Good to see you Jet. How are you doing?'

'Fine, what about you?'

'As well as you'd expect. Think I'm giving the authorities a bit of a headache. Did you see Shirley and Diane?'

'Yes, they're fine. I visited them, and they're worried about you, but other than that I don't think you've any reason to be concerned.'

'What about Trent's people?'

'Mark, I don't know if he has any people. I went to his home and spoke to his mother and it just doesn't seem to add up. His mother doesn't live the life of a drug baron's mother.'

'He must have stashed it away. He must have been making a fortune with the amount of gear he was shifting. I thought we hit it big when we caught him with that big stash. Is Diane all right?'

'She's confused. Worried about you. York put an alarm in the house, and I'll call and see them regularly. They've got my number. I promise I'll look after them. If there's any sign of trouble, I'll take them to my place and they can stay with me and Julia.'

'You're a good man Jet. Thanks.'

Jet looked at Groom and it struck him that he did not look as big as he had in the past. He looked tired and worn, and Jet guessed he had not slept much over the last few days.

'Mark.' Jet's voice changed and now had an earnest tone. Groom detected the change and did not reply but just continued to look at him.

'Mark, did you set Trent up?'

The question seemed to take Groom entirely by surprise.

'You wearing a wire Jet?'

Jet pulled his left trouser leg up exposing the small but still quite visible tape recorder secured to his ankle. Groom had used them often enough over the years to know what it was.

'York asked me to wear this for my own protection. I've disconnected it, so it can't pick up what we're saying. I thought it might be better if we have a private chat. I need answers Mark, if I'm to get to the bottom of this.'

'You always were too honest for your own good. That's why I asked you for help.' Groom seemed almost to smile as he finished speaking, and both men remained silent for a few seconds.

'Well?' Jet spoke quietly as he resumed the conversation.

'Well what?

'Was Trent set up?'

'I know what you think of me Jet, and I can't say that I've always lived up to your ideals, but no matter what anyone thinks, I've never set anyone up. And if I was going to, do you think I would risk my job by setting a little prick like Trent up?' Groom looked angry, almost hurt, that Jet had questioned his integrity. He paused for a second and with his eyes fixed firmly on Jet asked him a question he was not expecting. 'Do you know why I joined the police force?'

'No.' Jet's reply was accompanied by a slow, unwitting shake of his head.

'When I was a boy, I saved up my money to buy a Mother's Day present. It was a plant, a chrysanthemum it was – chose it myself. Not really much in the whole scheme of things, but it was special to me. My dad hid it for me in his car so my mother wouldn't find it in the house. I saw some little shit smash the car window right outside my house and nick it. I chased him and nearly caught him, but fell as I was grabbing him and broke this arm.' Groom's right hand gripped his left elbow across the point where the deep scar ran. He stroked it as if it still ached. 'Believe it or not, before that my mum had high hopes of me becoming a musician – I was a mean violinist – but my arm was never the same again. She was gutted; she'd spent a fortune on music lessons.'

Jet could see there was a deep intensity in Groom's face, as well as tone of voice. He was not sure how much the events of the last few days had also played a part in Groom's mood, but as he continued Jet could see what a profound effect this boyhood experience had had on him. 'Never did find out who stole the plant. Don't tell many people that story Jet, but that feeling of injustice stayed with me from that time. I'd never thought about crime before that day, but after that I hated criminals, and I decided to do my best to lock them up. That's why I joined the job, to see justice done and criminals stopped. I sometimes sail close to the wind to catch them, but I don't set innocent people up. Just like you Jet.'

Had Groom told Jet this story at any other time, he would not have known whether to take him seriously or not, but today, in a cell with Groom charged with murder, today of all days, Jet believed this story of a defining moment. A single event had shaped the future for one young boy and subsequently for a lot of criminals he had brought to justice. Jet could feel his opinion of Groom change and he realised that over the years perhaps he had done him some disservice. Groom continued to stare at Jet and after a few seconds the intensity seemed to relax slightly and Groom went on. 'We had intelligence of a shipment by a big dealer. All we had was the vehicle and location. We didn't even know Trent was going to be in the car. The squad plotted up and we waited for the car and then Trent turned up. We stopped him and the drugs were in the boot.'

'I knew Trent, a petty thief at best. This was a huge leap

for him and I just have a problem seeing it.' Jet was solemn.

'He was always into some scam or another; maybe he'd just got into the business and was unlucky to get caught the first time he made a big score. You know drug dealers; they probably fed us the information to keep the competition at bay.'

'Maybe,' Jet said but he was not convinced. 'Where did the information about the job come from?'

'I think it was an anonymous tip-off: just a call to the office. Most likely from another drug dealer. It's where we get most of our best information from.'

Jet stared at Groom as if he was trying to look into his conscience and assess whether he was telling the truth, but it was a fruitless search. Jet had seen good officers move into the dark and murky world of drug squad work, and they seemed to forget what they had promised to uphold when they joined the police. Keeping secrets and telling lies became second nature to them and he wondered whether Groom had gotten himself so involved in the business that he too had lost his way.

Jet had another thing on his mind. 'Does the name John Metcalf mean anything to you?'

Groom pondered the question. 'It rings a vague bell.' He took a few seconds as if searching his memory. 'Why, should I know it?'

'Another petty criminal. Ray Harris told me you'd asked him to speak to Metcalf on Saturday.'

'It's possible Jet. You know we spend most of our time talking to low life, so it's possible.'

'But you don't remember contact on Saturday?'

'Is it important?'

'I don't know.' Jet paused, then decided to explain further. 'Remember that assault you asked me to look at on Sunday?' Groom nodded. 'Well, he's a suspect for that, and the day before he was visiting the police station to talk to the drug squad.'

'If it was the day before, I don't see why it's bothering you Jet.'

Jet wasn't sure himself, but he knew it was.

'Maybe.' Jet's reply had an air of resignation about it.

'Listen, if it's bothering you that much have a look in my contacts book. I record everything in there.'

'I would imagine York will have that by now.'

'He might have, but not necessarily.'

'What do you mean?'

'In the locker room, 431, it's in there. Combination number 7390. Been the most secure place I've had for years. Safer than any desk, and now it's all yours.'

'I'll see if it's still there.' Jet suddenly felt a little more trusting of Groom, although there were still many things he was uncertain about. 'Is there anything else I can do for you Mark?'

'Just make sure Shirley and Diane are looked after.'

'I promise I will. Do you want them to visit? I don't

think there'd be a problem.'

'I'd like to see Shirley. I don't want Diane to see me like this though. Would you speak to Shirley and bring her in?'

'I'll speak to her and see what I can arrange.'

'Thanks. You're a good man Jet.'

There was a silence, and during that quiet few seconds Jet wanted to ask him why he had killed Trent; he wanted to know what had happened to trigger an event that could only ever have led to the destruction of both men. Jet wondered whether this life-changing event really had been caused by the presence of a photograph of Diane Groom, in the same way the theft of a plant had caused such a change in his life. He wanted to ask, he wanted some clarification, but Jet knew this was not the time and so the question, and all of the subsequent questions Jet knew it would solicit, went unspoken.

Jet sounded the buzzer and the young jailer quickly reappeared. Within a few minutes, Jet was heading north again back towards Newcastle. He was going to drop the tape off at York's office and hoped York would not want to listen to it right away. If he did, he was going to be disappointed, and Jet was in for a good shouting at. Another rocket for Jet, he thought, and not for the first time in his career, not by a long chalk!

He was not sure how York would react to his requests for future visits, but on balance, thought it had been worth taking the risk to have an honest exchange with Groom. He would just have to stick to his story. He did not like being dishonest, but he could not tell York the truth. Nor would he tell York that as soon as he had asked him to wear a wire and bring the tapes back to him, he had taken the sensible precaution of wearing his own wire. And that one had not been disconnected.

Chapter twenty-one

Jet had returned his secret tape recorder to the humourless technician and dropped the tape off at York's office before going in search of Detective Inspector Ormond to see what task was required of him in respect of the Gerald Goodman murder investigation. When he handed York the tape Jet did not suggest there may be a problem with it. He had decided the best thing to do was to give it to him, wait for the inevitable call demanding an explanation, and then plead ignorance.

Fifteen minutes later Jet found himself following Ormond's abruptly delivered instructions to return to the intensive care unit.

As he entered the ward corridor, the feeling of intruder came rushing back to him, but he was pleased to see a familiar face sitting in the office he had come to consider as the reception area. It did not offer any written notice to raise visitor expectations, but it did seem to be the office where staff gravitated when they were not performing other pressing duties.

'Hello Trish,' Jet spoke in a hushed tone to the nurse, who had not noticed his arrival. She raised her head and a smile spread across her face, which generated unexpected but welcome warmth in Jet. 'I was wondering how Gerald Goodman was doing?'

Jet's question changed Trish's smile into an expression he recognised as helpless sympathy: the smile broadened slightly but was accompanied by a frown as her eyes narrowed. 'Not good. All of the tests have shown him to be brain dead, I'm afraid.'

'How are Mr and Mrs Goodman?'

'They're with him now, saying their goodbyes. The machines are being switched off and they're staying with him until the end.' Trish's voice was soft and gentle. After a short pause, during which Jet's thoughts had wandered inappropriately off the matter in hand, she continued. 'It's so sad. He seemed to be recovering from the operation, but it looks like he suffered a massive haemorrhage early this morning.'

'How are they coping?'

'Mr Goodman's hardly spoken a word – in shock I guess. Mrs Goodman has been very distressed; she got a strange phone call about the time he suffered the haemorrhage, she's convinced it was him trying to contact her. She's angry that she didn't get to the phone before it rang off. I'm sure there'll be a simple explanation, but it does seem odd. It's a strange world isn't it…?' Trish looked at Jet, searching for a name.

'Frank,' Jet offered.

'It's a strange world, Frank.'

Jet thought his name sounded nice coming from the lips of this attractive nurse. He had never cared for Frank: it had a very old-fashioned feel about it. Francis belonged to his grandfather who had died just before Jet was born. The unfortunate timing of genealogy led to his sad inheritance, an act of remembrance to a man he was never to meet. Francis had thankfully been shortened to Frank by his parents for everyday use, but Jet still didn't think it was much of a name to be saddled with for life. It did not matter how many times Jet's father told him stories of the great man his grandfather was, and how proud he was of his name; he simply did not like the name Frank. Had it been possible for Jet to be consulted he would have said that he wanted to be called Max or Dan, something with an edge to it. Ian Fleming had not decided to call his famous hero Frank Bond, and in general, television and movie heroes called Frank were thin on the ground. Jet thought that was for good reason. His feelings about his name were probably the reason he had accepted 'Jet' so readily and, in truth, he had grown accustomed to it over the years. It was better than Frank. But occasionally, just occasionally, he liked the sound of it. Coming now, from the lips of this brown-haired slender nurse, it sounded quite pleasing and produced inside him something like a slight shiver which tingled and made him feel alive. Jet felt guilty that at this moment his heartbeat had been quickened by this nurse's warm smile. He could not help but notice the top button of her crumpled, trouser-suited uniform, was undone, revealing the soft, brown skin of her neck, and despite the bagginess of her uniform, he could also see the round curve of her breast. He felt rooted to the spot. He smiled, knowing that the moment would quickly pass.

'As you say Trish, it's a strange world.' And Jet meant this beyond the polite accord she may have thought he was expressing. He had no deep-seated beliefs in anything spiritual, but every time he thought he had a handle on life something came along to challenge him.

Jet smiled at Trish, and for a few seconds they remained in an unusual silence which Jet did not find in the least awkward. A wailing sound interrupted this moment of intimacy. It was unmistakably female and grew louder. Howls of anguish punctuated the loud sobbing on the deep breaths being expelled from the mouth of Mrs Goodman, who was clearly beyond consolation. As reboant bursts were expelled from her distraught body she was being guided by the contrasting figure of the silent Mr Goodman who looked ashen faced, confused and heavy with sorrow. Another nurse followed closely behind, and they were guided into a room where the door was quickly shut in a vain attempt to contain the sounds of grief.

No confirmation was needed. Jet knew this marked the passing of the Goodmans' only child. The result, Jet thought, of another senseless act, another inexplicable event inflicted by one human being on another. Jet had seen the results of many senseless acts and had stopped trying to understand why these things happened – he just stuck to the facts. They happened and it was his job to find out who was responsible and to gather the evidence to bring them to justice. Yes, he had stopped trying to understand why these things happened, but he could not stop feeling a sadness of his own when they did.

Trish gave a sympathetic smile. 'We'll do our best to look after them.'

'You must get a lot of this. Doesn't it get you down?'

'Sometimes, but we also save a lot of lives.'

'That must make it worthwhile.'

'It does, but it's still hard when this happens.'

'Would you assure the Goodmans that we're working hard to find out who did this, and I'll contact them soon?'

'Sure.'

'Thanks.' And with that last word Jet smiled and left the ward.

In the car park, Jet found Detective Inspector Ormond's number on his mobile phone and Ormond answered it promptly when Jet rang. Jet did not think Ormond sounded surprised at the news of Gerald Goodman's death. He did however sound anxious to hear about Jet's visit to John Metcalf's home which had been only two days ago but to Jet seemed a great deal longer.

'He must have done a runner.' Ormond confided his conclusion to Jet. 'There's no sign of him, and his neighbours say they haven't seen or heard him since yesterday.'

Ormond told Jet that Metcalf's shoes had come back from the lab and had revealed traces of Goodman's blood. They would now circulate Metcalf's details as the person wanted for the murder of Gerald Goodman.

'Let's see what the bastard has got to say about that when we get a hold of him.' Ormond sounded serious.

Jet explained he would be away for a little while as he had to attend to a job for Superintendent York. Ormond did not question it. Jet got into his car and headed to Prudhoe to see Shirley Groom. As he headed out of the car park in the Fiesta, Jet felt the sadness he had left in the intensive care unit hang over him like a long-cast shadow. He hoped that the further he drove away from the hospital the lighter he would feel, but he knew it was not so simple. And, as he drove, he considered the passing of the young man he had not spoken to, but had come to know, a passing few would mourn and most would not notice. Jet knew there was enough sorrow generated in the world every day to fill a thousand oceans. What he did not know was very soon he would face death himself.

Chapter twenty-two

What struck Jet about the Castlefields Estate, as he drove into it, was how quiet it was. He approached it from Low Prudhoe which made him appreciate the steep gradient of the hill the new houses were built on. The lack of individual boundaries between the open-plan front gardens gave the impression that the houses had been neatly placed onto a fresh green meadow at odd angles with each other. As Jet drove his car up the road which ran through the centre of the housing estate, it looked as if it had been abandoned. Perhaps, like a modern ghost town, it had experienced a supernatural event which had caused its occupants to disappear. He wondered whether there was a Prospero lurking somewhere behind one of the thick velvet curtains which dominated the large bay windows that were prominent on this new estate. He knew *The Tempest* would not be his favourite of Shakespeare's plays if Julia had not dragged him to the Theatre Royal in Newcastle at least once, and often twice, during RSC seasons. If she had not, he would never have seen enough Shakespeare to have a favourite. At first it had all seemed quite odd and inaccessible, but then a penny dropped and he began to enjoy the plays and admire the way the words of the work were carefully crafted.

Jet's mind jolted back to reality and, as he looked around the estate, he concluded that with big shiny new houses came big shiny mortgages, which meant that the time people had to enjoy their new homes was limited, as they were probably all at work in order to keep up the payments.

He parked his car on the fresh-looking Tarmac outside the Grooms' home. Shirley Groom opened the door after one ring of the bell. She smiled, and it occurred to Jet that, if appearances were anything to go by, Shirley was coping with the events of the last few days a good deal better than her husband. The last time he had seen Shirley her eye make-up had followed the course of her tears – thick, black smudges staining her cheeks – but there was no sign of that now.

Shirley opened the door wide. Jet understood the invitation to enter without a word being exchanged and followed her into the living room dominated by the white fireplace, and the word 'ostentatious' crossed his mind again.

'How are you keeping, Shirley?'

'OK I think, under the circumstances.'

'And Diane?'

'She's at school. It seemed best to try and get things back to as normal as possible.'

The response took Jet by surprise, and having not long left the pathetic figure of Mark Groom it actually struck him as callous.

'It must be very difficult to keep going at a time like this.'

'You're right. Have you seen him?'

'Yes.'

'Did he have much to say?'

'He's still worried about you and Diane more than anything else.'

'I don't know why. Nothing is going to happen to us, we haven't hurt anyone.'

'Mark's worried because of the photograph he saw of Diane. It does seem odd someone would go to all the trouble of taking the photograph and then making sure that Mark saw it at the police station.'

'Have you still got the photograph of Diane?'

'No. Truth is there seems to have been a bit of a cock-up. The man Mark arrested for shoplifting was cautioned and given all of his property back, including the photographs. He left, and we don't know who he was. The name and address he gave were false.'

'And for these photographs Mark went into the prison and murdered Geoffrey Trent?'

'I don't know exactly, but it looks like that's what happened. He must have thought they were some kind of threat.'

'Mark always was a hothead but to murder someone over a photograph?' Shirley shook her head slowly. 'It just seems so hard to believe that all of this is over a photo.'

It struck Jet that Shirley seemed distant again, as if

she was searching for answers in some place deep within herself. After a few seconds of silence Jet decided to change the subject. 'I think Mark would like to see you. Would you like me to arrange it? I could take you into the police station if you like.'

Shirley remained silent as she stared at the large lifeless fireplace and still lost in her thoughts. He decided to gently continue. 'He doesn't think it is a good idea for Diane to go and see him – not locked in a cell.'

'I don't want to go and see him yet.'

Shirley's statement took Jet aback, but he tried hard not to allow his thoughts to betray him. Jet could see she was clearly distressed, and he knew that people reacted in different ways when they were in shock.

'I'm sure Mark will understand; it's been a lot to take in. Would you like me to take a message to him?'

Jet was again caught off guard when Shirley changed the subject. 'You don't seem like one of Mark's usual friends.'

'I'm not on the drug squad, if that's what you mean.' Jet smiled. 'I work in the CID office at Newcastle.'

'I guessed that by the way you dress.'

Jet looked down at his grey suit and his sensible blue silk tie, with its small, red-diamond pattern; one of the many presents Julia had given him. It was his favourite tie, but he did not share that with Shirley.

'I see what you mean,' he replied still looking at his Marks & Spencer suit which he thought would not be out of place behind a desk in a bank or an accountant's office. 'It's not really necessary for me to make an effort not to look like a cop for what I do. All that undercover work was never really me.' And Jet sincerely meant this as no matter what he wore or where he was, he always looked like a policeman. Julia had told him this many times. Last summer they had gone to Corfu, and just after they had arrived he had changed in their room in the Hotel Potamaki, into a pair of new shorts he had bought himself for the occasion. As he had tucked his short-sleeved shirt into the waistband Julia had said, 'Frankie, I don't know how you manage it. Even here you look like you are going to investigate someone's burglary.'

He didn't know whether it was years of being a policeman that had affected his demeanour so he now automatically exuded the aura of a policeman, but he did know that he had resigned himself to his fate and had given up trying to change it.

'I'm sorry; I didn't mean to make you feel uncomfortable,' Shirley said.

'Don't worry about it, you didn't,' Jet said, not being entirely honest.

'Some of the people that Mark brings round here from work make me wonder how they ever became policemen.'

'I know what you mean.'

The uncomfortable silence returned for a few seconds, and it was Jet who broke it this time. 'Is there anything you'd like me to tell Mark when I go and see him tomorrow?'

Shirley took a deep breath and at the same time lifted her head to look at the ceiling, considering her response. After a few seconds her eyes returned to Jet. 'Just tell him we're fine and not to worry about us.'

'I told him you're more than welcome to come and stay with me and my wife Julia, and I mean that. It might make Mark feel better if he knew you were out of the house.'

'I'm quite all right here. I don't know what happened with the photographs, but I'm sure we were never under any threat from Geoffrey Trent.'

'I don't think we should be taking chances. Why don't you just come and stay with us for a few days?'

'You're very kind, but it's not necessary.'

'It might ease Mark's mind.'

Shirley appeared a little agitated by Jet's persistence. 'No, we're perfectly safe here.'

'You seem very certain about that.' Jet looked at Shirley and his eyes narrowed as he spoke, as if to impress on her the intensity of the situation, and perhaps get her to question her faith in this conclusion. 'Trent was quite a persistent criminal who'd been arrested many times; he didn't exactly like the police and Mark in particular. It's possible the photograph was meant as a threat and that it was delivered to Mark to show him how vulnerable his family was. I don't think we should underestimate it.'

Shirley looked solemnly at Jet. 'I don't just think that

Geoffrey Trent wouldn't hurt me or Diane, I'm sure of it.'

'How can you be so certain Shirley?'

'Because he's Diane's father.'

Jet had been startled a few times by Shirley's comments during the discussion, but this disclosure was a show-stopper.

'I don't understand.'

'We had a relationship, nothing too intense. I worked at a pub, he was a regular, Mark was away for months on one of his training course and Diane was the result.'

'Did Trent know?'

'He knew I was pregnant. That's when he cleared off.'

'Does Mark know?'

Shirley seemed to consider this question for a long time and then looked away from the fireplace and directly at Jet. 'You know,' she paused slightly again, 'I really don't know. Honestly I don't. He came back from training school and I'm not sure he ever questioned whether he was Diane's father. If he did doubt it then he never showed it, and he dotes on Diane.'

Jet paused for thought as all of this information circled around in his head. 'Shirley, you don't think Mark could have killed Trent because he knew that he was Diane's father do you?'

'I've asked myself that question a million times over the past two days, and I just don't know.'

'What if Trent told Mark this when they met in the

prison? It's a powerful reason to lose your temper and fight with someone.' Jet's voice slowed down as his mind processed the information, 'A more powerful reason than a photograph.'

'What have I done?' Shirley placed both her hands over her face and then slid them down so her fingertips crossed her forehead and rested over her eyes as she started to sob. It crossed Jet's mind to reach out and touch her shoulder in an attempt to console, but something within him prevented it.

'Shirley, I don't think you can blame yourself for what happened on Sunday.'

Shirley raised her head and dried her eyes with her fingers as if attempting to rally from her temporary display of distress.

'Do you understand why I don't want to see him at the moment? I just don't know what to say or do. If he's just found out Diane is Geoffrey Trent's child he's not going to be very pleased with me. I'm frightened of what he might do.'

'You don't think he would hurt you, do you Shirley?'

Shirley paused again. 'I don't know. I don't think so. I don't know what to think.'

Jet thought she was becoming more and more confused and did not know how to respond, and even though his instinct was to say something to reassure her, he could not find the words. It was Shirley who found the next ones. 'If he doesn't know Diane was Geoffrey Trent's child, then the news might destroy him. I need some more time to figure out what to do. Please tell him we're fine and I'll come and see him soon – when I'm up to it. Tell him I'm very upset and need some time to pull myself together. It's been a big shock.'

Jet thought Shirley was almost pleading with him as she spoke and had all the qualities of a desperate schoolgirl, as if Jet himself needed to be convinced of something.

'Don't worry Shirley, I'll tell him you are upset and need to look after Diane. I'm sure Mark will understand.'

Silence returned to the room as Shirley gazed at the white fireplace which had started to look like a monument to Jet: the thick, white columns of fluted wood actually had the qualities of a mausoleum, he thought.

'Shirley.' Jet's tone was soft, and the unnecessary use of her name told Shirley a delicate question was coming. She turned slowly to look at Jet again.

'Shirley, are you sure Diane is Geoffrey Trent's daughter?' They looked fixedly at each other for a few seconds in silence, and then Jet attempted to explain his question. 'I mean, there couldn't be any doubt could there?'

She lightly shook her head. 'No, there's no doubt – there never has been.'

Shirley's stare returned to the fireplace.

'Shirley, I think it would be a good idea if you and Diane came to stay with me for a little while. My wife Julia would love the company.'

221

A weak smile crossed her face. 'You're very kind, but I really would rather be here. I'd rather be at home, and I'm not sure it would do Diane any good being away from her home and school.'

Jet smiled back. 'I understand, of course you're right.'

Jet sensed that Shirley wanted to be on her own again, and he smiled a broad smile as he rose. 'I'll pass that message on to Mark. Please try not to worry.'

As they walked along the narrow hall towards the front door, Jet spoke again. 'I knew Trent, and I'm surprised he didn't use the fact that he was Diane's father to taunt Mark. He could be quite a tormentor when he wanted to be.'

'He wasn't stupid. Why would he do anything that might lead to him having to pay maintenance for his child? Anyway, I'm not sure if Trent ever gave us a second thought. It was all such a long time ago.'

'Suppose so.'

'You won't say anything to Mark, will you?' Shirley hesitated for a second, 'You know, about Geoffrey Trent and Diane?' she added unnecessarily.

'Of course not.' And with that, after one more sympathetic smile, Jet turned and walked down the driveway and back towards his Ford Fiesta.

Thank God he had Julia, he thought to himself as he slid into the front seat of the Fiesta. Julia who he knew he could always rely on and who would never have a secret to conceal from her beloved Frankie.

Chapter twenty-three

Some forty minutes after walking out of Shirley Groom's home, Jet entered the briefing room at Newcastle Police Station. It was now being used as an incident room by DI Ormond, two detective sergeants and four other detective constables. Together with Jet, they now constituted the enquiry team for the murder of Gerald Goodman. As he walked into the room, two detectives were sitting in front of computer screens punching at the keyboards.

'All right Jet?' said the detective closest to him as he entered the room.

'Yes,' was Jet's automatic reply although in reality it was not entirely accurate. Jet's mind had remained in overdrive since he had left Shirley Groom. He knew he was going to have to go back to see Mark in his cell soon, and he was not sure how the information that had been revealed to him had changed things. How significant was it that Diane Groom was in actual fact Geoffrey Trent's daughter? This question tormented him. It was not a simple question of whether Mark Groom actually knew or not but whether, if he did not know, should he be told? It could provide some serious mitigation to a charge of murder. It could even, Jet thought, lead to sufficient mitigation for a reduction of the charge to manslaughter and a much-reduced sentence. He knew Groom would have already been interviewed and asked for his account of events that led to the death of Geoffrey Trent. If Groom knew Trent was Diane's father, then that might have been the time for him to explain, but Jet suspected Groom would have been advised by his solicitor to say nothing during his interview. This was standard advice these days. 'Don't say anything and let's see if they can prove it,' was about as sophisticated as it got from solicitors who were paid handsomely from the public purse to protect the rights of criminals. Even when it was clear that an explanation might actually help a suspect, it was still given as the standard response for the arrested person to adhere to. Such was the uniformity of the mantra these days that solicitors had stopped coming to police stations themselves to deliver the advice in person but employed unqualified messengers to do it. It seemed to Jet to be the perfect arrangement: solicitors still charged their exorbitant rate, gave their messenger a small percentage and kept the rest for doing nothing. These 'runners', as they were known to Jet and his colleagues, spent their lives hanging around police stations being permanently treated with suspicion. Jet thought the worst ones were the ex-coppers who seemed favoured by defence solicitors for their inside knowledge and worked as runners to supplement their pensions. Traitors, Jet thought, collecting their thirty pieces of silver. It was sufficient proof for Jet to be convinced that the whole legal system was about the distribution of wealth and had very little to do with truth or justice. Truth was a word that was mentioned only when a witness spoke the oath in the witness stand, but other than that it served no purpose. Well-paid lawyers argued meaningless points in front of out-of-touch judges and the results were of little consequence to the real world, as criminals always returned to heap more misery on growing numbers of victims. Jet knew crime and criminals were of minor importance in the judiciary system. What was important, was it took money through taxes from predominantly poor people, and put it in the pockets of the solicitors and judges, who were predominantly rich people. That's what it was really all about. Jet thought the legal system was the world's biggest scam, and the main offenders were in more danger of being knighted than caught.

Jet moved close behind the detective who had spoken to him and looked at the computer screen that was the object of his attention. 'Anything new?'

'No not really.'

'Still no sign of Metcalf?'

'No. The others are all out looking for him, but he seems to have disappeared from the face of the earth.'

'He'll turn up somewhere.'

'Probably.' The detective had continued tapping on the keyboard as he spoke and went on. 'Did you check out Gerald Goodman's intelligence sheet?'

'No, I just looked at his convictions. Seemed to be all petty stuff.'

'Yeah, but there are one or two snippets on the intelligence updates that say he was probably quite active in the drugs trade.'

This was a surprise to Jet who moved closer to the screen as if this might help. 'Really? What sort of information was there?'

'A few confidential sources suggest he was getting into importing larger and larger quantities of cocaine into Newcastle, and he'd probably built up a distribution network.'

'You mean getting hapless goons to do the street selling for him?'

'Probably.'

'That could be a good reason for Metcalf to attack him. Drug dealers tend not to like up and coming competition.'

'Could be, Jet. Probably.'

Jet pondered this new bit of information for a few moments and then decided to share his thoughts. 'You know, I had a good look around Metcalf's house, and if he was in the drug game then he wasn't making much money out of it. His place was a pigsty – not even a decent telly in it. '

'You can't go by that these days Jet. It might just be used as a meeting or dealing place. He could be the Mr Big of the North East, you know, the one they're all after, the one pulling all of the strings. He's probably got a country mansion somewhere. Probably a yacht as well – he's probably on it now.'

'Probably.' Jet replied slowly, but he was not in the least convinced.

'Maybe he was just hired help doing a job for some other dealer?'

'That seems more likely to me. I guess we'll find out when we catch him.'

Jet walked the short distance across the room to a red felt noticeboard. Seven blue document holders were pinned to it in a neat column; each one had the name of one of the detectives written on it in bold black felt-tipped pen. Jet pulled at the edge of the folder with his name on and saw it contained two pieces of paper, both of which were messages. The first was from Superintendent York and simply consisted of one line asking Jet to go and see him in his office. Jet thought about this request for a moment. He felt certain when York discovered the tape of his last meeting with Groom was blank he would receive a telephone call on his mobile direct from him. This message did not contain the urgency or the anger that he expected from York once he made the inevitable discovery. He had known it was a risk to interfere with the tape but he had also known he needed to do it so Groom would talk, and he had not really wanted to give York any further ammunition to use against Groom. He seemed to be in enough trouble. Jet also knew he would have

227

his own tape of the conversation if anything went wrong or if Groom had said anything that did need to be disclosed to York. His tape was also good insurance, just in case he found himself to be expendable and needed protection from any spurious allegations. Jet had learned to be cautious. On balance, he decided not to make any sudden visits to see the superintendent. He had also harboured the anxiety that if the worst happened and York threw a fit, then he may actually prevent him from going to see Groom again. Yes, Jet thought, let's put this message back into the folder and pretend for the moment that he hadn't seen it! The second message was from the Crown Prosecution Service, asking the whereabouts of a file of evidence for a burglary case to be heard at the magistrates' imminently. 'Bollocks,' Jet mumbled to himself. He had forgotten all about that case and decided a quick visit in person to see one of the prosecuting solicitors was in order, so he could make a personal plea for an adjournment to give him time to get the damn thing done.

Jet was just leaving the office when his mobile phone rang and he saw the words 'Ju mobile.'

'Hi Ju, wondering if the carnival's coming to town?'

'Frankie….' The voice was rushed, emotional, and he knew she had been interrupted after she had called his name.

'Julia, Julia, are you all right?'

'She's fine.' The voice was deep, male and threatening.

'Who's this? What the hell…'

'Shut up and listen.'

Something inside Jet sank; he felt it, like an anvil dropping from his chest to the pit of his stomach. He felt rage growing quickly and wanted to scream down the phone, but experience took over from his emotion and he did as the alien voice on Julia's mobile instructed.

'If you don't want any harm to come to your wife, just do what I tell you to do. Are you listening?'

'Yes.'

'Say nothing to any of your piggy friends and go to your home. I will ring you there in thirty minutes. If you are not alone then that will be very bad for your wife. Do you understand?'

'Yes.'

'I'm told you've been looking at a videotape lately.'

'Yes.'

'Bring that tape with you. Do you understand?' The voice was without a trace of accent and was calm, measured and purposeful.

'Yes, I understand.'

'Remember, say nothing to anyone. You have thirty minutes.'

'Please let me speak to my wife, she's very frightened.'

Julia's mobile phone was quiet for a second and then Jet could hear the male voice mumbling something, which he took to be some sort of a warning to Julia, before he heard her voice. 'Frankie.'

'Julia don't worry, I'll be there soon – I'm coming now.'

'Please hurry Frankie.' She sounded anxious, but he could not detect a sob in her tone. 'They're not like you; they're not your type at all….'

The phone line went dead.

Jet screwed up the piece of paper in his hand, which had been of such importance sixty seconds ago, but now meant nothing. He put it in his trouser pocket and made his way quickly to his office. He unlocked the bottom drawer of his desk and saw the two videotapes. The voice had only asked for one but, without a great deal of thought, he picked up both and hurried out of the building towards the Fiesta.

Chapter twenty-four

He thought every red traffic light was a conspiracy and every slow-manoeuvring motorist a curse sent to persecute him. Why had so many elderly motorists decided to occupy the road at this particular time? Often Jet had dreams where he just could not make progress, in which he was running but couldn't get where he wanted to be, because the ground slipped from underneath his feet or because he sank up to his thighs in water, too deep to run in and too shallow for swimming. That feeling came back to him now, but this was not a dream. Every second passed in agonising slow motion and his mind raced as he heard the engine of his Ford Fiesta whining at a higher pitch than it ever had before.

He brought the Fiesta to a screeching halt outside his house and ran to the front door. It was locked, and he fumbled with his bunch of keys and cursed his own stupid clumsiness, Julia needed him now more than ever and he couldn't even find his own front door key. After finally turning the key in the Yale lock, he pushed the door open and immediately felt emptiness in the house; instinctively he knew Julia was not there. It wasn't just the absence of noise; it was a lack of warmth, of her presence.

'Julia!' He shouted her name, knowing no answer would

come, but desperately hoping that it would. 'Julia!' He ran up the stairs where he continued to feel the emptiness and the silence. He stopped running when he reached their bedroom – not because he wanted to, but because there was nowhere else to run. He looked around and could see the room was neat and tidy. He turned and hurried down the stairs. The usual order Julia kept in the kitchen and lounge still existed. After he had looked in every corner of his home Jet closed his eyes and screwed them up tight. In the darkness of his own mind he searched for something. He wanted to know what to do next; he wanted to know what he could do to help Julia. He wanted to be in control – but he was not.

Jet could feel the tightness in his cheeks and felt tears welling in his eyes. Not knowing what else to do, he lifted his head back and looked at the ceiling in total despair. After a few seconds the ringing of the telephone brought him back into action and he dashed to the cordless receiver which sat on the small table at the bottom of the stairs.

'Yes,' he shouted urgently into the receiver.

'So far so good.' The voice seemed calm and cruel to Jet, and he hated its owner, whoever it was.

'Where's Julia?'

'All in good time. Do you have the tape?'

'Yes.'

'Do you know a shop called "Nice" on Wallsend High Street?'

'No.'

'Hasn't been open long – it sells soap. It's near the library. Park in the car park next to the library, and walk down the High Street, stand outside the shop doorway and wait there.' The line went dead before Jet could ask to speak to Julia again.

He drove down Station Road and within a few minutes was on Wallsend's High Street. Jet parked the Fiesta untidily in a bay and ignored the signs on display in the car park instructing payment in return for a sticker to be displayed on the windscreen. He left the car, hurried to the pavement of the High Street and soon saw the blue front of a shop with the name 'Nice' in bold, golden letters above it. Jet walked to the shop and stood outside the doorway. He looked through the window and saw a small display of ornaments and vividly coloured, unusually shaped bars of soap. For the first time since he had received the phone call from Julia's mobile, Jet started to think like a policeman. He looked around the street and wondered why he was here. He looked across the road and saw an Indian restaurant. The pale-blue frontage, designed to give the appearance of an Indian palace, did not seem out of place in Wallsend High Street. Next to the restaurant was a discount motoring shop which was wholly dominated by silver wheel-trims. Jet noticed several people wandering from shop to shop but the High Street could not be described as busy; he imagined this was about the average for the place. He wondered whether that was the reason he was here, in a place quiet enough to be seen, but not so quiet that the people observing him would be spotted themselves. With that new thought in his head Jet again scanned the shops to see who was paying attention to him. He turned and looked in the door of the soap shop and inside he could see a corpulent middle-aged man behind a small counter. He was alone and looking at Jet. When eye contact was made the man smiled, no doubt the same round smile he gave many people every day, welcoming them into his shop, in the hope they would buy his goods. It certainly did not look like the expression of a kidnapper. Jet forced a false smile back and then continued to scan the rest of the street. Suddenly his mobile phone sounded and on the screen he saw 'Ju mobile'.

'Hello?'

'Listen carefully.' Jet listened to the calm deep voice and got the impression that its owner was enjoying this. He had absolute power over Jet and they both knew it. 'You came on your own and that's good. Keep doing what you are told and you'll get your wife back. Do you know Blyth Harbour?'

'Vaguely.'

'Follow the signs to the harbour. There is a building called the Greenwood Centre. It has a big car park. Leave your car there and walk towards the sea. On the dock there you will see a number of boats moored. Walk towards them and stand on the dock. Do you understand?'

'Yes.'

'One last thing.'

'Yes?'

'In the car park where you left your car there is a bottle bank. Do you see it?'

Jet looked towards the car park and could see the large, green metal bottle bank which had four circular holes cut high along its side.

'Yes.'

'Walk towards it now.'

Within a few seconds, Jet was standing next to the bottle bank.

'Right, I'm here.'

'Can you see anyone else there?'

'No.'

'Drop your mobile phone in there now, and then go straight to Blyth. If you stop or speak to anyone then you'll never see your wife again. Do you understand?'

'Yes.'

Something inside Jet told him this was a stupid thing to do. He knew he was placing himself in the hands of people who were clearly ruthless and judging by his experience so far, had no qualms about using any method to get what they wanted. He could feel himself sinking and becoming more and more vulnerable.

'Let me speak to my wife.'

'Later. Drop the phone into the bottle bank now.'

Jet took a deep breath and thought of Julia. He reached up to the hole in the bottle bank and dropped his phone into it. He heard the faint sound of glass being struck in the hollow vessel as his only means of communication hit the bottom. Then he got into the Fiesta. The engine screamed as he started it while pressing heavily on the accelerator, Jet could feel his heart pumping faster than he could ever remember. The tyres of the car screeched on the Tarmac of the car park as he quickly pulled out of the parking bay, and then he drove out of the car park onto Wallsend High Street and headed towards Blyth.

Jet knew Blyth was to the east of where he was and headed out of Wallsend and onto the Coast Road. He could not remember the last time he had been to Blyth, but he followed the signs and got to the Greenwood Centre with relative and welcome ease. The car park was half full, but there were no people about. Jet parked in the first available space and stopped the engine of the Fiesta. He grabbed the videotapes from the centre of the passenger seat. Jet knew he had not been thinking as rationally as he should have been, but he could not understand why these tapes were worth all this trouble to anyone. They were copies showing three cameras inside a police station. What did they contain that was so important, and why could he not understand what it was? After all, he had watched the tapes with Julia. Julia, where was Julia? He looked at the tapes in his hand and knew that, no matter what was on them, he would gladly exchange them in an instant for Julia. She was all he wanted and he desperately hoped he was getting close.

Jet left the car park and headed towards the sea which was only a few hundred yards away. Even on this summer day, the air from the sea was cool and raw. Seagulls screeched their unwelcoming reverberations as they circled above the surface of the water. Jet was struck by the huge wind turbines that were spaced evenly along the other side of the harbour. As he looked over the vast landscape before him, it looked desolate, and the only sign of human existence was the faint outline of two fishermen at the far end of the dock, their long fishing rods extended in front of them as they faced the grey sea.

Jet walked towards the harbour and saw four large boats moored at its side. There was no sign of activity on any of the boats, other than their gentle rising and falling on the sea's easy flap. Jet clutched the videotapes in his hand and looked around at the scene but could see nothing other than the boats at the dockside and a number of large concrete buildings which looked like storage buildings, standing in a row. They had big, heavy doors and resembled enormous garages. Several moments passed, and Jet's heart thumped inside his chest as he stood totally exposed on this open dockside without any clue to where Julia might be.

The sound of the seagulls seemed to change, and after a few seconds of concentration, Jet could hear an engine. He saw a small white van appear from the far end of the dock driving in his direction and towards the large buildings. The van was still a good fifty metres from him on the expanse of the concrete harbour, as it passed his position, and then drove away from him along the harbour. It then turned towards one of the storage buildings and stopped in front of one of its doors. Jet was about a hundred metres away as he watched a man get out of the driver's side of the van and unlock the building door, which seemed to slide open easily as he pushed it. Jet could hear the gentle rattle as the door moved along its runners and opened with enough space to allow the van to enter. The inside of the building was black, the bright sunshine unable to pierce the darkness of its solid construction. As the man got back into the van, Jet saw him put his arm out of the window and wave, beckoning Jet towards him. The van drove into the darkness of the huge building and was lost from Jet's sight. Jet walked across to the building, slowly at first and then he speeded up, anxious to find Julia. He slowed down again as he neared the large door, which was still open. As he got to the entrance, he found his eyes were having difficulty adjusting from the bright daylight to the darkness of the windowless warehouse.

'Julia!' Jet shouted, and the word echoed around the vast internal space.

'Shut up!'

Jet could not see where the voice came from, and he remained standing in the space of the open door.

Jet walked slowly, without caution, into the open doorway. As he did so, the shadow of the building covered his face and he could see the van's rear doors. The vehicle was approximately twenty metres inside the warehouse. The driver's door was open and the driver stood in the space between the open door and the van, his left hand was resting on the top of the open door and his right hand out of sight inside the van.

'Come closer, slowly.' The voice was unmistakably that of the man on the telephone. 'Stop there.'

Jet was now ten metres from the vehicle, and his eyes focused on the man facing him. Jet could see that he was tall and wearing a dark, workman's boiler suit and had a woollen hat pulled tight on his head.

'Where's Julia?'

'First thing's first. Have you got the tape?'

Jet lifted his right hand which was holding both. 'Yes. There are two. I didn't know which one was important.'

'It doesn't matter; just throw them on the ground in front of you.'

Jet obeyed. 'Don't you want to check them?'

'Not really. It's not important.'

Jet was bewildered by the response. 'If it's not important then why did you go to all of this trouble to get it?'

'You coppers are really stupid.' The stranger's voice was calm and betrayed no sign of emotion. Jet could see him lift his right hand from inside the van and saw the unmistakable shape of a semi-automatic pistol appear; the barrel quickly stopped, pointing directly at Jet.

Suddenly it dawned on Jet. At that moment, he realised what the last hour had been about, and he cursed his stupidity. 'You just want me?'

'I have a friend who would like the tape as well, but it's not worth all of this trouble.'

'What friend?'

'Never mind.'

Jet was rooted to the spot. He realised he was standing in the darkness provided by the cavernous building with no method of communication. He knew that even a shout for help was futile. His eyes had fully adjusted now, and he could clearly see the face that threatened him, nondescript, but with a smile growing across it – a face that was confident it was in control.

Jet said the first thing that came to him. 'Where's Julia?'

'Don't worry about that, you'll be with her soon.' As the man spoke, he raised and extended the pistol further. Jet said the only thing that was in his head.

'Julia.'

As he mouthed her name, he closed his eyes and heard the unmistakable blast of a gunshot. Then he felt a strange peace.

Chapter twenty-five

Jet stood still. There was no panic inside him; he did not know where this calm had come from. The echo of the gunshot rang through the building, bouncing off the empty walls and ceiling. A second deafening shot screamed out a split second after the first. Then there was silence. He opened his eyes and saw that the stranger was now slumped against the inside of the van door and was sliding down it. Jet could see he had been propelled violently backwards into the van door and now gravity was bringing his lifeless body to the bare concrete floor. The smile had been replaced with a vacant open-mouthed expression.

'Armed police! Stand still!' The shout was demanding, the Geordie accent was clear and purposeful.

Jet placed his hands on his head and slowly turned around. He could see uniformed figures running towards him carrying the standard police-issue semi-automatic rifles. He could see the fluorescent, chequered bands of their uniforms reflecting in the deep shadow of the warehouse. They ran past him, straight towards the stranger who had now completed his descent to the floor. Jet remained still as they continued to point their guns at the limp figure. The stranger's gun was now lying on the ground and one of the officers kicked it away. Blood seeped from under the back of the stranger onto the concrete floor. The officers continued to point their weapons as they looked into the front door of the van and then two officers, each holding their rifles single-handedly, used their free hands to pull the rear doors of the van towards them. They inspected the interior for a few seconds and then appeared to relax.

'Scene secure!'

The shout was as forceful as the first. The officers lowered their weapons, and as they did a number of other people ran through the open door of the building. Jet still had his hands on his head and started to feel dazed. Then he felt another hand gently take his right wrist and lower it slowly.

'It's all right Frank.'

Jet looked at the face and saw it was Detective Chief Inspector Anderson.

'They've got my wife.' Jet's instincts returned and he walked quickly to the fallen stranger. He could see two well-defined bullet holes close together in his chest, and it was obvious he was now well beyond interrogation. 'They've got my wife!' Panic rushed through Jet.

'Sir!'

The voice at the back of the van was speaking to Anderson. Jet got to the rear of the van first, and inside he could see a long black bag with a zip running down the centre of it. Jet's heart raced as he leant into the back of the van. Kneeling on its floor, he pulled at the zip of the body bag, quickly unfastening half of its length. As he pulled, the gap opened wider and he could see hair, dark-brown hair. He knew it, recognised it straight away, there was no doubt. He pulled the zip further down and pushed the bag open, revealing Julia's lifeless head. Jet had seen enough death to know its distinct pallor, to know when blood had stopped flowing, and all hope of it flowing again had gone. She was warm, and her head moved forward as he tugged it. He put his arms around her neck and, kneeling in the back of the van, pulled her head as close as he could to his. 'Julia,' he said but could say no more. As he hugged his wife he began to sob and then cry uncontrollably.

Anderson looked stunned as he stared into the back of the van. After a moment, Jet lifted his head slightly and then again hugged his dead wife, his cheek resting tightly on hers. 'Oh God Julia, no, God Julia.' Jet's words turned into the sound of muffled sobbing as his face pressed against Julia's lifeless neck.

Anderson stood at the back of the van and looked in helplessly. He placed both palms of his hands flat against his temples and said the only word that came to him. 'Fuck.'

Jet could not find it in himself to let Julia go. The armed personnel who surrounded the van were trained to deal with every kind of perilous situation, but now they did not know what to do and looked impotently on.

'Frank?' Anderson's voice was gentle. 'Frank?' He knelt inside the small van and had his hand on Jet's back. 'Frank, there are things we need to do.' He put his hand on Jet's shoulder and spoke close to his ear. 'Frank, you need to let her go. I promise you'll see her again soon, come on.'

Anderson gently pulled at Jet, and after a few seconds Jet released his grip and slowly left the back of the van. As he stood up, Anderson kept a firm hold of his shoulder, but none of the other officers standing around made eye contact.

'Come on Frank.' Anderson led Jet out of the building and into the strong sunlight.

Anderson removed his hand from Jet and they walked away from the building. Jet did not pay any attention to the army of forensic experts who walked past him into the warehouse. Both men walked slowly to the car park of the Greenwood Centre making their way towards the Fiesta. Jet got into the driver's seat and Anderson opened the passenger door and sat down next to Jet.

The two of them sat looking through the windscreen and said nothing, this being a moment in time when words would not come easily nor could ever be enough.

Eventually it was Anderson who broke the silence. 'It's going to take us a lot of time to work through the scene. Is there anything I can do? You shouldn't stay here.'

Jet shook his head but said nothing.

'Frank.' Anderson was speaking quietly. 'Look, I can see you're in shock, and I can't imagine how you must be feeling.' Jet thought Anderson was trying to get to a point and guessed it would be a suggestion to go home or seek the comfort of relatives. Jet knew there was no comfort to be found anywhere with anyone. 'Is there anything we can do? Is there anyone that we need to break the news to?'

Christ, Jet thought, he had not even considered having to tell Julia's mother, who lived in Gosforth, in the house that Julia had been brought up in, and where she had lived alone since Julia's father had died ten years ago.

'I don't understand.' Jet's words surprised Anderson and he did not have time to respond as Jet continued after only a very slight pause. 'How did you know I was here?'

'Do you think now's a good time to do this Frank? Wouldn't you rather wait until a better time?'

Jet turned to look at Anderson who was still staring out of the windscreen. 'Do you think there'll ever be a better time? My wife is dead, and I want to know what happened.'

'I'm not trying to keep anything from you Frank, I just thought...' Anderson paused, and Jet could see he was either having difficulty finding the words or reluctant to tell him the truth.

'Just thought what Sir?'

'Just thought this might be even more upsetting for you. I think there's little doubt that the man who murdered your wife is the man we've killed. I don't think there's any need to go through things now.'

'How did you know I was here?'

Anderson turned his head and looked directly at Jet.

'We've had you under surveillance since Groom asked to see you.'

'Why?'

'We think Groom is importing drugs into the region, in a big way.' Jet stared at Anderson as he spoke. 'We've known for a long time now that there was a well-organised operator moving all of the drugs into the region, but we couldn't get close. We knew that the two main criminals in the North East, David Waters and Richard Patterson, were using their network to distribute drugs, but we couldn't get anywhere near the people bringing the stuff in. We've thought for a while there must be some inside work going on – how else could we have no idea who it was? We've had our suspicions about Groom for a while. Then Groom killed one of his drug rivals in prison and then he asks to see you.'

Jet continued to stare at Anderson. 'And you thought I was dealing drugs with Groom, is that it?'

'We couldn't be sure about anything.'

'Who's the man who killed Julia?'

'Don't know for sure yet, but it looks like he's hired help. Looks likely the drugs were coming in by sea: small vessels, fishing boats, that sort of thing. He was probably involved at that end of the business. It's a good way to bring drugs in and also a good way to dispose of bodies: take them out to sea and weigh them down in a body bag never to be seen again.'

Jet turned his head away from Anderson and stared back

out through the windscreen. 'Why would Groom want to hurt Julia?'

'To get to you – to get you here quietly and kill you too.'

'Why would he want me dead?'

'I don't know Frank, but he must be frightened of something you know. There must be a reason. Do you have any idea what it could be?'

'No. None of this makes sense.'

'Look Frank, maybe now's not a good time.'

'And you thought I was working with him and had me followed?'

'I know it sounds ridiculous – we know you're not his sort – but we just couldn't be sure.'

Jet heard Julia's voice in his mind. 'They're not like you; they're not your type at all.' He repeated it slowly to himself and then paused. 'That was the last thing Julia said to me.'

'Frank, let me arrange for someone to take you home. I'd really like the force doctor to see you.'

'She was telling me, and I didn't see it. She always was cleverer than me.' Jet gripped the steering wheel and leaned forward, his forehead touching the top of the wheel. 'Christ Julia, I'm so sorry.' He closed his eyes and for a few seconds remained in the same position. Anderson lifted his hand and was moving it towards Jet's back in an attempt to offer some comfort when Jet suddenly sat bolt upright as if rallying himself. 'Julia has an elderly mother; I'd better go and see her myself. This isn't the sort of thing a stranger should do.'

'Do you want me to arrange someone to take you down there?'

'I'd rather just head down there myself thanks.'

'If you're sure?' Anderson reached into his jacket pocket and produced a card. 'My mobile number's on there. Just give me a ring at any time if there's anything I can do.'

'Thanks.' Jet took the card and, without looking at it, put it in his pocket.

As soon as Anderson got out of his car, Jet started the engine and drove out of the car park. But he was not heading to see Julia's mother; he was heading somewhere else. He had seen how mindless violence had taken the life of Gerald Goodman and destroyed the lives of his parents. He had seen the death of the only person he truly loved, and he had himself stared death in the face today. But this was no time for reason, no time to learn all the lessons around him which proved violence brought only misery. For the first time in his life, Jet was on his way to commit a crime himself and that crime was going to be one of murder. The tempest which had just overwhelmed Jet's life was now about to find another victim.

Chapter twenty-six

The Fiesta screeched to a halt in the car park of the police station at Newcastle and Jet was oblivious to the fact that his parking now made it impossible for some of the other cars to get out. He turned to look at the back seat and saw his bright yellow thick metal steering wheel crook lock. It had been a present from Julia when he had bought the Fiesta. 'A wise precaution given the type of people you choose to associate with,' she'd said when presenting it to him. The heavy metal frame felt cool in his hand as he picked it up before getting out of the car. He walked into the station.

Jet went up the stairs and along the wide corridor that led to the drug squad office. The crook lock hung in his right hand, the bottom edge of it almost touching the floor. He walked purposefully and ignored the glances of the few people he passed. He entered the office quickly and recognised the back of Ray Harris who was alone.

'Thought I'd find you here.' Jet said as he made towards him, the comment caused Harris to turn his head. Before Harris had time to speak Jet swung the crook lock swiftly. The heavy metal lock connected with the side of Harris's head and the force of the blow knocked him off his chair towards the wall which abutted his desk. There was a clang as Harris's head hit the radiator on the wall.

Harris was disorientated by the strike and made no attempt to get up from the floor. He groaned as he turned his head to look at Jet and muttered, 'What the fuck?'

Jet lifted his metallic weapon above his head and left it hanging menacingly in the air. Harris appeared to have regained his senses but remained on the floor as Jet stared at him intensely. 'What better place for an alibi than a police station. I bet you're surprised to see me. I should be dead shouldn't I?'

'I don't know what you mean.'

'You should know that I'm going to smash your skull in. You had my wife killed just to get me out of the way, just because I was getting too close to you and the truth. Isn't that right?'

'I don't know what you're talking about Jet.'

'Don't lie to me. Do you want to spend your last seconds on this earth telling lies?' Jet's voice was loud and menacing. 'Maybe it's fitting for a little piece of murdering, lying, drug dealing shit like you to die pathetically like this.'

Jet raised the yellow weapon slightly, making Harris wince and draw his hands up to his face in an attempt to protect himself from the blow he was clearly now expecting.

'Julia recognised you; she'd never have left the house with a stranger. What did you say when you told her you were a police officer? Did you tell her I'd been hurt and you were going to take her to me? Well you made a mistake because you were seen – not just by Julia but by others in the street,' Jet lied.

'I can explain. I was just doing a favour for someone. I didn't know she was going to be hurt, honestly Jet.'

'You lying twat. York thinks that Groom's the big drug dealer around here, but it's you isn't it? You ruthless bastard.'

Harris remained helplessly still as Jet, wild eyed, persisted. 'You had Goodman attacked. What did you tell Metcalf? Did you say that Goodman had been grassing him up? Setting the drug dealing competition on each other, that's good business.'

'I didn't know Goodman was going to die.'

'I suppose that was just a bonus. I bet you nearly shit yourself when I started sniffing around. You knew Metcalf would tell us why he'd attacked Goodman when he was arrested for murder.'

Harris did not speak.

'Where's Metcalf now?'

Harris continued to stare at Jet.

'Is he at the bottom of the sea? How many people have you disposed of during your career as a drug dealer Harris? Was it all worth it?'

Harris looked up at Jet helplessly.

'Were you there when Julia was killed?'

Harris remained silent.

'You were there weren't you? You had her killed to protect yourself didn't you? Just like that, a woman who wouldn't

251

hurt a soul.' Jet lifted the metal bar above his head. Harris winced again and hurriedly spoke.

'I never meant for your wife to get hurt; let's talk. We can sort this out between the two of us. I have money Jet, a lot of money, it's yours. Let's work out a deal, it will benefit both of us.'

'You must be mad. Do a deal with you after what you've done?'

'It just got out of hand Jet. I didn't want anyone to get hurt, honest.'

'You lying shit. You arranged for people to get hurt.'

'I've enough money to see us both right for the rest of our lives – more than you could imagine.'

'Do you think your filthy drug money means anything to me? You murdered Julia and now it's your turn to die.'

Jet lifted the bar as far above his head as he could, and Harris closed his eyes and placed his arms over his head. The rage inside Jet overwhelmed him, and he started to move the bar down towards Harris's head. It had moved just a few inches when he heard a voice. 'You're not their type Frankie.' As he heard the voice, Jet halted his movement of the metal bar. 'You're not their type.' The voice spoke again. It was Julia. Her voice was unmistakeable; Jet could hear the soft tone as it spoke somewhere inside him. As he heard her voice he felt tears, like molten metal, sting his eyes as they welled and he tried again to bring the bar down onto Harris, to avenge the death of Julia. It was only what he deserved, maybe less than he deserved. The bar moved only a few inches and it stopped as Jet heard Julia's voice again. 'You're not their type Frankie.'

'She was my wife.' Jet raised the bar up straight in the air and Harris flinched as the bar quivered in Jet's hands.

'You're not their type Frankie.' Julia's voice repeated. Jet could feel the words bite into his head.

Harris remained cowering on the floor as Jet brought his left hand down and picked up the telephone on the desk beside him and dialled York's extension.

'Superintendent York.' The phone had been picked up quickly.

'Yes, it's Whittle. I'm in the drug squad office. I've got your drug dealer here; he is also responsible for the murder of my wife.'

'Whittle, are you all right?'

'I'd come down here now, if I were you.'

The phone went dead and Jet put down the receiver. He kept the metal bar above his head with his right hand, and for a few minutes he just stood until York and Detective Inspector Ormond came in through the door of the office.

'Easy Frank.' York and Ormond slowed and then came to a halt as they entered through the doorway, apparently uncertain about any sudden movement. York continued to speak. 'What have we got?'

'You were right about a cop being behind the drug smuggling but you had the wrong one. It wasn't Groom, it was him.'

'How do you know that?'

'He took my wife. Isn't that right Harris? He told me he didn't know she was going to get hurt, but he knew what he was doing. He arranged it.'

Harris did not speak but remained trembling on the floor as the bar remained hovering above him.

'Julia told me when she spoke to me. She said they weren't my type. She recognised Harris.' Jet looked down at the figure on the floor. 'You probably told her your real name; you knew she wasn't going to be around to tell anyone about it. Didn't you Harris?'

Harris remained silent.

'I saw Harris talking to John Metcalf on the station video before he attacked Goodman. It was a mistake that wasn't it Harris? Forgetting about the cameras? He told me he hadn't seen Metcalf, and I couldn't work out why this happened before the attack. But it was Harris who set Metcalf onto Goodman. Goodman was starting to get into dealing in a big way, and Harris got rid of the competition. He told Metcalf that Goodman was grassing him up to the drug squad. Wasn't that how it worked Harris? How many other people have you had sorted to protect your business? You piece of shit. Probably just wanted Goodman to get a good slapping and even if Metcalf was arrested Harris knew he'd just say nothing; but when Goodman died, that changed things. A murder meant a full enquiry, no stone left unturned.' The bar was again raised and Harris flinched.

'Easy Frank.' York's tone was conciliatory and he did not move.

'I found the videotape and Harris realised I was getting close to him. He couldn't risk any suspicion. He's just admitted to me that he's got a fortune stashed away. He didn't want anyone making enquiries about him, looking at his lifestyle and bank accounts. So he decided not to take any risks and to get rid of Metcalf and me. Nice and simple – no mess and no evidence. You piece of shit. And to get to me he took Julia. Expendable wasn't she? A small sacrifice to protect yourself.' Jet straightened the bar in the air again. 'You know, before you joined us, he offered me money to keep quiet. Can you believe that? He kills my wife and he thinks money is going to solve it.'

The bar still shuddered menacingly in Jet's hands. York slowly moved towards him.

'The kidnapper asked me to bring the videotape I'd been watching but there were two of them. But Harris didn't know that, he only knew I'd been watching one because I'd only asked him about one. He's the only person who could have asked the kidnapper to get the tape.'

York was now standing next to Jet as he spoke. 'Frank, let me take over now. I'll sort it from here.'

Jet remained still and did not resist when York lifted his hand and took hold of the yellow bar. He lowered it, leaving it in Jet's hand but removing the threat to Harris. Jet stood still with the bar now in his right hand at his side.

York nodded his head towards Ormond and then moved his eyes to look at Harris. Ormond understood York's gesture and he moved towards Harris and gripped him by the arm, guiding him as he stood up. A slight trickle of blood ran down the back of Harris's neck and he winced as he touched it with his right hand. No one expressed any interest in the injury and Ormond spoke to him. 'You do not have to say anything. But it may harm your defence if you do not mention, when questioned, something which you later rely on in court. Anything you do say may be given in evidence. Harris, you are under arrest on suspicion of the murders of Julia Whittle and John Metcalf.'

Harris stood motionless in the grip of Ormond but now stared intensely at Jet. The threat of Jet cracking his skull had been removed, and his attitude seemed to change – he became more confident, even cocky, Jet thought.

'You've got fuck all on me; just this crazy arsehole's word against mine. I didn't say anything to him; he just came in here and attacked me for no reason. It's him you should be arresting.' Harris nodded towards Jet as he said this.

Jet placed his hand in his pocket and removed the tape recorder, which was still recording as he held it. 'Had this wire fitted myself, the microphone is in my belt buckle. Clever, isn't it?'

Jet disconnected the wire from the rear of the tape recorder and gave it to York. Harris's face changed expression as he was led out of the office.

Jet still held his car crook lock in his right hand. He looked at it and said to York. 'I suppose you'll want this?'

'I think you've lost enough today. Why don't you take it with you?'

Jet attempted a weak smile, but it would not form on his face and he walked out of the office. He soon found himself sitting in the Fiesta and as he sat gripping the steering wheel he moved forward, rested his forehead on the top of the steering wheel, and started to cry.

Chapter twenty-seven

Four days after Julia's death, Jet found himself straightening his tie in the hall mirror. It was his sensible blue silk tie with a small red-diamond pattern, his favourite; the one Julia had bought him. He looked at his face in the mirror and he could see it had changed: he looked tired, pale and old. He had barely slept since Julia's death. The bed felt cold and empty and only sheer exhaustion had caused him to drift into unconsciousness for a few hours through the night, as he lay, thinking of her. The pain which gnawed away in his chest showed no sign of easing. The pills prescribed by his doctor remained in the paper bag the chemist had placed them in and Jet now wondered why he had paid the prescription price. Julia would have chastised him for the wastefulness. The last four days had seen him think twice about breaking his abstinence from spirits but, when he came close to putting his coat on and going to the off-licence, he thought how profoundly Julia would have disapproved and the temptation passed. Jet knew Julia was gone forever. He knew that he would never feel the warm curve of her body or the familiar sweetness of her breath on his face as they embraced, but he also knew that she still dominated his life and always would.

Jet left the house and walked into the garden towards the Fiesta. He noticed the lawn looked long and the garden had started to look untidy. He decided he would have to do something about it when he got back home. Julia would not have forgiven him for allowing things to slip. He knew he had to carry on.

He started the engine of the Fiesta, reversed out of the small driveway and headed towards Durham. After a gentle forty-five minute drive, Jet arrived at Durham Police Station, for his appointment with Mark Groom. York had arranged it. There had been no requirement for him to attend the technical unit this time; there were no hidden microphones or tapes.

Jet reported his arrival at the station's front desk and was soon ushered into the cell block. He thought he could detect a different attitude towards him from the custody staff, as if they were less suspicious of his presence. The sergeant gave Jet a forced smile and spoke to a young, uniformed jailer who followed the instruction to lead Jet to Groom's cell. The jailer wrestled with the large key in the lock and then pulled the heavy door open and stood back, allowing Jet to walk straight into the cell.

As he walked into the cell Jet thought Groom also looked tired.

'All right Jet?' Groom's familiar greeting was ill-considered.

'No.' Jet's reply was abrupt and honest.

'I know, I heard. I'm sorry.'

'How are you?'

'Fair to say we've both seen better weeks.'

'I've spoken to Shirley – she and Diane are fine. I don't think there's any need for you to worry about them.'

'I don't suppose she said anything about coming in to see me?'

'No, I'm sorry Mark, but I don't think she's going to.'

Groom's head was bowed like that of a man trying to come to terms with his loss. 'I thought that.' Jet did not know whether Groom was being truthful about this or not, but thought there was a distinct air of resignation about him.

Jet changed the subject. 'Did you have any idea about Harris?'

'Anderson came to see me and took a statement. I'd no idea, but now I think about it, it makes sense. He always had good information and we took a lot of dealers out. Little did I know that we were actually taking out his competitors. From what Anderson said, he was bringing shiploads in and supplying across the whole of the North East. He must have been making a fortune.'

'I gave York your contacts book.' Jet looked directly at Groom and almost looked apologetic.

'Don't worry about it.'

The exchange between them was remorseful. Two men resigned to their fates. Broken men.

'It ties Harris in with times and dates. After what he did to Julia, I want him put away for the rest of his life.'

'I understand.'

'The day you arrested Trent, Harris must have planted the drugs on him.'

'That's what Anderson said he thought had happened.'

'Poor Geoffrey Trent – innocent after all. Just like his mother always told us.'

Groom was silent and sat on the cell bench staring at the floor. Jet carried on, 'I still find it hard to work that out because I don't think Trent was ever a dealer. I don't know why Harris would see him as competition and want him put away.' Groom remained silent, head bowed. 'But I still reckon the drugs were planted and that must have been done by Harris.' Jet looked directly at Groom but Groom did not look up. 'Either he planted them,' Jet paused for a second, 'or you did.' Groom remained motionless. Jet continued. 'Why did you kill Trent?'

'I just lost it after I saw the photos of Diane.'

'Are you sure that's all it was about?'

Groom stared at the floor.

'You knew that Shirley had an affair with Trent didn't you?'

Groom remained cowed and then quietly spoke. 'Can you imagine it? Shirley and a low life like Trent.'

'We all make mistakes.'

'I just didn't want to believe it; shut it out of my mind

— bottled it up all these years. Every day I looked at Diane, and I could see she was growing up and getting less and less like me. I knew she wasn't mine.' Groom had still not moved his head. 'Low sperm count, did Shirley tell you?'

'No.'

'After a few years, I had some tests done. Shirley tried to tell me that Diane was extra special, our miracle child, one chance in a million, and I wanted to believe it. I wanted to believe it so badly that I nearly did.'

'Did Trent say anything about this when you last saw him?'

'You mean when I killed him? No. Even if he did know, he obviously didn't give a shit. Bet he didn't have a low sperm count. I'll bet there are hundreds of little Trents out there.'

'You need to tell your solicitor about Diane and Trent. It will make a difference. You need to tell the truth about that Mark.'

'Tell the world that Diane is Trent's daughter, not mine? What will that do to Diane, to me and her, when she finds out I'm not her father?'

'You carried this burden around with you for years and suddenly you snapped when the balance of your mind was disturbed — understandably disturbed and that's manslaughter. You keep the reason why you killed Trent to yourself and you'll get life, and for a cop killing someone in prison that will mean life. You'll have no relationship at all with Diane if you spend your life locked away.'

Jet could see tears rolling down Groom's face and falling onto his shirt. 'Anyway, I think you underestimate your Diane.'

'Don't you see, she's not my Diane?'

'Oh yes she is.' Jet's voice was raised. 'You've brought her up, given her everything including your love, especially your love, and that's what being a father is. It's not just the sperm bit, it's everything else, and nothing can erase that.'

The tears were now flooding down Groom's face.

'It makes sense now to bring this into the open – it doesn't make sense not to. Mark, you must tell your solicitor about this. It could make the difference between you having no life in here or a chance to rebuild your life outside.'

Both men were silent for a while. Jet stared at Groom and watched as the tears continued to teem as he bowed his head slightly.

'If you like I could go and see your solicitor and explain to him what happened in the past. I'll ask him to come and see you again. Should I do that Mark?'

Groom nodded, the tears still streaming.

'I'll do that now Mark.'

Jet walked towards the door of the cell. As he did Groom raised his head and wiped his eyes. He inhaled a deep breath. 'Thanks Frank.'

Jet pushed the button inside the cell door to attract the attention of the jailer and had his back to Groom. 'Only

Julia ever called me Frank, and when she did I knew I was in trouble.' Jet smiled at the thought this brought to him.

The loud noise of a key being placed in the outside of the cell door rattled around the stone walls of the cell. Groom spoke as the door was just beginning to open. 'Jet?'

'Yeah?'

'Do you want to know how the drugs got on Trent?'

The door was fully open as Jet took a long deep breath. He had his back to Groom and looked out of the open door. He did not turn around as he spoke. 'No. I don't.' And he walked out of the cell.

Chapter twenty-eight

The first weeks of August had seen the sun shine brightly. The combination of warm weather and school holidays had brought more than normal activity to the street outside Jet's home. Children, some with their parents, rode bicycles past his house. He also saw young boys kicking footballs backwards and forwards to each other. He did not feel any hatred or dislike towards them but, watching them enjoy their simple pursuits, he felt a sense of injustice. He heard the laughter of many people – perhaps he was just more aware of them now – and he felt it was unfair that Julia was not here to witness their joy. In his darker moments – and there had been many of them – he had even thought about shouting outside and chastising people for their lack of respect, as if they should be feeling guilty that they were here enjoying themselves while Julia lay in the mortuary.

He looked at the clock on the kitchen wall and saw it was almost ten on this fine summer morning. The shafts of sunlight were forcing their way through the blinds. The first to arrive at the house were Julia's sister Heather, her husband Craig and her mother Catherine. They were all dressed in dark clothing which appeared too heavy for this warm day but was expected for the occasion of Julia's funeral.

Jet thought Julia's mother looked older and frailer than she ever had. She wore a dark two-piece suit and underneath it a white blouse. The collar of the blouse was fully buttoned but hung loosely around her thin neck.

Something had changed between Jet and Catherine since Julia's death; he did not know exactly what that was. Jet had gone to her home to break the news himself, and as she had answered the door to his knock he could see that his presence had brought an immediate look of concern.

'Hello Frank, don't often see you here by yourself. Everything OK?'

Jet had not known what to say, he walked up the two steps in the doorway and embraced her. 'Oh Catherine, it's Julia – I'm so sorry.'

The two had stood for some time in the same pose, crying together. Jet had spoken to Heather before he had gone to see Catherine. She had arrived just a few seconds behind him and joined them in the embrace. Something had changed between the three of them in the sorrow of that hug, some barrier had fallen. When Jet had explained what had happened and done all he could to answer Catherine's questions, he had not felt the blame he thought might have been natural. Perhaps she had seen the intense pain on his face and could not bring herself to torture him any further with recrimination, or perhaps she had felt he did not require forgiveness for an event she thought was not of his making. It had never occurred to him before to consider where the gentleness of Julia's soul had emanated, that power she had to see the good in everything and forgive, but the source of this now became clear.

As Catherine entered the house for Julia's funeral, she embraced and kissed Jet, as did Heather who followed. Craig waited awkwardly behind and his handshake lacked the warmth of the previous two encounters. After that not a great deal of conversation was exchanged, other than some irrelevant pleasantries, they seemed content with the silence. Jet could see in their eyes they were surprised at the tie he was wearing, it was his blue silk tie with the red-diamond pattern, and he knew it looked incongruous with his black suit. But today it seemed to him to be the right choice and he knew Julia would have approved.

Soon others began to arrive: friends of Julia's – she had many of them – distant relatives and neighbours who she had always helped when she could by taking in parcels or closing curtains during holiday time. Jet could not remember or even imagine Julia ever refusing to do a favour asked of her. As the people gathered, Jet was struck by how many people Julia had come to know. In the evenings, after work, he had often listened to her tales of her encounters through the day, but this was the first time he had collectively seen the number of people she had touched with her natural warmth. She had a special way of communicating with people, of getting to them. After all, she had even got to him – what more proof was needed?

The noise did not increase with the number of people – words were not easily found as they congregated in Jet and Julia's home. In this gathering, among all these people to whom Julia meant a great deal, Jet had a strong feeling of isolation. An only child whose parents had died a long time ago, and whose job consumed his life, he had only Julia. It had been enough. But now, surrounded by all of these people, he felt painfully alone.

Jet stared out of the front window and watched a family of blue tits feeding on a mesh nut holder which Julia had hung from a low branch of the cherry tree in the garden. He had topped the feeder up every day since Julia's death and had been surprised at how quickly the birds devoured the nuts. He wondered whether the birds were the same ones that had nested that spring in the bird box at the bottom of the garden, the ones that Julia gave him progress reports on every night when he got home from work, no matter what time that was. She had taken to leaving a broom next to the back door and would use it to frighten off the cats she saw near the tree. Jet remembered how worried she had been when the activity in the box had suddenly stopped, and he eventually had to go and examine it, levering the top off to reassure her that the chicks had survived their ordeal and left the nest.

In stately silence, the hearse arrived and pulled up outside the front door. Flowers surrounded the coffin, and on the top of it lay the wreath of chrysanthemums, Julia's favourite, which Jet had insisted on. Everyone made their way in respectful silence to the combination of funeral and private cars that now cluttered the street. Soon all the mourners were accommodated, and the procession snaked its way up the street towards the nearby St Peter's Church. Jet could see York and Anderson standing outside the entrance of the church as the cortege glided to a halt. Carefully, the coffin was removed by the pall-bearers as they carried out their well-practised routine. It was gently raised shoulder high and slowly, feet first, it entered the silence of the church. Steadily it was carried up the aisle and placed with efficient care on two wooden trestles at the front of the church. The mourners, who followed, took their reserved seats in the harsh wooden pews, joining the rest of the congregation. Jet had selected the order of service and it began with Julia's favourite hymn, *Rock of Ages*. Julia had not been much of a religious person, but the hymn had stuck with her from her schooldays. Jet knew she liked the tune.

While making the arrangements for the service Jet had been struck by the patchwork nature of funerals. They seemed to be a series of odd compromises. He was not even sure whether the venue would have received Julia's approval, but the options had been limited. It had been sensible to stick with tradition rather than do something along the humanist lines, which might have been more akin to Julia's character. He had tried to take into consideration Catherine's, Heather's and even the vicar's opinions, but the most important person was not here to direct events. He had wondered how different the service would have been if Julia had written it herself and guessed the truth was it would have been very different. As they sang the hymn, Jet wanted to be able to ask Julia whether she knew what the lyrics meant. Why would anyone harbour the desire to hide in the cleft of a rock and what dreadful imagery it was. He would have enjoyed the discussion, like those they had after she had taken him to the theatre to see the Royal Shakespeare Company; she always had a better handle on these things. But she was not here and he was, singing the mystifying words to *Rock of Ages*.

When the hymn ended, the vicar welcomed the mourners to the service and said a short prayer. He then invited Craig to speak on behalf of Julia's family. There had been some debate between Jet, Catherine and Heather about who should speak at the service and Jet had felt a strong urge to do it himself. He had not been able to bear the thought of Julia's funeral passing without words from someone who knew and loved her, and he knew, of all creatures on earth, he had loved Julia more than anyone. But he had listened to the reason of Heather and Catherine and had reluctantly agreed Craig was the best person to address the congregation. Craig walked the few paces from his front-row pew to a lectern at the front of the church. As he turned to face the congregation, he took a piece of paper out of his jacket, placed it on the lectern and took a deep breath. He looked out at the sea of faces, each one belonging to someone whose life had been touched by Julia.

'Frank, Heather and Catherine felt this service would not be complete without some words from Julia's closest family. They are sure that Julia would understand why they have asked me to speak today. We know Julia's sudden death has deeply affected everyone in this church and indeed the word tragedy seems inadequate to describe what has happened or how we all feel.'

As Craig spoke, Jet looked to his left where Heather and Catherine sat. Heather had her arm across her mother's shoulders and both held handkerchiefs to their faces to wipe the tears that rolled down their cheeks.

Craig's words seemed to steady as he continued to speak. 'Julia loved music. She often told Frank of her earliest memories of her mum playing records when she was a toddler and both of them dancing in the front room to *The Beatles* or *T Rex*. It was always clear that she was grateful for the loving upbringing she had, for the care her mum and dad gave her and the freedom they gave her spirit to fly free. We know that, in return, they were ever-grateful for the love she returned to them and, of course, to her sister Heather with whom she was always close. Heather and Julia enjoyed a special relationship, and I do not recall a day passing when they did not have some contact with each other. Heather wanted me to say that she deeply loved Julia and will always treasure the time they spent with each other.'

Craig lifted his head from the lectern and smiled towards Heather. 'When Heather said that, I told her it didn't really need to be said because anyone who knew anything about either of them couldn't fail to see that the bond they enjoyed was very special.' Craig snorted a laugh. 'You know, when Heather and I were abroad on our honeymoon, they still managed to speak to each other every day on the phone.' There seemed to be a gentle, muffled laughter across the congregation, as if the warmth of the bond between sisters was breathed in by all present.

'Julia also loved words and collected endless numbers of novels and books of poetry. She soaked up information and derived a great deal of pleasure from it, but typically not just for herself, she also shared this with others and Frank reckons that most people here will have a book on loan either to or from Julia.'

The warmth returned to the atmosphere of the church, and Craig paused to allow the restrained laughter to subside.

'Most of all Julia loved people. She always wanted the best for them, for everyone that she loved, and Julia was one of those special people who had plenty of love. She touched all of our lives and we give thanks for every minute that we enjoyed with her. We are better people for knowing Julia and all of our lives are richer because of her. Julia will always be with us, in our thoughts and in our hearts.'

Craig paused for a second and there was absolute silence. Craig took a deep breath and everyone in the church heard him inhale and exhale. He continued, 'The tragedy that has hit us has understandably left us all in shock. The passing of someone so young and with so much more to give is enough to make the most devout believer question their faith. But we ask you to look around the church and examine the evidence: evidence of a much-loved friend; evidence of a much-loved daughter; evidence of a much-loved sister. As a wife, Julia could not have been more loving or more loved. All of us here know of the bond Julia and Frank shared and indeed still do share. So when you examine the evidence of the life Julia led, you see a life lived to the full and enough to fill several lifetimes.'

It seemed to Jet as if the whole building was sobbing and an unexpected feeling of admiration for Craig, who had remained steady and confident throughout, swept through him, he had been a good choice after all. Jet knew he could not have spoken the words, even though he had written them and knew every one by heart.

'Given Julia's love of words and poetry, we wanted to finish with one of her favourite poems. You probably know it. Frank said it was one she returned to quite often and today it seems especially appropriate. For those of you who are familiar with it, please forgive the slight amendment that we have made.

Not, how did she die, but how did she live?
Not, what did she gain, but what did she give?

These are the units to measure the worth
Of a woman as a woman, regardless of birth.
Not what was her church, nor what was her creed,
But had she befriended those really in need?
Was she ever ready, with word of good cheer,
To bring back a smile, to banish a tear?
Not what did the sketch in the newspaper say,
But how many were sorry when she passed away?

Craig steadied himself for a second at the end of the poem. 'Julia, we love you. We all look forward to the day when we will be together again.'

Craig picked up the paper from the lectern and walked back to his seat. As he did, he passed Jet who smiled and nodded.

The remainder of the service seemed to pass in something of a haze for Jet. As the coffin was led out, one of Julia's favourite songs *Keep the Faith* performed by Bon Jovi was played. Jet had worried this rock anthem might sound out of place, but as it played, he could imagine Julia singing to it and it seemed a perfect choice.

The short trip to the cemetery and the graveside ceremony passed quickly, and soon Jet found himself back at his home. He had felt it would be expected of him to cater for mourners and had paid for this service to be provided. Dutifully, most had accepted the invitation, but they did not stay long and not much was eaten or drunk.

Soon Jet, Heather, Craig and Catherine were the only people left. Catherine sat on the settee nursing half a cup of tea, oblivious to the fact it had gone cold. Heather and Craig stood beside her chair as Jet returned from the front door having seen out the last of the guests.

'It was a nice ceremony,' Jet offered, and all nodded. 'I was really grateful for your speech Craig, thanks.'

'They were nice words Frank. I'm pleased you thought it went well.' Craig wore a weak smile.

'Very well, thanks.'

The silence returned, and Craig looked at his watch. 'Well I suppose we should really be making tracks. It's been a long day. I'll go and get the car – had to park it halfway down the street.'

Craig reached out his hand which Jet gripped and shook before Craig walked out of the door.

'Come on mum, I suppose Craig's right.' Heather reached her arm out to help Catherine to her feet after lifting the cup from her hand and placing it on the coffee table. Once Catherine was on her feet, Heather stroked the creases out of the front of her skirt – daughter and mother roles reversed. She turned to Jet. 'Will you be all right Frank?'

'I'll be fine.'

'It must feel lonely here, all on your own.'

Jet looked around the room. 'The strange thing is, everywhere I look I see Julia. I could almost hear her voice this morning telling me to put my tie on straight.'

Heather returned Jet's smile. 'I'll pop in tomorrow and see how you're doing if that's OK?'

'You're always welcome, but there's no need to worry about me.'

'It'll do me good too.'

'She's a big miss.' Jet's smile had slipped off his face.

'Such a waste.'

'When I think of what she must have gone through, I could explode.' Jet moved his hand down his face and rubbed tears from his eyes with the ends of his fingers.

'There's no sense in torturing yourself.'

'Don't worry. When those dark thoughts happen I make an effort to think of all the years I spent with her and the simple beauty of her spirit, about the love that we shared. Then, as ever, she makes me feel better. She's looking after me even when she's not here.'

'I try to hold onto the good thoughts as well. It's all we can do.'

Catherine lightly gripped Jet's arm, then moved towards him and gently kissed the cheek which he slightly lowered. 'Goodbye Frank. Take care, I'll see you soon.'

'Thanks Catherine, please take care of yourself.'

Heather's arm circled Jet's neck, and she held on to him for a few seconds in a firm embrace. Both of their faces were warm and moist with tears, and Jet could feel the skin of their cheeks stick together.

Soon Heather and Catherine had left the house, and Heather guided her mother into the front passenger seat of the car which was now standing outside the garden gate. Jet waved as it pulled away. Once it had disappeared up the street, he closed the front door and felt the emptiness of the house. He walked into the front room and collected the many plates that had been left around it. As he cleared up napkins and poured away the contents of half-empty glasses, he realised he had never been so alone in his life.

Chapter twenty-nine

York and Anderson were sitting in Jet's front room, perched uncomfortably on the settee. Jet had not been alarmed, or even surprised, when he had received the telephone call from Anderson asking if they could come and see him. After all, it was only two days since he had buried Julia. No doubt his senior officers thought, under the circumstances, there would be many welfare issues to consider.

York and Anderson had politely accepted Jet's offer of coffee and two cups stood carefully placed on mats on the small table in front of them. Julia would never allow any risk of heat rings scarring the furniture, a habit Jet now strictly adhered to as sole guardian of the home.

'Looks like the murder charge against Mark Groom will be dropped and he'll plead to manslaughter.' York said, turning his coffee mug so the handle was facing towards him. Jet noticed he did not lift it.

'That's good news. How did Trent's mother take it?'

'Not well.'

'I made a promise I'd go back and see her.'

York nodded. 'It can't do any harm, but I would leave it for a while.'

'Does she know she has a granddaughter?'

'Yes, but I don't think she knows what to make of it given the reason Groom killed her son.'

'She was very close to Geoffrey.'

A silence fell after Jet spoke. York was looking at the carpet and Jet thought he was having difficulty finding his words. After a few seconds York looked directly at Jet. 'We've been consulting the Crown Prosecution Service about the case against Harris, and they're not confident we've got enough to convict.'

It was an unexpected hammer blow.

'What are you talking about? He admitted taking Julia out of the house! Surely you've got all the circumstantial evidence you need to tie him into the drug dealing, and what about Goodman and Metcalf?'

'We can't find any trace of Metcalf and all we have is a video of Harris talking to him on the day Goodman was attacked.'

'He'll be at the bottom of the sea, you know that.'

'Difficult to prove murder without a body.'

'You've got Julia's body, and Goodman's.'

'Julia was killed with the same gun that was going to be used to kill you. The murderer, an ex-mercenary, was killed in the process of doing it.'

'You know he was hired help. It was Harris, he was behind all of this.' York could see the emotion rising at great speed inside Jet and could well understand his exasperation. 'I'm sorry Frank, I'm just telling you what we have.'

Jet silenced himself, and after a few seconds York continued. 'You know that conversation you recorded with Harris wasn't exactly standard procedure. You were threatening to club his brain with a metal bar at the time. The prosecutors don't think we can use it.'

Jet was on his feet and walked towards the window of the front room. The light-coloured curtains were fastened back neatly to the wall with the ties that Julia had spent so much time making, with material she had bought to match the curtains. He looked out of the clean glass, and as he breathed in deeply he could smell her. 'What about a link between the shooter and Harris? Have you found one?'

'We found the flat where he was staying. Looks like he'd only been there for a few days. Probably brought in to do a job, get paid and go. All very clean and no evidence. His neighbours didn't even know he'd moved in.'

'Where was he from?'

'Born in Surrey, joined the army and left after a court martial for assaulting an officer. He was a mercenary in Africa for a long time, until he came back to this country three years ago. Looks like he has been making a living as a professional hit man since.'

'That must prove he was here just doing a job for Harris?'

'It proves he was a paid killer and not likely to be here without direction from someone. Doesn't prove who was paying him.'

Jet turned from the window and looked at York. 'Well

it's early days, there must be a lot of avenues to follow yet. The mercenary must have been paid somehow, and there might be some links with the flat.' As Jet spoke York turned his head to glance at Anderson, and then he looked at the floor again. Jet continued. 'Don't you think there's still a lot more we can do to prove Harris was the person responsible?'

York lifted his head but did not look directly at Jet. His eyes were still fixed on the carpet. 'Harris's solicitor has said he will plead guilty to conspiracy to kidnap and drug supplying, and if we accept that plea, Harris will give us the details of all his associates. The whole network. Not just the dealers here but the international links as well. The whole shooting match Frank, enough to bring all the main players down for a very long time – the people we haven't been able to touch.'

'No doubt you told them to piss off!'

York did not move or reply to Jet's angry comment.

'You're really thinking about making a deal with that murdering bastard?' Jet could feel the rage inside swell, and his voice began to rise. 'That man had my wife murdered! She didn't even know him, she was no threat, but he had her murdered because it suited him. How can you be thinking about doing deals with him?'

York looked intimidated by Jet's outburst and remained silent for a few seconds, then spoke. 'Look, I know how difficult this is, that's why we wanted to come here and speak to you personally. It's a matter of proof, you know that. This way at least we get Harris in prison and a lot of other people as well. If we don't do this then there's a real risk he could be acquitted and could come back to work as a policeman. Can you imagine that?' Jet thought York was bordering on tearful as he spoke. 'Frank, with Harris's testimony we can bring down both of the big criminal families in the North East.'

Jet fixed his eyes on York. 'What does Harris get out of this deal?'

York maintained eye contact and spoke softly. 'Two years.'

'Which means he'll do less than twelve months.'

'It's the best we can do. In return for that, he's agreed not to make any complaints about you assaulting him.'

Jet shook his head. 'I should have smashed his skull in when I had the chance.'

'Then you'd have been in prison instead of him.' York continued to stare at Jet. 'This way at least we get him inside, and a lot of criminals with him, and you get to keep your job.'

'What about justice for Julia?'

'The man who killed Julia is dead.'

'The man who was paid to pull the trigger might be dead, but the man who killed her, the man really responsible, he's going to get away with it!'

'Look Frank, I can see how upsetting this is for you and I'm sorry. I wish it were different as well, I really do.'

'Upsetting? For fuck's sake, upsetting?'

Jet returned to looking out of the window. He could feel tears forming in his eyes and he did not want to betray this to York. He continued to look out of the window in silence. As he did, he could see a small blue tit pecking at food on the table in the centre of the lawn. An image of Julia tending to the bird table flashed so vividly into Jet's mind that he could see her smiling, as she broke up a slice of leftover toast.

'Listen Frank, is there anything we can do to help you? How about the force doctor?'

Jet shook his head, there was only one thing he wanted and he knew nothing was going to bring her back.

'No. I'd just like to be on my own please.'

'Of course.' York and Anderson got up from the settee. Two full cups remained on their coasters on the small table and both men walked to the door and quietly left. Jet did not move as he heard the front door gently close. As he saw the figures of York and Anderson walk down the garden path, he turned away and looked into the room. Julia's sweet odour filled his nostrils and, as the tears coursed over his cheeks, he looked at the rug in front of the fire and remembered how, just a short time ago, he had been locked in Julia's arms as he had entered into her pretend world of the carnival and their real world of mutual and total love.

Jet's mind was spinning. Images flashed around his brain. He could see Julia's face – his beloved Julia who he would never see again – and the vision of Harris, who he saw smirking confidently at literally getting away with murder. Jet did not doubt he would have huge sums of dirty money stashed away to enable him to live in luxury after his short stay in prison.

Then with the jumbled thoughts of good and evil crowding his mind and the aroma of Julia being breathed into his body, he fell to his knees. This time he felt no need to hide his tears.

Chapter thirty

Jet sat in the driver's seat of the Fiesta and stared out of the windscreen. For three hours now he had been pretending to be interested in the newspaper he held in his hands, every now and again turning the pages back and forth. It had been three days since York visited his home and broken the news about the deal negotiated by Harris. At first Jet thought his own life was over and he would never be able to recover from the blows he had taken over the past few weeks. He had found it almost impossible to come to terms with how much his life had changed and he lay in his house with no inclination to do anything other than lie still and fade away. Then he heard Julia's voice. Exhaustion had caused him to doze and somewhere in that place between sleep and consciousness he could hear her talking to him, telling him not to give in. 'Pull yourself together Frankie.' He had heard her voice in that scolding way she had of saying things, but also encouraging and determined.

Now he was sitting in his car on the main road that ran through the Castlefields Estate and he watched. He watched Mark Groom's house, the house that Groom himself would not be seeing for some time.

It was early in the afternoon and he felt uncomfortable

sitting in the car. It was a clear and warm summer's afternoon and he felt his shirt sticking to his back as he rested on the fabric-covered seat.

There had been little movement of people in the street and even though he had been sitting feigning interest in his copy of last night's *Evening Chronicle* for far too long, he doubted he had been noticed by anyone. He had read the front page article, written by their chief crime reporter Barbara Hickson, about young offenders being taken on holiday to the Lake District as part of their rehabilitation and, not for the first time today, thought the world was going mad. He looked at his watch for the umpteenth time and began to wonder whether he was just wasting his time. He started to question his own judgement. He had found it impossible to stop his mind turning over the events of the previous devastating weeks, and he still could not make sense of everything. It was not just the unfairness of what had happened; it was also the detective in him searching for resolution, trying to put things in order. He had mulled over all of the events many times and convinced himself that a vital missing piece could be found here. But now he was having doubts. Now he wondered if he was ever going to entirely understand all of what had happened. Now he was questioning the course of logic which had caused him to sit in his warm, sticky Fiesta – the car Julia had never liked. Ironically, one of the main sources of her dissatisfaction had been its lack of air conditioning. But here he was.

After a few more moments' thought, Jet decided it would be a good idea to leave and perhaps return later. Even if he were wasting his time, at least he would be able to satisfy himself of that fact. Just as his fingers reached the key inserted in the ignition, he saw Shirley's four-wheel drive go past him and pull onto the Tarmac drive. He was sure she had not spotted him. He lifted the newspaper to his face and looked over the top of it to see Shirley Groom get out of her car and walk to the front door of her home. Within a few seconds she closed the door behind her and the street returned to its normal state of inactivity. Jet reclined in his seat as far as he comfortably could and continued to watch. After a few more moments another car arrived and parked on the road outside the house. It was a new saloon car, a typical family car Jet thought. As soon as the sole occupant got out of the car, Jet recognised him. There were at least thirty metres between him and this man, and even though he had only seen him before on his television screen, in a still from a CCTV videotape, he recognised him – there could be no mistake. He watched as the man walked at a leisurely pace up the drive, put a key in the lock of the front door and entered the house.

Once the front door was closed, Jet got out of the Fiesta and headed towards the house. He rang the bell, and after a few seconds he impatiently pushed at the button again. As the bell was still sounding the door opened. Jet could feel his heart racing and as he saw Shirley Groom's face he moved forward and pushed the door open. 'Hello Shirley, don't mind if I come in do you?'

As he said the words he had a brief recollection of saying something similar to John Metcalf as he conned his way into his flat, but he did not dwell on this. He had things to do and say.

Shirley appeared startled, and she stood back as the door was firmly pressed opened. Jet thought he might surprise her further. 'I really would like to be introduced to your friend Shirley, where is he?'

'What is the meaning…?' But Jet was not listening to Shirley and he moved into the house so quickly that she realised the futility of finishing her statement.

Jet followed the hall to the lounge he was familiar with and left it when he saw it was empty. 'I hope he hasn't run out of the back door Shirley. There's no point in hiding now,' he said to her as she followed behind him and he walked through another door and found the kitchen. The room was bright and clean, the tiles above the units seemed to sparkle and there, standing next to the bench, he saw the face of the man he had last seen on a videotape. The man who, six Sundays ago, had been caught on the police station video camera being led into the back door of the police station by Mark Groom.

'I know your real name isn't Jack Wagstaff, so what is it?' Jet thought the stranger might make a bolt for the door. 'It's no good running now. I don't think there's any point, do you?' The stranger looked frightened as Jet angrily continued, 'I want some answers!' The two men stared at each other and for a few seconds, there was a silent stand-off, neither man knowing what to expect next. Jet raised his voice again. 'So what's your real name?'

'What do you want from us?' The stranger's voice was trembling.

Jet looked at Shirley. 'There's an us?' As he spoke she bowed her head slightly, like a schoolgirl caught smoking behind the bike shed. 'You did something that led to people being murdered. One of those people was my wife.'

'Shirley didn't do anything.'

'I think others will have to be the judge of that.'

'Look, I didn't mean for anyone to get hurt. I didn't know Mark would go and kill Trent.'

'So what did you mean to happen?'

'I just want me and Shirley to be together. We knew Mark would never allow that – you know what he's like. I knew when he saw the photos he'd go off it. I thought he'd do something hot-headed and get himself into trouble, but I didn't think he'd murder Trent.'

'So you hoped he'd go and thump Trent in prison and end up getting sacked and maybe even get put in prison for a while?'

'I didn't know what would happen. I just thought it would bring things to a head. I just wanted us to be left alone so we could start a new life together.'

'You mean it was the only way you could think of getting him out the way and avoid getting thumped yourself?'

'He's not the sort of person to take things like this rationally.'

'You must have realised he'd see you eventually and he'd find out what you'd done?'

'If he did, it would be a long time from now and Shirley and I would be together.' The stranger's voice was quiet, but he appeared to be a little more confident now. 'Shirley told me about Diane's real father and even if Mark didn't know who Diane's father was, I knew he'd overreact when he saw the photos. But honestly, I never thought anyone would die.'

'You know, a cynic like me might think things couldn't have worked out better for you. After all, Mark's going to be out of the way for a long time.' Jet's voice rose as he spoke. 'This was a well thought out plan, shoplifting where you knew Mark would be and getting him to arrest you.'

'It wasn't that difficult. He's a creature of habit.'

Jet stared at the stranger as he thought about what he had just learned. He always had trouble working out where the mysterious shoplifter fitted into the scheme of things and his thoughts had always returned to Shirley. Somehow there had to be a logical explanation why a stranger had appeared with a photo of Diane Groom with Geoffrey Trent's name on it, and at last it was beginning to make sense. As he was considering all of this, the stranger spoke. 'Look I'm really sorry about what happened to your wife. It had nothing to do with me, you know that. I'm so sorry.'

Jet did not respond to the stranger's comment. In truth, he did not know how to. He had experienced so many emotions over the past weeks that he was starting to feel confused himself about who he was angry with and why. In his darkest moments he hated everyone, but when the mists cleared in his mind he knew he hated Harris.

'So what are you going to do with us?' The stranger sounded pathetic, as if Jet held in his possession the gift of life or death.

Jet continued to look at him and was silent for a while as if he had not heard the question. Then he made a comment that instantly confused the stranger. 'Jack Wagstaff has one more performance to make.'

Chapter thirty-one

It was ten o'clock on Wednesday morning and Jet was sitting in the Fiesta in Merchants Wharf, a street in St Peter's Basin, a private and exclusive estate on the River Tyne. As he sat looking at the newly built houses, he thought this was another place where Julia would have loved to live.

Jet had learned that Shirley Groom's lover was in fact James Harrison, a computer programmer, and he was now waiting for him outside his house. It had briefly occurred to Jet that Harrison might not turn up for their appointment, but on balance he was comfortable he would appear as arranged. Jet knew relatively little about Harrison, but it was enough to make his disappearance very unlikely. Jet did not think he was going to abandon his whole life to escape from him now.

The day was overcast, and although the air was still mild, it had more a feel of autumn than summer. Jet knew Harrison lived on his own and felt only slight relief when he saw the front door open and he appeared, wearing the same bulky coat he had worn when arrested several weeks ago for shoplifting.

As Harrison opened the passenger door of the Fiesta there was a brief exchange and very quickly they were travelling out of the estate towards North Shields and the offices of the solicitors Smith, Boar and Wren.

As they turned right at the traffic lights heading out of St Peter's Basin and then onto the main road that would take them to North Shields, Jet broke the awkward silence. 'How did you meet Shirley?'

'I was a singing sailor.'

'What?'

Harrison laughed. 'I was in the Wylam Amateur Dramatic Society's production of the *Pirates of Penzance*. Shirley and I have a mutual friend, Adelle Pearson, who lives in Stocksfield. She was one of the captain's daughters and Shirley came to see her. We met at a party after the show.'

'You're obviously a man of many talents.'

'You haven't heard me sing. The *Hexham Courant* review said the performance was "cheery if slightly off-key". That was the best review we had. I was smitten with her from the first time I saw her and Adelle helped me engineer a few more meetings. Things worked out well from there.'

'Not for everyone.'

'Sorry, I just meant that me and Shirley. You know.' Harrison had stopped smiling.

'Yes I know.'

The silence returned for a few more seconds and then Harrison spoke. 'Shirley was so unhappy with Mark, she was terrified of him. The only way we'd have any chance of being together and building a life was if he was away. You know what a bully he is. We wouldn't have had a hope otherwise. Shirley was never going to leave; he controlled every part of her life.'

'So you delivered the photos to him personally and you knew he'd react violently and do something stupid enough to get put away for a while?'

'I'd read in the paper about Trent being arrested and I knew from Shirley that he was Diane's father. It just seemed to be a chance worth taking, but I didn't think anyone would get killed.'

'It was a clever plan. Did Shirley know what you were doing?'

'I told her afterwards what I'd done. She went mad, but we agreed to support each other. We love each other very much. I'll make her very happy.'

I'm sure you will.'

The silence returned for a few more seconds then Harrison spoke. 'I'm sorry about your wife. You don't think I had anything to do with it, do you?'

'Don't worry, I know who killed Julia.'

The silence returned again and this time it was Jet's turn to break it. 'I know this firm of solicitors very well, but the strange thing is I had to use the A to Z to find out where their office is in North Shields.'

'How come?'

'Because when I've dealt with them they've always been

with their clients at the police station. They represent most of the serious criminals in the North East.'

'I still don't know why you want me to do this.'

'Don't worry about it; it's just our little deal. I think you owe me the favour, don't you?'

Harrison nodded in agreement.

A few minutes later they were in North Shields and found the building without difficulty with a little time to spare. Jet looked at the large office block which had a bold sign with the firm's name above the door and this was repeated in gold lettering on all of the upstairs windows.

'Who says crime doesn't pay?' Jet said to Harrison, as they sat in the stationary Fiesta some fifty metres away from the office block on the opposite side of the road.

He looked at Harrison. 'Are you clear about what you need to do?'

'We've been over it a hundred times.' Harrison seemed weary rather than nervous.

'Well in that case go and put your acting talents to good use.'

Harrison left the car, walked over the road and disappeared into the building. Inside he saw a chest-high mahogany reception desk behind which sat an attractive woman in her early thirties. Her hair was neat and she wore a smile that looked well-practised and displayed a set of radiant white teeth that were just a little uneven, but this slight imperfection could easily be forgiven.

'I've an appointment with Mr Boar. My name is Wagstaff.'

'Please take a seat and we'll be with you soon.'

Harrison looked at the leather sofas which stood against the two available walls and decided not to make the descent to sit. He could see himself being consumed by the soft leather and feared the contents of his trouser pockets would quickly disappear down the sides of the sofa.

He had been standing for a few minutes when he was summoned to what appeared to be a large meeting room and invited to take a seat. After a few more minutes a man in his early fifties appeared and shook his hand. 'Good morning, Mr Wagstaff. I'm Edward Boar.' As he spoke he pulled out the chair at the head of the large conference table. Boar wore an expensive, dark-blue, pinstripe suit, and the same well-practised smile as his receptionist. A sky-blue silk tie was neatly knotted around the collar of his pristine white shirt. He placed his elbows on the table and gently clasped his hands together, as if in some informal praying position. 'And what can I do for you Mr Wagstaff?'

'I'm grateful you've taken the time to see me. I've brought an important message which couldn't be delivered in any way other than personally.'

'So you said on the telephone, and I'm most intrigued. Please continue.'

'I've a friend who is a police officer and he's currently awaiting trial for a number of serious offences.'

'Do you want us to represent him?'

'No. He's represented by another firm and it is important that there's no connection between your firm and his.'

'Why is that?'

'He and his solicitors have made an arrangement that will reduce his sentence considerably.'

'That sounds like a sensible arrangement.'

'It is for my friend, but he's worried about some of the people you represent.'

'Really, why should that be?'

'Because part of the deal he's made involves him giving evidence to bring prosecutions against two of your clients, a Mr David Waters and Richard Patterson.'

'Who's your friend?'

'His name is Ray Harris.'

'Why does he want my clients to know about this?'

'Well he feels really bad about letting them down and he wants them to know he's sorry, but he's sure they'll understand that he'd little alternative, given the fact that he's looking at life imprisonment.'

'Yes, I see.'

'He knows that if they know in advance, they can make arrangements to alter their business activities – perhaps a temporary move to another country or a nice long holiday, and when he gets out of prison, he promises he'll make it up to them both.'

'Really, that's very good of him.'

'Yes, well he's really embarrassed by this. But he was careful to make it part of the deal that before he gives anything away, they actually sentence him first. He doesn't want the police doing the dirty on him and getting a life sentence after he's told them what they want to know.'

'Very sensible.'

'So in a few weeks he should be sentenced, and he'll do what he has to after that. It gives your clients plenty of time to put their houses in order.' Harrison paused but continued when it became apparent that no response was coming from Boar. 'So do you think you could pass the message on? It's important to Ray that Mr Patterson and Waters don't think badly of him, and he fully intends to carry on business with them when he gets out of prison in the not-too-distant future.'

Harrison could see Boar had been scribbling notes on the pad in front of him during the discussion, using the gold-nib fountain pen he had removed from the inside pocket of his jacket. As he had removed it, Harrison got a flash of the bright-red silk lining of his jacket.

'I'm not sure I can be of any assistance. I've lots of clients and they call me when they need me to represent them. I'm not a deliverer of messages. Why don't you contact them yourself?'

'Ray was very particular about that. He said he didn't want any misunderstandings and it was best if you dealt with the situation.'

'Well I really don't think I can help. I'm sorry you've wasted your time, Mr Wagstaff.'

Harrison rose to his feet and shook Boar's outstretched hand. 'Never mind. I did what Ray asked me to do, I can't do any more than that. I'm sorry I wasted your time.'

'Don't worry about it. Goodbye Mr Wagstaff.'

Harrison turned and left Boar in the large meeting room and soon he was outside of the building.

Within a few minutes he was again sitting in the Fiesta, which Jet had now turned around so that the car faced away from the solicitor's building and was a few more metres away.

Harrison spoke as he got into the passenger seat. 'It was a waste of time. He said he couldn't help.'

'Did you deliver the message the way I told you?'

'Word perfect.'

'Good.'

'I still don't understand why you are passing messages for Harris.'

'Don't worry about it. As long as you passed the message.' Jet looked Harrison straight in the eye. 'Don't forget our deal, you never tell a soul about this, and I'll never tell anyone about you and your shoplifting.'

'Fine by me;' Harrison said, and Jet thought he sounded a little puzzled.

There was no need to explain to Harrison that his meeting had been the equivalent of lighting a blue touch paper, and now they should stand back at a safe distance and see what happened.

He knew Julia would never have condoned his actions, and he knew what he had done was a poor second to justice. That was the difference between him and Julia, she would never have settled for second best. There had been a time when he would have agreed with her, but today, Jet thought, second was better than last.

He also knew that Justice was a myth.

Chapter thirty-two

It was Friday morning and the late summer sun was shining as Jet parked in the police station car park. It was just after eight o'clock by the time Jet was sitting at his desk, a cup of hot coffee gently releasing steam into the air. He always came in earlier on weekdays, to enable himself to get sorted out and be at his desk while the rest of the office sprang to life around him. It meant he didn't have to become entangled with rituals of tea making, gossip and accounts of out of work activity. It was the kind of detachment he preferred.

Jet had been back at work for two days following his compassionate leave and had seen more people smile at him than he could ever recall in the past. He had also noticed the people around him were choosing their words very carefully, as if any reference to wives and families would cause great offence. It had occurred to him that he could explain that the pain of what had happened could not be eased by denying Julia's existence, but on balance he decided against it. He could also have told people that Julia still spoke to him, he still heard her voice, but he knew he could not share that with anyone. He remembered the comment of his mother when the doctor had suggested a psychiatrist after the death of Brian Edwards: 'That's all we need, people thinking he's mental as well.' No, this was information he would not even share with Julia's sister, Heather, who had called in to see him at home many times since Julia's death. He had often thought in the past that Julia and Heather were chalk and cheese, but during these more recent visits he had realised the similarities that existed: the shape of her nose, the slender build and her small feet. He smiled as he thought of Julia's size-three feet and the indignity she expressed as she looked around the children's shoe department to find something fashionable to wear.

The office was beginning to stir into life when the phone rang, and Jet found himself obeying an order to go to York's office.

'Sit down Frank.' York smiled, and Jet thought he too was giving him the kid-glove treatment and wondered how long it was going to last.

'I've received some bad news this morning, and I wanted you to know rather than hear it by rumour.'

'Bad news?'

'Ray Harris was stabbed to death in a prison exercise yard yesterday afternoon.'

Jet felt nothing as he absorbed the information and then he felt his stomach starting to turn.

'You'll forgive me if I don't feel so sad about that.'

'I understand, I just thought you should know.' York smiled. 'It's a good job it happened in a prison in Hull or you might have been the chief suspect.'

Jet's stomach turned more quickly now and he started to feel light-headed. He tried his best to breathe deeply and compose himself. 'Do you know what happened?'

'He was in an exercise yard with a number of other prisoners when he was found by a warden lying on the ground. No one saw anything of course.'

'Guess prison just isn't a safe place for a copper.'

'I guess so.'

Jet's mind was whirling and his stomach continued to spin. 'Had he told you what you wanted to know about his criminal contacts?'

'We'd spoken to him, but it's of no use now without his testimony. It's a real shame because we could've put a lot of big names out of business.'

'Maybe they found out and had him killed.'

'There's no way that could have happened – we were so careful. He wasn't even in strict segregation so as not to raise suspicion. We were waiting until he received his sentence and then we were going to act. We didn't want the big players to start moving out of the country to escape. It was all going to be a big surprise. When we struck, it was going to be swift and hard.' York shook his head. 'But that's all out of the window now.'

'Sounded like a good plan. I hadn't really thought about it.' Jet's words were not coming easily to him now; he could feel beads of sweat burning through his forehead and his stomach churned.

'Don't suppose you had.' York was silent for a second and stared at Jet who tried to remain poker-faced while everything inside him twisted and he felt more and more faint. York continued, 'Well at least we'll be spared Harris's trial and all of the bad publicity that it would've brought us. And as he's still a serving police officer, it means his wife gets his pension.'

'I suppose every cloud does have a silver lining.' Jet could now hear his own voice, the words echoing around the room, as they had all those years ago at Brian Edwards' inquest.

'Yes, indeed.' Jet thought that York was looking quizzically at him as he spoke. 'Are you all right Frank? You look a little pale.'

'Fine, thanks,' Jet lied. The sweat felt like red-hot needles piercing through the skin on his forehead, and his stomach was now a washing machine on fast spin over which he had no control. He felt dangerously close to losing consciousness.

'Anyway, as I said I just wanted you to know.'

'Thank you Sir.'

Jet rose quickly and left the office. Once in the corridor, he felt his legs weaken. He reached his arm out and touched the wall. He staggered as he guided himself along the wall down the corridor and found his way to the men's toilets. Once inside he pushed open a cubicle door and turned to fall back onto the plastic toilet seat. As he sat, he reached up and locked the cubicle door. The sweat poured profusely from his forehead.

'Well, are you pleased with yourself?'

Jet's mind seemed hollow. His light head felt empty, as if he was barely in control of his own faculties. 'What?' he replied instinctively to the voice.

'Are you pleased with yourself?'

Jet knew the voice, he had heard it many times. Julia spoke to him again. 'Are you pleased you've killed Harris?'

'I didn't kill him.'

'You knew fine well when you got Harrison to pretend he was a messenger what would happen. That's why you did it.'

'I didn't know what would happen.'

'You knew they'd think Harris was trying to warn them, but they'd really think he was just being naïve. You knew they were ruthless criminals and that they'd make sure Harris wasn't going to be a threat to their business or their future. You arranged his death. They weren't going to take any risks over Harris.'

'I didn't know what would happen.' Jet bent forward on the toilet seat, his hands holding either side of his face; his voice was now nothing more than a mumble.

'It was really clever using Jack Wagstaff again. You knew if there'd just been a telephone call they'd have just dismissed it as a pathetic hoax, but a personal messenger, that was smart.'

'I didn't know what would happen.' Jet lifted himself back onto the toilet and he slumped, the back of his head touching the smooth Formica wall.

'You knew they'd think the message was genuine. It would be the only way they'd think it was. After all, they'd know Harris couldn't have made direct contact from prison because all of his calls were being monitored.'

'I didn't know what would happen.' Jet was sobbing.

'And using Boar was really clever. You knew Boar would never say he was going to help, and you know he'll never admit to anyone that he passed the message on. He might live off the proceeds of criminals, but he's never going to put himself in a position where he's vulnerable.'

'I didn't know.'

'It was a perfect link. Harrison doesn't know the effect of his performance and Boar's never going to say a word – no one will ever make the connection with you. I always said you were clever Frank, and now you've committed a clever murder.'

'I didn't do it.' The small cubicle was spinning around Jet's head and his stomach was now nothing more than a tight knot.

'Harris didn't pull the trigger himself either.' Jet felt tormented by Julia's unrelenting voice.

'I didn't know.' The tears flowed in torrents down Jet's cheeks.

'Maybe you're their type after all Frank.'

'No Julia, please no. I'm sorry Julia.'

Julia was the last word that left Jet's mouth before he slumped back against the toilet cistern and lost consciousness. His head fell back and rested on the Formica of the cubicle. He remained seated, his buttocks fastened in the hole of the toilet seat.

The tempest that had raged through Jet's life had now engulfed and shattered him. He was not in a position to appreciate the irony of what had struck him, or why, or understand the poetic injustice involved. As he slumped on the seat of a toilet, collapsed and tortured, he had lost everything dear to him. The most important person in his life, the woman he adored, and he had now sacrificed the principles that were once at the core of his being. He knew that. What he could not possibly have known was the storm was still far from over.

Chapter thirty-three

A cheerless January morning witnessed Jet park the Fiesta and trudge into the police station.

'Is it raining out there?'

Jet looked up the stairs as he walked and saw Jean the cleaner polishing a brass plate on one of the double swing doors on the first floor landing. The doors led to the corridor which ran the length of the building, off which ran many offices, including that of the CID constables.

'No, it looks like it might though.'

'Bloody hell, that's all I need.'

'You going out?'

'Billy's at hospital this afternoon, gets his fizzy-o-ferretty – daft bugger.'

It took Jet a second to comprehend Jean's translation of physiotherapy but he was not in the mood to smile. 'At least he's out of plaster.'

'Daft bugger. I told him it's the last time he gans up that ladder, don't care how bloody big that hedge gets.'

'I'm sure after the fall he must have learnt his lesson.'

'Have to watch him like a hawk, he's a daft bugger that one.'

'Well I hope it stays dry for your trip.'

'You never get parked at that hospital you know, and they've got a man that clamps you if you don't park in a proper space. Last time we hast to bloody well leave the car in Eldon Square multi-storey and walk to the hospital – took us bloody ages.'

'That is a long walk.'

'Bloody right. Better than getting clamped though.'

'Right.'

'I seen them clampin' up there. Poor bloke just left his car a minute and they was there puttin' a bloody big clamp on his wheel. Don't expect it on the national health do you?'

'No.'

'You ever been clamped?'

Jet had reached the doors Jean was working on and placed his right hand on the one she was not polishing. He paused for a second. 'No, not that I remember,' he lied and then continued as he pushed the door open. 'Hope it all goes well this afternoon.'

He walked into the corridor and took the third door on his right into the main CID office.

It was just after eight o'clock on Tuesday morning. He always came in early on weekdays, to enable himself to get sorted out and be at his desk while the rest of the office sprang to life around him. It meant he didn't have to become entangled with rituals of tea making, gossip and accounts of out of work activity. It was the kind of detachment he preferred.

316

It was five months since Jet had been hospitalised after having been found unconscious in the police station toilet. The autumn had disappeared in a blur. Doctors had prescribed pills he had not taken, and he avoided the recommended bereavement counselling with as much vigour as he had shunned the Christmas festivities. Returning to his work routine had been his only salvation.

He picked up the electric kettle and, assessing it to be half full, flicked the switch which started the water boiling. The office was completely empty. Jet walked to his desk, pulled a copy of last night's *Evening Chronicle* from his jacket pocket and threw it onto his desk. He unfolded it and read the headline again. 'Gang Land leaders Caught in Drug Swoop'. He left his paper, returned to the kettle which was now ejecting steam into the air, poured the water into a large mug, stirred the contents, carried the mug to his desk and sat down. He read the story underneath the headline as he had already done several times since buying the paper on his way home the previous night.

David Waters and Richard Patterson, two men reputed to be leaders in the North East gangland network, are behind bars having been remanded in custody this morning by Newcastle Magistrates' Court. Both have been charged with conspiracy to supply drugs. The offences relate to the mass distribution of illegal drugs across the North East over the past three years. Both men spoke only to confirm their names and heard their application for bail being refused. If convicted of the offence, both men could expect life sentences. The arrest is seen as a major breakthrough for the police who have struggled to stem the massive flow of drugs into the area.

Jet pulled open the top drawer of his desk, folded up the newspaper and rested it on the other documents inside. As he closed the drawer he was lost in his own thoughts. The newspaper report made him feel uneasy. It had been over five months since he had arranged for the message which led to the death of Harris to be passed on, and he was sure that nothing could ever be traced back to him. But the news of the arrests still made him feel on edge.

The office phone sang its alarming tune; Jet picked it up and spoke his name into the receiver.

'Thought I might find you there Jet.' He recognised Sharkie's voice at once.

'Nothing if not predictable Sergeant.'

'One of the uniform is at a burglary at Squire Towers, number 316, can you have a look up there?'

Jet did not think this was really a question and wrote the address on the pad on his desk. 'Do you know any more details?'

'No. It's been confirmed as a burglary so it needs CID. John Dawkin's up there at the moment.'

'I'll get up there soon.'

'Good man Jet.'

Jet picked up his jacket and walked out of the office and down the corridor. As he got close to the door that led to the stairs, he could hear Jean's voice. 'Billy's fizzy-o-ferretty, got to get up to the bloody hospital.'

As Jet headed down the stairs, he could see that Jean's remarks were aimed at one of the women who worked in admin on the second floor. She smiled at Jean as she was being spoken to and continued with her ascent.

'Have to park at the multi-storey, or we'll get bloody well clamped.'

Jet walked out of the building into the car park and unlocked the Fiesta. He removed the bright-yellow crook lock from the steering wheel and within a few seconds had joined the traffic on Market Street on the short journey to Squire Towers.

The traffic was its usual stop-start and the tower block, which was a fifteen-minute walk from the station, took a fifteen-minute drive. Jet could see that all of the resident's parking bays were taken and mounted the pavement outside the tall tower block, parking the Fiesta with both nearside wheels on the path. He cast an eye over the offside of his car to make sure he had left enough space for passing traffic and knowing the local traffic wardens knew his car, he locked it and walked to the front of the building. Jet looked at the slip of paper in his hand which said 'flat 316' and then up at the huge building. It seemed nothing more than a colourless construction of boxes heaped high into the sky, its formation of large drab grey square concrete blocks casting long unfriendly shadows.

Jet walked into the front of the tower block and was pleased to discover that 316 was only as high as the third floor. He pressed the button on the elevator panel which, he quickly realised, did not merit anything to happen in haste. He looked at the sign above a door which said 'stairs' but decided to wait by the elevator, and after a few minutes the doors slowly opened and he entered the lift. He was feeling impatient as the elevator doors closed behind him and it slowly made its way to the third floor. The lift stuttered as it reached its destination and the last ten centimetres of his ascent were at a snail's pace. Once the doors opened, Jet marched out of the lift as if trying to make up time and, looking at the numbers on the doors, made his way to 316. He saw the uniformed figure of John Dawkin walking down the corridor towards him. Dawkin was not a tall man, and as he got nearer Jet was struck by how big his uniform helmet appeared. It seemed to rest uneasily on his head. His thick grey hair hung scruffily, and Jet thought it looked as if it were attached to the edges of the helmet rather than his scalp, like some pathetic hat bought from a joke shop.

'All right John, what we got?'

'Old woman, seems a bit dotty to me. Says her locks have been tampered with and someone has been moving her stuff around – blames the council.'

'Anything stolen?'

'Says she's lost her husband's war medals, but they could have been lost years ago judging by the state of things.'

'You knocked on any doors?'

'No, door to door's a CID responsibility.'

'I forgot you'd been elected the federation representative – no going the extra yard for you these days.'

'Fair day's work for a fair day's pay. You get paid to do the house to house enquiries.'

'Thought we both got paid to catch criminals?'

'We have to stick to the rules otherwise the bosses will take advantage of us.'

'Whatever you say John. Is the old woman in the flat alone?'

'Yes, Mrs Juliet Rodgers. Knock loud, she's a bit deaf.'

Dawkin walked away down the corridor, and Jet turned his head and watched him nearing the elevator. 'Tit,' Jet said to himself as he saw Dawkin's back disappear.

There had been times in Jet's service when he had been grateful for the support of the Police Federation. Their central office had access to legal representation, and he understood why it was important. But the position of part-time local representative often seemed to attract a certain type of character with their own axe to grind: the canteen-lawyer types, whose lack of knowledge did not prevent them from offering strong opinions or dispensing advice. He had seen it go wrong many times and he thought Dawkin was the sort of loose cannon who epitomised the problem. Dawkin had been the subject of a disciplinary enquiry when he had apparently misplaced some found property: cash that had been handed to him. He had been reprimanded for his dereliction of duty. After that he stood for election to the federation and was now a representative who seemed hell-bent on being counterproductive. Yes, Jet thought, 'Tit' was an apt description.

Jet knocked hard on the flat door. After a few moments he heard the door lock turn and a face appeared. The old woman's skin was pale, her short, grey hair thin, but brushed neatly back. She wore a cream cardigan and a dark-blue tweed skirt.

Jet produced his warrant card and waved it as the door opened.

'I thought you were going to have the door down there. I'm not deaf you know.'

'Sorry. I'm a detective. I understand you've reported a break-in?' Jet's voice was raised.

'What's the matter with you policemen, you got to be shoutin' all the time?'

Jet lowered his voice. 'Sorry, may I come in?'

'That's better. Come in. I don't know how many times I told that last policeman he didn't need to shout, but I gave up in the end. Expect he's got a deaf old grandmother or somethin'.' The old woman was talking as she walked into the flat, and Jet followed. The short passageway led to another door and into a room which was crammed with furniture. It looked well preserved but old and out of place in this small abode. The old woman sat down on a high wooden-framed armchair and pointed to a sofa. Jet quickly sat down as directed.

'I understand you've had some medals stolen?'

'Yes, they were my husband's. He fought in the Second World War, fought in France and Germany.'

'Campaign medals?'

'Yes, and the Military Medal for bravery. Hero he was.'

'He's no longer with us?'

'No, passed away over twenty years ago; heart attack.'

'Where did you keep the medals?'

'In the bedroom through here.'

The old woman gripped the wooden arms of the chair, lifted herself up and walked towards the door at the rear of the room. Jet stood up, negotiated his way past the cluttered furniture and followed her into the bedroom. She pulled the top drawer from a dressing table. 'They was just here.'

'Best leave that alone for the moment, I'll get someone to check for fingerprints.'

Jet saw the surface of the dressing table was cluttered: a brush and mirror lay alongside a number of boxes and trinkets. At the back of the table, there was a black and white photograph of a man in military dress. 'Is this your husband?'

'Yes, that's Walter when he was in the army.'

Jet picked up a photograph frame that stood next to it.

This man in uniform was in colour. 'Who's this one then?'

'My William. He's a prison warden.'

Jet stared at the impeccably dressed prison warden who had allowed himself only the slightest of smiles and then again at the soldier. 'No mistaking the family resemblance.'

'Yes. My Walter would have been ever so proud of our William.'

Jet returned the photograph. 'Did you give the last police officer a full description of the medals, which medals they were?'

'Yes, I had a photograph of them which he took as well.'

'Good, that will be helpful. Was there anything else taken?'

'Just some odd bits of jewellery; a brooch and a pendant, nothing much.'

'Has anything else been disturbed?'

'Some of the furniture has been moved about.'

'Where?'

'These pieces.' The old woman pointed to a small table and some chairs in her front room which stood near to the bedroom door.

Jet walked back to the door and looked at the cluttered living room. He saw that one of the four dining chairs was pulled away from the table while the remaining three were tucked neatly into the table. 'I see. Any idea when this happened?'

'Just popped out to get some milk this morning, only away twenty minutes.'

'Did you see anyone when you left?'

'No, just some kids at the lift. It'll be the council whose done it.'

'Why do you think that?'

'They want the flat. The social services keep saying I should be in a home. I can look after myself, but they want the flat. Who else would have the key to get in?'

'The door wasn't forced?'

'No, just the way it is now.'

'Excuse me a second.' Jet left the bedroom and walked through the living room into the small front passage to the front door and inspected the Yale lock. He turned the lock, opened the door and then closed it again. The old woman had followed him the short distance through the flat. 'The lock looks OK. Are you sure you locked the door properly when you went out?'

'Course I did. It was locked when I got back as well.'

'Did you recognise the kids you saw near the lift when you went out?'

'No.'

'I don't think the council would come in and steal your husband's medals Mrs Rodgers, but if the door hadn't been properly closed someone could have dashed in and just grabbed them.'

'Will you get Walter's medals back? They mean a lot to me.'

There was a knock on the door as the old woman spoke.

'Should I get that for you?'

The old woman nodded, and Jet turned and opened the door. He recognised Peter Logan, the scenes of crime officer. Jet turned back to the old woman. 'It's just another policeman to look for fingerprints.'

'Oh.'

Jet looked back at Logan and spoke. 'There's a jewellery drawer in the bedroom, and it looks like whoever's been in has knocked some of this furniture on the way in or out. And could you check for prints on the outside of the front door and around the lock?'

'No problem Jet.'

Jet stayed at the front door and turned back to Mrs Rodgers. 'This officer is going to check for fingerprints. I'll go and make some enquiries and I'll come back to see you later.'

Jet left Logan opening his case, ready to remove his brush to sprinkle aluminium dust over the chosen areas, and walked into the communal corridor. He looked down the broad hallway and choosing the direction that appeared to have most doors he walked. Jet knocked on the first door he came to but, after a short period of silence, went onto the next door which was on the opposite side of the corridor. He got the same lack of response there so moved to the next door, which he noted was 319. Again Jet knocked and was just about to walk away when he heard a rustling sound from inside and the door lock turned. As it opened he reached into his inside jacket pocket, and by the time the door was half open he had unfolded his police identification. 'I'm from the police, there's been a break-in a few doors down, and I was wondering if you'd seen anything.'

The figure behind the door was silent for a few seconds, as if registering what had been said. Jet could see the woman was standing with her body behind the door, and her head was at an angle peering out at him. She was wearing a dressing gown and he guessed his knock on the door had woken her up. 'Sorry to knock on the door so early, but it's just happened and I'm trying to find out who did it.'

'Sorry, I'm on late shift, I was sleeping. Which flat was broken into?'

Jet could see the woman's thick brown hair was untidy, with a number of strands leaving the rest at unusual angles.

'316.'

'Juliet, oh dear. Is she all right?'

'She's fine. Looks like someone has sneaked in somehow and stolen some of her jewellery and her husband's medals.'

'Not the medals – she treasured those.'

Jet could see the face was more alert now and felt there was something familiar about it. 'Don't suppose you saw anyone?'

'No, I got home from work late last night and I've been in bed until you knocked on the door.'

'She mentioned to me some kids hanging around the lift this morning – don't suppose you've any idea who they might be?'

'There are always kids coming and going from the flat right at the end of the corridor of late, since a young man moved in. They go back and forwards a lot but they don't seem to stay long.'

'You don't think there could be something illegal going on?'

The woman smiled. 'Why don't you step in for a moment?'

She pulled the door open and Jet walked into the small hallway. The layout of the flat was a mirror image of the one he had just left, but this one smelled fresh and felt bright.

'Let's just go in here for a moment.' She walked past the door Jet knew led to the living room and through another one which led to a small kitchen. The room was narrow with units running down both sides. She reached out and flicked the switch on an electric kettle. 'Coffee?'

'If you're having one.'

Jet could now see that she had a thick tartan dressing gown tied tightly around her waist. He noticed a brown leather bag resting on one of the units close to the door and resting beside that was a dark-blue jacket, part of an informal uniform which he recognised. As he looked at it he realised why the woman's face was familiar. 'It's Trish isn't it? I think we've met before.'

'I thought so, a few months ago at the hospital.'

'Yes. The Goodman boy, very sad.'

'Dreadful.'

They smiled politely at each other for a few seconds in silence and then Trish turned to a cupboard and brought out two mugs and put a spoonful of coffee into each.

'You were saying about the flat up the corridor?'

'Yes, I didn't like to say too much in the corridor – you never know who's listening.'

'What do you think is going on?'

'There does seem to be a constant stream of people.'

'Drug dealing?'

'Wouldn't surprise.'

The kettle boiled and Trish poured water into the mugs and handed one to Jet. He refused the offer of sugar but added a dash of milk from the jug which she had placed on the bench.

'Mrs Rodgers seems to think the council broke into her flat.'

'She has a thing about social services – they're trying to help her but she thinks they want her flat.'

'Why?'

'She's a tad forgetful: left the gas on one day and went out. The neighbours called the fire brigade. The social services are concerned about her living on her own. She thinks they're making trouble.'

'So she could have gone out and left her front door open by accident?'

'I've found it open before.'

'That would explain things a bit better.'

The smiles and the silence returned and Jet could not remember when he had last felt so at ease with himself. Trish took a sip of her coffee and lowered the cup from her lips. 'I read about what happened to you. I'm sorry. It must have been a terrible time.'

Jet slowly nodded, his eyes looking down to the floor. 'World's full of sadness.'

'Sorry I didn't mean to…'

'Don't worry,' Jet smiled, 'it makes a change. Everyone at work is still giving me the kid-glove treatment – lots of smiles but frightened to say anything.'

There was a gentle silence and then Trish spoke. 'I have some idea what you went through – I lost my husband recently.'

'Sorry to hear that,' Jet's face straightened. 'Illness, accident?'

'No, dental receptionist: perfect smile and huge breasts.'

Jet laughed warmly, and as he did it felt odd, as if he were practising a foreign activity. 'He must be mad.' The unguarded comment led to a pause and then Jet changed the subject. 'Suppose I'd better make tracks.'

'Of course.'

Both smiled and Jet walked out of the kitchen, opened the front door and turned as he stepped into the corridor. 'Thanks for the coffee.'

'Welcome. I'm late shift all this week If you're back to see Mrs Rodgers and have a moment, the kettle's always on.'

'I'll do that, thanks.'

Jet walked along the corridor and heard Trish close her door behind him. He walked as far as he could to the end flat. He knocked hard on the door and waited. A few seconds later he knocked again. After a moment he pulled the notebook out of his inside pocket, wrote the flat number down and then turned and walked away.

Chapter thirty-four

'Eddie, see what you've got on flat 347 Squire Towers, young man just moved in. I think he might be dealing.'

'I'll see what we have and let you know.'

Eddie was sitting at his desk in the local intelligence office. He was surrounded by files and only looked up briefly. As soon as he had recognised Jet his eyes returned to the papers on his desk. Whilst Jet spoke Eddie scribbled '347 Squires' on the corner of one of the pieces of paper on his desk. Jet watched him scrawl. 'You're not going to lose that in your filing system?'

'Don't worry Jet, I'll not forget.'

'Look, I'm going down to Durham now, be back in a few hours – I'll check with you then.'

'OK.'

Jet left Eddie sitting in his cluttered office and walked out of the back door of the building into the cold winter air of the car park, quickening his pace as he made his way to the Fiesta. Within a few minutes he was working through the gears and heading across the Tyne Bridge south towards Durham. The sky was grey and it did not improve as he drove. As he arrived at the rear yard of Durham Police Station, a light shower of rain greeted him. He parked and walked around the building towards the front door. The drive to Durham, like the station, had become familiar to him over recent months, and as he approached the front desk the young woman behind the counter smiled in recognition. 'Take a seat. We're a bit busy at the moment – someone will be through soon.'

Jet returned the smile as he followed the instruction. A few moments later a solicitor entered and after he explained he was here to see his client, was also asked to wait. He took up a seat opposite Jet in the waiting area. The two short rows of blue plastic seats were fixed to the floor with heavy bolts and had not been designed for comfort. They reminded Jet of seats in a football stadium. The two men sat facing each other avoiding eye contact and a middle-aged woman came in with a slip of paper in her hand, which everyone within earshot quickly learned was a parking ticket. 'Bloody ridiculous, I'd only been gone for a minute.'

'It says here the traffic warden waited for ten minutes and you still hadn't come back by the time she'd issued the ticket.'

'Well it's a lie. I've never seen such incompetence. I demand to see an inspector immediately.'

Jet sensed the woman was just getting into full flow when a side door opened and a head peered around it. 'DC Whittle?'

Jet got up and followed the young jailer through a familiar corridor and three sets of doors. Within a few minutes he was speaking to another person he had become accustomed to, one of the custody sergeants, and soon was being ushered through the heavy metal door that led to a small corridor containing four separate cells. They were signposted as the female cells, but all of the doors were open and the cells, as well as the secure corridor which joined them, were now the entire domain of Mark Groom. Jet walked through the heavy door and it was locked behind him. Jet knew the four-cell complex well, as it had become Mark's home whilst he awaited his trial. There had been considerable debate over Groom's detention, and eventually agreement was reached that the best place to keep him was here. The consensus had been that as he was a police officer accused of murdering a prisoner in a prison, then this makeshift secure accommodation in a police station was the place he was safest. Jet had often wondered what arrangements would be made after Groom was convicted, as he inevitably would be, and he feared his personal safety would become less of a concern for the authorities once he was a convict. He had not shared the full extent of this thought with Mark but knew from the snippets of conversation which touched on the subject that Groom had arrived at the same conclusion. Jet wondered whether Ray Harris's demise had also played a part in the decision to keep Mark away from the prison population until he had faced trial.

Mark looked out of the cell that had been chosen as his main living area and smiled as Jet entered. Jet's eyes swooped around the magnolia-painted concrete walls. Two plastic chairs stood facing the fixed wooden bench. On the bench sat a small portable television. Jet had brought it in on a previous visit. The electric cable which ran from the television was attached to the wall by thick tape and led out of the door into a socket in the corridor. Mark moved one of the chairs so it leant against a wall and faced the other, which Jet pulled back and sat on.

'It gets more like the Hilton every time I come here.'

'You should see the cell next door: I've got an exercise bike and some weights – my own personal gym.'

Jet was struck by the staleness of the still air but realised the absence of any opening windows meant little could be done to change this, and the broad smile he could see on Groom's face made him believe that Mark had acclimatised himself to the atmosphere.

'Is there anything I can get you?'

'Don't think I have room for anything else, thanks. How are things in the outside world?'

'All right. What do you think about the news on Patterson and Waters?'

'Good to see them get it. Hope they do as much time as me.'

'You'll be out long before those two.'

'Not so sure.'

'You plead to manslaughter and you'll be out in no time.'

'My brief was just in to see me. The trial has been listed to start next Monday.'

'That's good isn't it? Get it over and get on with your life Mark.'

'He told me they're going to run with the murder charge.'

'What?'

'They want to put it to the jury, let the world see the wheels of justice turning – no deals for murdering coppers.'

Jet was silent for a few seconds and as he was thinking his eyes wandered around the meagre contents of the room. 'I thought the murder charge had been withdrawn?'

'No, it was talked about by the lawyers, but I think the politicians have got hold of it. They try me for murder, with an alternative charge of manslaughter. The trial is reported in the papers, if I get off the murder they still put me away for the manslaughter. If I don't get off, I go away for life.'

'What did your brief say?'

'The prosecution case is I went into a prison under false pretences with the sole intention of killing Trent. He said, being realistic, there's a fifty-fifty chance they'll convict with the murder charge.'

'But you went there to talk about the photos, not with intent to hurt him.'

'State of mind Jet, impossible to prove – the jury will decide.'

'So a full trial?'

'Listed for two weeks.'

'Are they going to call Diane?'

'I hope not. They have the DNA result.'

'You need to stay positive Mark.'

'I know; I'll do my best.' Mark summoned a weak smile as he spoke. 'I need another favour.'

'Name it.'

'Will you have a look over the file and make sure everything possible is covered?'

'What about your solicitor and barrister? They must have been through it.'

'I told them I was going to ask you. Another pair of eyes can't hurt. Between you and me, I'm worried I'm just another case. They are good people Jet, but if I get convicted of murder, you know I'm not going to see the light of day again.'

'It's bad Mark, but surely not that bad?'

'Life in prison for a cop who murdered a criminal? At best I'll spend my life in solitary, but you know that even then they can't watch me forever. I won't survive, you know that.'

'It's not that bleak.'

'Yes it is Jet. Once I'm convicted and out of the news, I'll not be such a problem to the authorities. Life for me will be twenty-five years at least. I can't survive that long. Truth is, I'm not sure I want to.'

'Come on man. You've got to think positive Mark,'

Mark's weak smile returned. 'Ever the optimist.'

'I'm not sure how York is going to take me getting involved in your defence.'

'No reason why it should be a problem – just go through the evidence and make sure that everything's covered.'

'I'm due some days off – don't suppose it matters what I get up to.'

'Thanks.'

Jet rose from his chair. 'No problem. I'll come and see you before next week. Anything else I can do?'

'I think that's enough, don't you?'

Jet walked back to the heavy door at the end of the cell passage and it took just a few seconds for him to attract the attention of the jailer. Within a few more seconds he was outside the police station and in the Fiesta heading back towards Newcastle.

Thirty minutes later, Jet walked into the local intelligence office and it appeared to him that Eddie had not moved since he had left him. 'Anything on that address Eddie?'

'Jet, yes. I checked with the local authority and it was taken by a Robert Crompton. His previous address was in Middlesbrough. I checked with the police there and he was last thought to be a small-time dealer operating in their area.'

'Any idea what brought him up here?'

'The local intelligence officer at Middlesbrough said he thought he'd been threatened by some of his competition down there, and he'd just disappeared off the face of the earth. When I told him he was here, he said he must have taken fright and moved here to set up business.'

'I might see if I can frighten him a bit myself.'

'Middlesbrough reckon he's only been missing a few weeks. You did well to catch up with him so early. How did you get on to him?'

'Informant – you know I have my sources.'

'That one's obviously a good one Jet, you want to hold on to him.'

'Yes, I was thinking about speaking to her again soon.'

'Her?'

'We live in changing times Eddie.' Jet smiled and then changed the subject. 'What have you heard about the arrest of Patterson and Waters?'

'Very little. It's being kept very tight – some crime squad from headquarters brought them in. DCI Anderson was in charge. Strange that they were taken to the nick at North Shields and not here.'

'That does seem odd.'

'What's even stranger is that they seem to have been charged very quickly. The evidence must have been there already. It's not like them to be caught with any gear in their possession, but they must have been caught with something.'

'I wonder why all the secrecy?'

'Don't suppose it really matters does it Jet? Let's just hope they go away for a long time.'

'With you there Eddie.'

Chapter thirty-five

Jet still felt a rush of excitement with early morning starts and dawn raids. After a quick briefing at the police station, it was still only 6.00am as Jet drove the Fiesta towards Squire Towers following the large Transit Van which contained the police task force. The magistrate's warrant which authorised the search of flat 347 for drugs, lay on the front passenger seat of the Fiesta as both vehicles swiftly moved through the empty streets. The van pulled up outside the front of the building. Jet saw the rear doors open and officers jumping out before he had even pulled on his handbrake. He waited for a second, making sure they had all left the van, before he followed them into the main entrance and again followed them as they made off purposefully up the stairs. It crossed his mind to use the lift but he decided against that and followed the eight task force officers, all of whom looked fit and menacing in black body armour. His legs felt heavy by the time he reached the third floor, just in time to hear a thud as a door ram sent the flat's door crashing open accompanied by shouts of 'police!' There seemed to be an uneasy silence in the flat as he entered and noticed the remains of a Yale lock lying on the passage floor. Through the short passage he walked into the main living room where two officers had already begun their systematic search. He walked into the bedroom and there saw two more officers. One of them was standing with a young man who wore only a pair of boxer shorts. The semi-naked youth shivered, looking dazed and intimidated by the officer who stood over him, ensuring he did not make any sudden moves, perhaps to reach for a concealed object or, as seemed most likely, to follow his instinct to run like hell.

'Is he on his own?' Jet asked.

'Yes, no problems – we've started the search.'

Jet almost felt sorry for the bare-skinned youth who had been pulled from his warm bed and now seemed to be hugging himself, his arms crossed over his chest as he shook in the cold air of the flat. 'Are you Robert Crompton?' Jet was straight-faced.

'Yeah.'

'We have a warrant to search the place.'

'Why are you picking on me?'

'Because you're a drug dealer and we pick on drug dealers. Do you want to tell us where the gear is or do you want us to find it?'

'I don't know what you mean.'

'OK, you stay where you are. We'll not be long.'

'Jet!' The shout came from the living room. Jet raised his eyebrows, turned his head away from Crompton and walked towards the voice. In the living room, an officer held open the door of a sideboard with his right hand, and in his left he held the wooden base that had formed the false bottom inside it. Removing this wood had revealed a small set of scales and a bag of white powder lying underneath.

'Didn't you mention war medals at the briefing?'

'Yes.'

The young officer pulled open a drawer which was above the small cupboard of the sideboard. Two medals were lying discarded in the corner, their ribbons crumpled as one lay on top of the other in a small, uncared for heap. Two open cases also sat in the drawer.

'Got a bag?'

The young constable produced a clear polythene bag into which Jet carefully placed the medals and the cases.

'Should I bag the drugs?'

Jet shook his head. 'No. Better leave it to forensics, get it photographed *in situ*, give the court something to look at, and we'll get it tested to see what it is.'

Jet walked back to the bedroom with the plastic bag in his hand. 'You don't look like a military man. Want to tell me where you got these from?'

'Someone brought them in a while ago, said they got them from a pub – they're just there until he comes back and gets them.'

'And who would that be?'

'Don't know his name.'

'I'll bet you don't. Put some clothes on, and we'll continue our chat at the station. You're being arrested for burglary and possession of illegal drugs with intent to supply.'

'I don't have any drugs.'

'Then what's that under your sideboard?'

'If you've found stuff under there I don't know how it got there – you probably planted it.'

'I can see we're going to get along well. Just get ready.'

Chapter thirty-six

The phone on Jet's desk rang.

'CID, DC Whittle.'

'Jet, it's Sharkie. Your man Crompton is expecting his solicitor in about an hour so you can start interviewing him then.'

'Thanks Sharkie.'

As soon as the phone was returned to its cradle, Jet picked up his keys and headed out of the building. Within a couple of minutes he was driving back to Squire Towers. The roads had been transformed in the few hours since his last journey and the traffic stopped and started, doubling the travelling time. As he pulled up outside the tower block he lifted a polythene bag from the passenger seat and walked into the building. He pressed the button and this time waited for the lift to arrive. As the lift slowly carried him to the third floor he again examined the medals through the clear plastic bag, wondering what deeds had been performed to earn the small metal decorations. The lift doors opened and he walked to the old lady's flat and knocked on the door. As the door slowly unlocked and opened, he smiled at the pale lined face that appeared.

'Mrs Rodgers, DC Whittle again. Can I come in?'

The door was pulled fully open and Jet followed the old woman into the small living room.

'I would like you to have a look at these for me and see if they are yours.'

Jet placed the bag on the dining table. Mrs Rodgers picked it up and after a second's glance clutched the bag to her chest and, closing her eyes, stood still, as if unable to do anything else. Jet did not need any further reassurance that she recognised the contents of the bag, but after a few seconds of silence the old woman exhaled loudly. 'Walter's medals!'

Jet saw a tear leave her left eye and roll quickly over her puffed cheek.

'We executed a warrant this morning at 347 and found them. I take it there's no doubt they're yours?'

'I've looked at them every day since Walter's death. I'd know them anywhere. Can I take them out of the bag?'

'Yes. They've been checked for fingerprints so there might be some dust left on them, but they look OK.' Jet did not add that after they had been examined he had spent a good ten minutes polishing them to ensure they were as presentable as possible and had placed the medals in a small clean bag, straightening the ribbons as well as he could. 'I'm afraid I'm going to have to keep them for a little while longer as evidence. I've got someone in custody, and now you've identified them I've got some difficult questions to ask him.'

The old woman held the medals in her hand and gently rubbed them between finger and thumb. After a few seconds she carefully placed them back into the bag and slowly returned it to Jet.

'Don't worry Mrs Rodgers, I'll look after them and return them as soon as I can – at least you know they're safe now.'

The old woman nodded and rubbed her hand in the crease below her left eye.

'I'll come back and get a statement from you soon and I'll let you know what's happening to the man I've got in custody for your burglary.'

Jet smiled and then made his way to the door. As he opened it he spoke. 'Have you lived here long?'

'I moved here not long after Walter died – over twenty years ago now.'

'Is there anyone who comes to help you?'

'My son comes over when he can, and Trish across the corridor pops in every now and then, to see if I need anything. I manage fine.'

'I'm sure you do Mrs Rodgers. Do you think you might have left the door open on the day you were burgled?'

'I don't think so.'

'I don't think it was the council who broke into your flat Mrs Rodgers – more likely opportunists, kids probably, who saw your flat door open and ran in and grabbed the first thing they saw.'

'You know what it's like when you're in a rush with things to do – sometimes you can be forgetful – but it doesn't mean I need to be in a home.'

'Course not, Mrs Rodgers. Don't worry; I'm not going to tell the council about any of this.'

Jet walked out of the flat. As the door closed behind him he stood still for a few seconds and looked up the corridor to the door of flat 319. He looked at his wrist and saw it was a little after nine o'clock. He hesitated and then slowly started to walk towards the elevator but after a few footsteps he stopped, turned, walked back to 319 and gently knocked. After a few seconds the door was pulled open and Jet was surprised to feel his heart race as it did. His smile was returned and neither was quick to speak.

'Hello again, come in.' Trish pulled the door open wide, and as Jet passed her, he was aware of a subtle scent. He thought about complimenting the very pleasant aroma but decided against it. What would Julia have said if she had heard such impertinent intimacy? He noticed her hair was neatly tied back, and she wore a light-cotton shirt tucked into black denim jeans.

'I'm not interrupting am I?'

'No, I was just getting ready to go out. I need to do some shopping before I go to work, but I've got plenty of time.'

'Just called in to say thanks.'

'Really, what for?'

'You were right about the flat down the corridor. We

paid it a visit early this morning and, among other things, we got Mrs Rodgers' medals back.'

'That is good news. They mean so much to her. Coffee?'

'Thanks.'

'She was really down when I saw her yesterday. I'll bet you're her hero today.'

'She did seem pleased.'

'They mean the world to her. Her husband died suddenly some years ago. I suppose she told you about it?'

'No.'

'Really? I've heard the story dozens of time. He was chasing some villain who had stolen his wallet whilst he was playing bowls and he had a heart attack. She'll often say to me – what Hitler's Panzers couldn't do in wartime Europe, some thug did in the park at Wallsend.'

'That's poignant.'

'It is. I don't think she's ever gotten over it. Every time I speak to her the subject drifts onto her Walter.'

'Death of a loved one can be hard to get over.'

Trish smiled and looked awkward. She lifted a cup from the kitchen bench and offered it to Jet who took the handle. 'She has a son that she's always going on about as well. He's in the prison service, she dotes on him. I think he's tried a few times to get her to move in with him, but she's so independently minded.'

'I think you were right about the door being left open. I think someone just saw it open, took the chance and ran in. They probably just grabbed the first thing that looked valuable.'

'I don't know what things are coming to, stealing from an old woman. And what would anyone do with medals? They can't be worth much to anyone else.'

'You're right. Probably some junkie trying to raise money for his next score.'

'Was it not the lad from the flat?'

'We found the medals in his flat, but he's saying someone brought them in and left them there. My guess is he took them as payment from someone.'

'Not much of a businessman then?'

'He's not been long in the area and is building up his customer base.'

'Will you be able to put him out of business?'

'I'll do my best.'

'I hope you do. There've been a lot of strange characters hanging around here since he moved in, it's quite frightening sometimes, especially when you're on your own.'

'How long is it since your divorce?'

'I've been here nearly a year now.'

Jet sipped his coffee and smiled as a silence fell. He looked at his watch and then placed his cup on the kitchen unit. 'Must rush. His solicitor will be at the station now and I'll have to interview him, see what story he comes up with and what evidence I can use to get him charged.'

'Of course, good luck.'

Jet moved purposefully towards the door of the flat. 'Thanks for the coffee.'

'Any time you're passing.'

'Thanks. I'll be back to see Mrs Rodgers to keep her updated.'

'Pop in if you have the time.'

'Thanks Trish, I'll do that.'

They smiled at each other and then Jet made his way out of the flat, Trish closing the door behind him. Jet made his way along the corridor to the lift. He pressed the button but soon decided to use the stairs for his descent. As he walked down the stairs his mobile phone rang and after a few moments of scrambling around in his pocket he placed it to his head.

'Yeah?'

'Jet, it's Sharkie. Where are you?'

'Just leaving Squires. What's the matter, is the solicitor working himself?'

'No, York is after you – wants you to go and see him as soon as.'

'What for?'

'Search me.'

'Guess I'd better do what he says.'

Jet put the phone back into his pocket and dashed out of the building. The roads were still busy but the rush hour congestion had passed and soon he was walking up the stairs of the station towards the superintendent's office. The door was open and he walked straight in. 'You wanted to see me?'

York looked up as Jet walked towards his desk. 'Shut the door.' Jet obeyed. 'Sit.' York pointed to a chair in front of his desk and Jet thought the command would not have been out of place in a kennel. 'You've seen the news about Patterson and Waters?'

'Yes.'

'They've been running most of the big crime syndicates around here for years. It's a major breakthrough getting them charged with drug supplying: if they're convicted, they'll go down for years, and we'll have broken up the biggest organised crime network ever.'

'It's a good job.'

'Just think of the lives that will be saved and the victims spared with them put away.' Jet could sense the emotion in York's voice. Clearly this was a landmark in his career, and Jet thought a big feather in his cap. 'Things like this don't happen by accident, they need planning, care and sacrifice.'

Jet was confused by this outpouring and said nothing.

'There's a brief hearing at court tomorrow. We've been working closely with the court and in the circumstances we hope for a quick trial.'

Jet remained silent.

'They'll find out at the hearing tomorrow about the evidence we have to prove the charges.'

'Must be good.'

'It is. The best we could hope for. Someone who worked

with them and knew their business inside out. They'll go away for life.'

'Really, a witness? That's good.'

'That's why I wanted to talk to you.'

'Really? What can I do?'

'Nothing, I want you to do nothing. I just wanted you to know about the witness before it hits the press tomorrow.'

'What's it got to do with me?'

'It's Ray Harris.'

Chapter thirty-seven

It was 9.00am on Thursday when Jet walked into the office of Sanderson, Robson and Reece Solicitors. The young receptionist was thumbing through a large pile of unopened mail and settling down on her swivel chair as Jet spoke. 'My name's Whittle. I'm here to see a Mr Russell.'

'Please take a seat.'

The young woman made a brief internal telephone call as Jet paced the reception area – he was not in the frame of mind to sit.

A man came through a door into the reception. 'Mr Whittle?' An arm was thrust at Jet and he shook the hand offered to him. 'Jeff Russell. I've found you an office, come in.'

Jet followed. 'I hope this is not causing any inconvenience?'

'Not at all, although I'm not sure what good it will do.'

'I realise that, but I promised Mark I would do what I could to help. He's desperate.'

'I know. I've been through every piece of the evidence myself and I've briefed our barrister for the trial on Monday. All I ask is that you keep everything in the order it's in now.'

As Russell spoke, he pushed open the door of a room

that appeared to be a small interview room. A square table was in the corner and on it stood two boxes each with *R v. Groom* written on the side.

'All the evidence is in these. Take your time. My office is the second door on the left if you need anything. Let me know when you're done.'

Russell left the room as Jet pulled out the hard wooden chair from under the table and sat down. He pulled the first box towards him and removed its lid. Although he was not surprised at the quantity of paper the box contained he now felt quite daunted at the prospect of reading the contents. Jet took a notebook out of his jacket pocket, placed it on the table and started to go through the documents.

Jet soon became immersed in the detail of the case and had lost track of time. A voice interrupted his train of thought. 'You managing all right?'

Jet turned and now noticed the door was open and saw Russell. 'Yes thanks.'

'You not sick yet? You've been there for over five hours.'

'Nearly finished for the day. I've promised Mark I will go and see him this afternoon.'

Russell looked at Jet's notebook and could see several pages of scribbling. 'Found anything of interest to you?'

'No. As you said, it seems pretty straightforward – just got to hope that the jury can be convinced Mark didn't go there with the intention of murdering Trent.'

'We'll do our best.'

'I know.' Jet placed a tidy bundle of documents back into the box in front of him. He replaced the box lid before closing his notebook and returning it to his jacket pocket. 'What did you make of the pathologist's report?'

'There isn't much to it: cause of death asphyxiation. Just as Mark said, he strangled him to death.'

'Yeah, I suppose so. He made mention of a lot of bruises across Trent's neck.'

'Something obviously got caught on Trent's neck during the struggle – it was a very violent outburst. Mark's a powerful man.'

'Suppose so.'

'Not a good way to go.'

'No, definitely not.'

'Do you need to see anything else?'

'Don't think so. I've been through the main witness statements. If anything does occur to me, would you mind if I give you a call?'

'No problem.'

Russell walked with Jet back to the main entrance and they politely shook hands. The feeling of being an intruder began to ease as Jet returned to the Fiesta and headed towards Durham.

The familiar journey passed in a blur as Jet's mind ran through statements, post-mortem reports, and then inevitably went back to the thought of Ray Harris still being alive. Jet could see his face and imagined a broad, smug smile across it – it burned inside him.

Jet went through his usual routine in the police station and ten minutes later Groom's cell passage door was unlocked and Jet walked in.

'Good to see you Jet.'

'How are you feeling? Nervous about the trial starting on Monday?'

'Terrified.'

'At least it'll be over soon. I've had a look through the file – it's pretty straightforward. I don't see how anyone could prove that you went there with the intention of murdering Trent. You've just got to stick to your story.'

'You know it all depends on what the jury think about my state of mind Jet. There's no evidence to prove either way what my intentions were, it'll be just down to what the jury want to believe on the day.'

'You've got to think positive Mark. Trent was a convicted criminal and you're of previous good character, a cop, one of the good guys Mark. Your barrister knows what to do.'

Groom smiled. 'I hope so Jet.'

'It'll work out, I'm telling you.'

'Are you coming to the trial?'

'I've taken some leave, so I can be there.'

'Thanks, it'll be good to have some support. I can't see Shirley being there.'

'Heard anything from her or Diane recently?'

'Only from solicitors, about Shirley wanting a divorce.'

'What about Diane?'

'Nothing.'

'Do you want me to go and talk to them? I'm sure Diane would want to come and see you.'

'No. I don't want her in here. Let's get the trial out of the way and see what happens. Maybe after that.'

'Whatever you want Mark, just don't go underestimating your Diane.'

'Don't worry, I won't.'

Jet took a deep breath as the conversation paused and then exhaled slowly before he spoke again. 'Got a bit of a shock myself yesterday.'

'Yeah?'

'You know that case against Patterson and Waters?'

'Yeah.'

'There's a preliminary hearing at the magistrates' court, when they're going to have the evidence disclosed to them. Guess who the star witness is?'

'Haven't a clue.'

'Ray Harris.'

'Taking his evidence by seance?'

'He's alive.'

'What?'

'York told me yesterday: they faked his death so Patterson and Waters wouldn't get nervous and do a runner before they got arrested.'

'So he wasn't attacked in prison?'

'York reckoned he was knifed but a warden saved him. They took him to hospital and told everyone he'd died of his injuries.'

'The sneaky bastards.'

'So the deal's back on. Harris gives evidence, they get Waters and Patterson, and Harris walks.'

'He walks, after what he did?'

'New identity, new home. He'll have a fortune stashed away – looks like he's coming out of this smelling of roses.' Jet shook his head.

'Devil looks after his own Jet.'

'Never a truer word said. I look forward to the day when I see him again.'

'What you gonna do?'

'What are the options?'

Mark nodded. 'Look at me.'

'What?'

'This is what happens when you look for revenge.'

'He's not getting away with it Mark.'

'For Christ's sake Jet, don't do anything stupid.'

'I wasn't thinking of doing anything stupid, I was thinking about doing something smart.'

'Nothing is smart Jet, do nothing.'

'He killed Julia.'

'He's taken a lot from you, I know that. You go and do

something stupid and you'll lose the rest. It's not worth it, believe me.'

'Told you Mark, I'm not thinking about doing anything stupid, I'm thinking about doing something smart.

Chapter thirty-eight

Jet stopped walking outside Newcastle Crown Court and looked up at the tall multi-storied modern building. It boasted an impressive stone stair entrance, a huge tinted glass frontage and scenic elevators running up the centre of the building. It stood on the Quayside among the trendy wine bars and apartments, and Jet could not help feeling that it was hopelessly misplaced. Perhaps it was a sign of the times that the jewel in this modern development crown was the place where criminal trials took place, but it just did not seem right to him. If Jet had been a city planner then this spot might have been reserved for a theatre or cinema, to reflect the spirit of entertainment and leisure which existed everywhere else on the Quayside. The court would have been hidden somewhere else in the city, concealed, like dirty washing ought to be.

Jet made his way up the grand stairway to the entrance and walked into the foyer. He stopped at the noticeboard and looked at the list of all the day's hearings. His eyes stopped at '*R v. Groom court three*', and he made his way into the building. Two security guards stood at a counter at the foot of the stairs, and Jet nodded to them as he approached. One moved a plastic container towards him and asked him to put all of his metal objects inside it. Jet was very familiar with the procedure and complied quickly. After a few seconds of the guard running a hand-held metal detector across Jet's body, he returned the items to his pockets and walked up the stairs. The first floor was a huge space, designated as a waiting room for each of the ten courtrooms, whose entrances were uniformly marked along the length of the waiting area. The room reminded him of an airport departure lounge, without the anticipation of being flown to some far-flung exotic location. A strong sense of Julia's presence ran through his body as he remembered dragging two large suitcases to a check-in counter. On their last holiday, Julia had, as usual, packed for both of them and it wasn't until they had arrived at their hotel in Corfu that he discovered she had packed herself eight pairs of shoes.

'We're only here for two weeks!' Jet had complained, as the contents of the cases were placed in drawers and a wardrobe.

Jet could see courtroom three and walked past a number of people who were untidily scattered around the blue thinly-padded seats which were fixed to the floor. Others were pacing nervously and they all looked as if they would have preferred to be somewhere else. Jet pushed the swing door of courtroom three and stared at the empty room. It was dominated by the prisoner's dock, which stood in the centre, encased by huge glass screens to ensure no defendants were going to vault to freedom. The judge's bench was elevated high on the opposite side of the room, the tall chair where the judge would soon be enthroned standing in the centre of the rear wall. A short distance away, to its left, was the witness box which was directly opposite the jury's enclosure. Even empty, the room had an intimidating quality about it, despite its modern design.

Jet left the room and returned to the fixed seats of the waiting room. As he sat down, he rued the fact that in all of the hours he had spent sitting in court waiting rooms, he had never found a comfortable chair. He pulled the notes he had made from the court file out of his jacket pocket and flicked through the pages. He heard voices and looked up to see two uniformed men taking seats on the row facing him as they continued to chat to each other. The rows of seats were only a few feet apart.

'Shouldn't you be inside the court?' Jet smiled at the two officers, realising from their uniforms they were prison wardens. Their bright-white shirts and black clip-on ties looked uncomfortable and both had long chains hanging from their belts, which looped low below their knees and then led into their pockets, where Jet assumed their keys rested.

'Wish we were.' One of the wardens smiled as he spoke and the other remained grim faced.

'Not looking after prisoners today then?'

'No, giving evidence.'

'Not as bad as it seems, I wouldn't worry.'

'You with the police?'

'Yeah.'

'We were asked to come here for ten o'clock, but no doubt they'll keep us hanging around for ages.'

'Better than working for a living though.'

'I can think of better places to be.'

Jet smiled as he gently nodded towards both of the officers, and as he gazed at the straight-faced warden, a thought occurred to him. 'Haven't we met before?'

The warden looked back at Jet and shrugged his shoulders as he spoke for the first time. 'It's possible. I seem to have spent a lot of time hanging around these places.'

'Yeah, know what you mean.' Jet smiled. 'You here for the Groom trial?'

'Yeah, we have walk-on parts. We'll probably have to hang around here for days and then not be required after all.'

Jet continued to smile as a silence fell. After a few seconds he returned his eyes to his notes and flicked the pages. Jet had written and underlined the name of each witness, whose evidence he had been through, as he sat in the uncomfortable surroundings of the offices of Sanderson, Robson and Reece. After each name he had summarised what they had said in their statement. It was all straightforward. He looked at the first page of his notes and saw the pathologist's evidence and then he turned the page over and saw what the investigating officer had to say. He turned another page and saw the content of the statement of the first of the two prison wardens who had spoken to Groom on the fateful day when he had squeezed the life out of Geoffrey Trent. Prison Warden William Rodgers had shown Groom into the room and left him there as another colleague had gone to get Trent. He looked at the notes under the name of Prison Warden Terry Richards who had led Trent into the room for his meeting with Groom and left them both together. As the meeting was an official and authorised police interview there had been no reason to supervise it. Both wardens had been standing together, not far from the room when they thought they heard a strange noise and had looked in, and saw Groom with his hands around Trent's throat. They had managed to pull Groom away but attempts to revive Trent were futile as he was clearly already dead by the time they got there.

The two wardens continued to chat to each other and didn't notice Jet rise and walk towards the floor-to-ceiling windows which overlooked the Tyne. Again the thought occurred to him that the stunning view across the river was wasted. The people who came to this building were too nervous and distracted to appreciate the Millennium Bridge or the newly opened live music venue, The Sage Gateshead, which looked to Jet like a huge glass slug, but for all that was still very impressive. Then another thought crossed Jet's mind and he picked his mobile phone out of his pocket and within a few seconds was speaking to Eddie in the intelligence office at the station. 'Eddie, Jet. I'm at the Crown court. Pull some files for me and I'll come straight up.'

It had taken Jet two hours to check the files that Eddie had retrieved for him and then to look through the details on Trent's computerised records. When he came back into the court building, it looked like nothing had changed. The two prison wardens sat in silence in the same chairs.

'Not been in yet?'

'No chance, they're arguing about some of the members of the jury. We could be here all bloody day.' It was the cheerful prison warden who replied to Jet's enquiry.

'Never mind, it'll be over soon.'

Jet looked at his watch as he gently pushed open the courtroom door and saw it was now twelve thirty. As he entered, he could see the judge stand up and walk towards the private exit near his seat.

'What's happened?' Jet asked the usher, who stood next to the door.

'They've adjourned for lunch and will start hearing the evidence soon.'

Jet could see Mark through the glass screen of the dock being led away to a room below it. Jet looked over to the lawyer's bench and saw Mr Russell standing with a barrister. He walked quickly over to them. 'Mr Russell.'

'Hello, pleased you could make it. This is Mr Green, Mark's barrister.'

'Could I have a few minutes of your time? I think I have some information that might be of use.'

'Sure.'

It was almost two o'clock before the first witness was called to give his evidence. Much to the two prison wardens' dismay it was Dr Norman Frisk, the pathologist, who was called first to explain his findings from the post-mortem examination of Geoffrey Trent. Jet sat at the rear of the court and noticed Mrs Trent sitting in the public gallery. Jet had an urge to talk to her and suggest that she might want to give the gruesome details of Dr Frisk a miss, but he knew that she would never be inclined to take his advice. No matter what his intentions, Jet was one of the enemy as far as she was concerned. Even during the emotion of their discussion after Geoffrey's death he had been unable to pierce the armour of her hate for all things law enforcement. If the police had just left her son alone he would be alive and happy, it was as simple as that.

Dr Frisk's evidence was undisputed by either barrister. Trent had died of strangulation. His throat had been squeezed with considerable force and unconsciousness and death would have taken just a few minutes once Groom had applied pressure to Trent's slim neck. Green asked Dr Frisk about the unusual bruises on Trent's neck, but there was no conclusive explanation. The pathologist was unimpressed by the marks which could have occurred during the violent confrontation in any number of ways.

'Did you examine Mark Groom's hands?' Green enquired of Dr Frisk.

'Yes, of course.' The doctor was indignant at the thought that he would have overlooked such a simple procedure.

'The bruises are in a straight line, like a little string, was he wearing a ring or anything else that might have caused the bruises?'

'No.' It was not in the doctor's nature to speculate without invitation.

'Thank you, Dr Frisk,' was Green's last remark to the doctor who quickly left the witness box and the court, uninterested in hearing anything further of the proceedings.

The first of the two prison wardens was called and the prosecution barrister gently led him through the events of that fateful afternoon. He had heard a noise and entered the room where he had seen Groom with his hands around the neck of Trent, who by then had the look of a rag doll. He had managed to pull Groom away from Trent and manhandle him out of the room. Jet thought the prison warden looked relieved when he was thanked for his efforts and allowed to leave the witness box.

The second, stern-faced prison warden was called to the witness stand and again the prosecution barrister gently led him through his statement. He had entered the room immediately after his colleague and had helped him pull Groom from Trent. He had spent some time attempting to revive Trent, but it had been a forlorn effort. Trent was clearly beyond help by the time Groom had been pulled out of the room. The prosecution barrister thanked the prison warden for his evidence, but his smile was not reciprocated as he sat down and Green stood up.

'Prison Warden Rodgers, how well did you know the deceased, Geoffrey Trent?' Green's question clearly surprised the prison warden.

'Not well at all. He was a prisoner on remand. He hadn't been there very long.'

'Trent was a regular in prison. Had you never come across him before?'

'No.' The prison warden remained straight faced.

'So you had never met him before?'

'No.'

'Had you heard of him before?'

'No.'

'Your Honour.' The prosecution barrister rose to his feet as he spoke. 'Prison Warden Rodgers is not on trial here, I don't see any relevance to this.'

'Your Honour, the purpose of this point will be clear in a second, if I could prevail on the court.'

The judge seemed irked by the proceedings, and Jet thought he probably wished he was on a golf course somewhere, rather than in his bright-red regalia, overseeing these proceedings, perched high on his throne.

'Get to the point quickly Mr Green.'

'Thank you, Your Honour.' Green turned to the witness

stand and the prosecution barrister returned to his seat.

'Had you ever heard of Geoffrey Trent?' Green's question was directed to the prison warden.

'No.'

'Is your father still alive?'

Jet thought he could see the prison warden's already pale face drain of what little colour it had.

'No.'

'How did he die?'

'Your Honour!' The prosecution barrister was back on his feet again, and there was urgency in his voice.

'This is important Your Honour.' Green interrupted the prosecution's pleadings.

'Continue Mr Green, but get to the point.'

'Your father had a heart attack in Wallsend Park, when he was chasing someone who had stolen his wallet. Is that correct?'

'I don't see...' All eyes were on the prison warden as his words stumbled.

'Please answer the question.'

'Yes.'

'There was a young man arrested for stealing that wallet wasn't there?'

'Yes.'

'I understand your father was a decorated war hero. It must have been a great loss.'

The warden nodded but did not speak.

'Deserved to be treated with respect didn't he?'

'He was a hero.' The warden's voice was faltering.

'Who was arrested for stealing the wallet?'

'I don't know.'

'Come on, you know who it was don't you? After all, it was the person responsible for your father's death. Who was it?'

The warden looked confused, and Jet thought he looked distressed as he stood in the witness box, apparently unable to respond to Green's enquiry.

'It was the deceased Trent wasn't it?'

The courtroom was deathly quiet as everyone waited for a response from the warden, but he remained silent.

'You know, you could be forgiven for thinking that Trent was responsible for your father's death, couldn't you?'

The warden remained speechless.

'Do you blame Trent for your father's death?'

The warden shook his head. 'I don't know what you're talking about.'

'Really?' Green looked down at the bench in front of him, picked up a photograph and then walked towards the witness stand. 'You said in your evidence that your colleague pulled the defendant out of the room, and that you stayed with Trent to administer first aid. Is that right?'

'Yes.'

'How long were you with Trent before other help arrived?'

'Don't know, a few minutes.'

'A few minutes, that would make sense.' Green continued to walk towards the witness stand and lifted the photograph he was carrying towards the warden. 'This is a photograph of the deceased. Perhaps you could help the court to solve a little mystery. Can you see the bruising around the neck?'

'Yes.'

'It's an unusual little string of bruises isn't it?'

'Yes.'

'The pathologist has already told us that it must have occurred during the assault on Trent, before he died. People don't bruise like that after death, so it must have happened while he was being strangled.' The warden looked at the photograph. Green continued, 'I couldn't help notice that you and your colleague are both wearing long chains on your uniforms. Is that where you keep your keys?'

'Yes.'

'Standard issue to all prison wardens?'

'Yes.'

'That chain is easily long enough to put around someone's neck and choke them isn't it?'

Jet could feel an electrical charge in the air, the same uneasy feeling before a tropical storm was about to erupt. In the silence all eyes were on the warden.

'Trent wasn't dead when you got to him, was he?' Green looked at the warden who did not respond. 'Groom didn't kill Trent, you did, didn't you?' Green paused, but there was no response. 'You had the opportunity to take revenge on the man responsible for your father's death and you took it didn't you?' The warden was gently shaking his head.

Jet looked up and saw Mrs Trent staring at the proceedings, her mouth was open and she looked confused. The tension stretched across the courtroom and Jet thought it almost unbearable.

'Look at the defendant.' Green demanded. 'You are a good man. Are you really going to watch an innocent man go to prison for the rest of his life for a crime you committed?'

The warden continued to shake his head.

'It will be possible to match your chain up to the bruises on Trent's neck you know. There are probably still fibres on the chain. We will be able to match it up. You know that don't you?'

Jet watched in the silence that followed Green's remark and thought the warden looked dazed.

'It's over, you know that don't you?'

'My dad was a hero, and he killed him for an empty wallet – he was scum!' The warden's outburst was loud and angry. Jet looked on and could feel the air tingle as the warden stared, now wild-eyed, at the barrister.

'I understand, he killed your father.' Green's voice was quiet and reassuring. 'Was Trent still conscious when you reached him?'

'He was groaning.'

'What did you do?'

'I put the chain around his neck and just pulled.'

The whole courtroom seemed to be holding its breath.

'You strangled Trent?'

'I paid him back for murdering my dad.'

All eyes were on Rodgers who looked down at his feet. Green looked away from the warden and at the judge. 'Your Honour, in view of the circumstances, I think it wise if this examination cease now. I think we've heard enough.'

The judge nodded towards the officers in the court, and within a few seconds the warden was being escorted away out of the witness box.

'Your Honour.' Green's voice was clear and purposeful – the tone of a man who had the taste of victory. 'In view of the last witness's testimony, I submit that the defendant Mark Groom has no case to answer.'

The atmosphere was now pure electricity, and Jet could feel his heart thumping. He looked at Groom who appeared bewildered and was staring at the judge.

'Do the prosecution wish to comment?'

Jet thought the prosecution barrister looked as shell-shocked as Groom as he rose to his feet. 'No representations Your Honour.'

The judge turned to Green. 'This court finds the defendant has no case to answer.' He lifted his head and directed his next comment towards Groom. 'You're free to go.'

The courtroom erupted. The agonising silence became

a widespread roar. The numerous members of the press ran out to file their reports, while other spectators shrieked with surprise. Jet could see Mrs Trent watching the back of the warden as he was led out of the courtroom. She looked astounded and unable to speak.

Groom stared open-mouthed at the judge and then turned his head to look at Jet. Jet smiled at Groom and winked, he could see the tears streaming down his cheeks. Groom walked to the door of the dock which was opened by the prison warden who had been escorting him. Now free, he walked down the steps into the courtroom. He headed towards Green and Russell, quickly shook their hands and continued to walk past them as he muttered, making his way towards Jet.

Jet stood still as the huge figure of Groom put both his arms around him in a firm bear hug. Jet could feel Groom's breath on his shoulder and the warm moisture of his face as the tears flowed freely. 'You clever bastard, how did you know?'

'I recognised him from a photo I saw at a house. A bit of luck, that's all. The gods smiled on us.'

'About fucken' time!'

Chapter thirty-nine

It was two thirty on Tuesday afternoon, and the winter sun shone brightly on all the graves in St Peter's Cemetery in Wallsend.

Jet looked tired. The skin under his eyes was dark and lined, leaving permanent shadows. His grey suit was baggy and untidy; his belt was pulled up a couple of notches tighter to hold the crumpled trousers around his diminishing waist. His jacket pockets gaped open, like the hungry mouths Julia had always complained of.

He stood at the foot of the grave and stared at the black marble headstone that was so smooth and polished he could make out dark reflections. The gold lettering read simply, '*In loving memory of Julia Whittle, beloved wife and daughter,*' followed by her dates of birth and death. When he read it, Jet was again hit with the harsh reality of what had happened, and he felt the now familiar pain in his chest.

'Thought I'd find you here.'

Jet turned and saw Groom holding a bouquet of white lilies. He thought Groom looked very different compared to the last time he had seen him. His clothes looked clean and fresh, and in the sunlight he appeared a much different person to the man he had come to know incarcerated in his Durham cell. Jet could see that a huge burden had been lifted from him and detected an air of optimism, a return of the hope that had been absent for many months.

'Creature of habit.' Jet tried to smile but it would not form around his lips.

Groom took the few steps needed to stand beside Jet and they stood in silence for a few seconds, the sunlight pouring down, whilst they stared at the coal-black gravestone, which looked cold despite the effort of the low winter sun. Groom stepped forward and placed the flowers on the surface of the grave before returning to stand next to Jet. 'A terrible waste.'

Jet nodded gently, but did not speak. In his hand he held a plant in a plastic pot. It was a favourite of Julia's, a chrysanthemum. The full rounded bright-yellow flowers of the 'butterball' variety were in perfect bloom, forced unnaturally to do so at this time of year, by their grower's strict regime of darkness and light, to simulate the autumn days when the chrysanthemum would itself have chosen to display its natural beauty to the world. He knew the plant would not fare too well outdoors, but as Julia had always been fond of them, he had taken to buying and replacing the plants each week.

'Did you see your solicitor today?' Jet's thoughts had momentarily returned to the living.

'Yes, it looks like I'm going back to work now I've been acquitted. He thinks it's unlikely they'll want to resurrect any other charges. Embarrassing for them, that they didn't work out the link between the prison warden and Trent.'

'That's good news Mark.'

'You really came through for me. I'll never forget what you did.'

'No problem.'

Groom turned his gaze from the headstone to Jet. 'What are your plans now?'

'Try to get my life back into some order.' Jet continued to stare at his wife's grave as he spoke and Groom thought his comment lacked conviction.

'What about Harris?' Groom still stared at Jet.

'What about him?'

'You going after him?'

'He's in prison.'

'What about when he gets out?'

'Won't the taxpayers look after him? New identity, home, life?'

'They'll protect him from Patterson and Waters. But I'm not so sure they can protect him from you.'

'You worried about his welfare?'

'I'm worried about you. Rebuild your life Frank, don't give it away.'

'Don't worry. Maybe you were right; maybe doing nothing is the smartest thing.'

'I'm sure of it.'

Jet moved forward and held out the plant in his right

hand. As he did so he spoke quietly. 'Maybe.' Groom did not hear this.

As Jet placed the new chrysanthemum in the marble pot which stood just in front of the headstone, he realised the one he had previously left was gone altogether. The only remaining evidence of its existence was a single dying bloom which lay on the earth. Jet thought it most likely that the plant had been stolen from the grave. He did not give this any great thought as he placed the new plant in the holder. After all, in the grand scheme of things, what did the theft of a plant matter?

ACKNOWLEDGEMENTS

Thanks to Andrew, Adelle and June, for their invaluable help and support during the writing of this novel.

I am also very grateful for the encouragement and guidance of Sheila Wakefield.